WRONG Turns

Jackie Calhoun

Bella BOOKS
2009

Bella Books, Inc.
P.O. Box 10543
Tallahassee, FL 32302

Printed in the United States of America on acid-free paper
First Edition

Editor: Cindy Cresap
Cover Designer: Linda Callaghan

ISBN 10: 1-59493-148-8
ISBN 13: 978-1-59493-148-2

Who has not made wrong turns along the way?

Acknowledgment

My first reader and good friend, Joan Hendry.
My partner, family and friends for their support.
Those at Bella Books who do such good work.

About the Author

Jackie Calhoun is the author of the following Bella Books—*Roommates, The Education of Ellie, Obsession, Abby's Passion, Woman in the Mirror, Outside the Flock, Tamarack Creek, Off Season and Seasons of the Heart* (reprint). She also authored *Crossing the Center Line*, a Windstorm Creative, Ltd. book, and wrote ten novels published by Naiad Press. Calhoun lives with her partner in northeast Wisconsin. Take a look at her Web site at www.jackiecalhoun.com, or contact her at jackie@jackiecalhoun.com. She loves to hear from her readers.

Chapter 1

Callie parked her Saturn wagon behind the small cottage and carried her bag and cooler to the back door. Her tiredness fell away as she unlocked the door. She had sworn she'd never return, yet here she was. Inside, she threw open windows and put the food in the fridge as the familiarity of the place threatened to overwhelm her. Even the slightly musty smell from being closed up reminded her of years past. She thought she'd kept the excitement at bay, but now that she was here, it began to take over.

She hurriedly changed into her swimsuit and headed down the sandy steps to the water. Ankle deep, she looked out over the lake she'd considered her own when growing up, and noted the changes. Many of the small cottages that once nestled among the trees had been replaced by sprawling two-story log homes with matching boathouses and elevated stairs. Almost all had docks with covered lifts for boats and Jet Skis.

The hot wind ruffling the water lifted her hair off her forehead. Minnows nibbled on her ankles and feet, making her smile. She unlocked the boathouse and dragged the small Sunflower sailboat to the water, then carried the mast and sail, keel and rudder out to it. A gust caught the fabric of the sail as she clambered into the tub-shaped fiberglass shell. The sun canted toward the west, its rays dancing on the water, nearly blinding her. Her heart soared.

The little craft sped across the lake, sail straining and boat heeling in the wind. Like ballast, she stretched across its width, feet braced against the gunnels, head and shoulders leaning over the other side, both hands holding the sheet tight as the sail and boom skimmed the lake. The sailboat rounded a jut of land and the wind dropped to nothing, just like that. The sail flapped aimlessly as the boat stopped dead in the water. She glanced up at the white triangle with its yellow stripe and sunflower against the blue sky and let go of her worries—the failing business, the loss of the cottage, the pittance that was her income, her life that was going nowhere—and lived in the moment. It was enough to dangle a hand in the cool water and relish the heat of the sun and the rock of the boat.

From nowhere, an enormous horsefly buzzed her. She tried to ward it off by wildly waving her arms around her head. When that failed to work, she grabbed the rope attached to the front of the sailboat, slipped overboard and sank into the water. When she came up, the fly was gone.

She floated on her back then, propelling the boat toward her with each kick, an unwitting joy filling her chest. She'd swim the sailboat into the wind or back to the cottage, whichever came first. The water, heavy and deep, slid over her like a caress. When she turned to check her bearings, she saw the speedboat.

Caught like a turtle on a road, the next few moments seemed larger than life so sure was she that they were her last. The clear sky, the cool water and the boat speeding toward her etched themselves in her mind. She had a fleeting thought that this might not be a terrible way to die, in the lake that held her best memories. The driver was looking away, eyes on the skier riding outside the craft's wake.

She began screaming and waving her free arm, the one that wasn't clinging to the rope attached to the sailboat. As the speeding craft bore down on her, she plunged into the depths, lungs and heart bursting. Overhead, she saw the underside of the speedboat, turning, the prop spinning. She surfaced and gasped for air. The sailboat seemed to have disappeared. Had it been sunk? But then she spotted it bottom side up floating away.

The speedboat—a MasterCraft—rocked next to her on its wake. A woman leaned over its side, asking, "Are you all right?"

"You damn near killed me." Her voice came out thin, high and hysterical. Her body trembled. Her heart, which had lodged in her throat, now thudded with anger. The water, no longer friendly, seemed a dangerously deep, opaque place.

"I know. I'm sorry." The woman's face appeared ashen beneath her tan and around her sunglasses. "Let me tow your boat home. Okay? You aren't safe out here." She turned toward the skier who was climbing back into the speedboat. "Go get the sailboat, Brady, will you? Turn it right side up."

The boy slid back into the water and swam toward the small boat that was drifting toward shore.

Callie jabbed a finger at the boy seated next to the woman. "He's supposed to watch the skier so that you can pay attention to where you're going. Non-motorized boats have the right-of -way." She shook as the rage spilled out of her.

"I know. Get in. I'll tie your boat to mine," the woman said.

Brady returned with the upright sailboat in tow—the sail dripping, the keel and wet life jacket she hadn't worn floating inside the shell.

"No." Callie slithered into the sailboat headfirst and awkwardly turned right side up, belatedly realizing how foolish she must look. She bailed with one hand, while reaching for the sheet with the other.

"I'll stay with you then."

"I don't need an escort, certainly not you," she said, slamming the keel back in its slot.

The woman flipped her thick blond-highlighted hair back.

She said something to the boys, which was impossible to hear over the purr of the motor. When all three laughed, Callie became furious all over again.

As if to rescue her, a breeze sprang up. She pulled the sheet tight with one hand and turned the rudder into the gust with the other. The sailboat leaped forward, the wet sail straining, as the small craft slid through choppy waves past the speedboat. Callie turned her face skyward, trying for calm.

As she tacked across the lake, the speedboats and Jet Skis began to disappear. No-wake hours went into effect at five thirty. How quickly the day was going. If only she could hold it back.

The boat headed toward shore at an alarming rate—the gusts always seemed to pick up speed in the shallows. She dropped the sheet, pulled up the keel and turned out of the wind just before jumping overboard in waist-deep water. After mooring the boat, she climbed the steps with legs still shaking from the scare.

The cottage at the top of the hill was one story and wood sided, with an enclosed sleeping porch that faced the lake. There was one small bedroom used mostly for storage, one bath with a shower, a kitchen and a bigger room that opened onto the porch. The view of the lake lay framed between tall red and white pines and some scrubby oaks. The cottage faced south, capturing the sun and the summer breezes. That was how her grandfather had planned it.

In the kitchen she mixed a vodka and tonic and took it down to the lake where she sat on the beach, sipping the drink, occasionally looking up from her book at the lake. A kingfisher chattered as it flew low across the water. The voices and laughter of kids swimming across the lake carried over the surface. Fishermen's boats appeared. A couple of kayakers paddled past the beach and waved. A feeling of peace settled over her, and she put the book down.

Drawn to the water, she set her drink on the pier and dove off the end. When she shot through the surface, she found herself facing a boat. A beat of fear electrified her. She looked up to see her distorted reflection mirrored in a woman's sunglasses, the woman in the MasterCraft that had nearly run her down. There was no one else in the boat.

To put some distance between herself and the craft, she sculled backward. "Are you trying to kill me or what?"

"I wanted to see if you were all right."

Acutely conscious of how she looked, having seen herself in the bathroom mirror—hair wet and tangled, face red from wind and sun—she said, "Yes, no thanks to you."

"For what it's worth, I am sorry. I'll never take my eyes off where I'm going ever again." She put a hand over her heart. "Want to go for a ride? It's that time of day." After five thirty, the boats often began circling the shore slowly. The woman held up a beer bottle and raised her eyebrows in question. She was attractive, slender with broad shoulders like a swimmer's. When she'd leaned over the side of the boat after the near accident, her breasts had nestled against each other, catching Callie's eye despite her fear and anger.

"I already have a drink."

"Bring it with you. My name is Victoria." She smiled, her teeth white against her tan.

"Callie," she said, still treading water. Her feet touched the sandy lake bottom, and she pulled herself up on the pier.

The boat bumped the dock and Victoria took hold of a post and held on. "Come on. Climb in." She gestured with her head.

"I'd rather have my drink here," she said, unwilling to get into the boat that had nearly run her down.

"Would you like to ski tomorrow? I'll come by and pick you up."

"I'm not a skier."

"You can spot for me then."

Callie sighed and all resistance drained from her. "All right. Just for an hour or two, though." She got bored and hot sitting backward in a boat, watching someone ski.

"I'll be here around ten," Victoria said, but she didn't leave. Instead, she twisted off the beer cap and leaned back, holding the pier post with one hand, drinking with the other.

Victoria was downing her third beer, the boat now fastened to the pier. Callie had mixed another vodka and tonic and taken it down to the beach where Victoria was sitting on a chair next to hers. When the breeze died and the sun sank toward the lake, coloring it purple, Callie slipped into the water and Victoria followed.

It wasn't until the stars popped out of the dark sky that Victoria fired up the engine and left. "Remember, tomorrow at ten," she said. "I have to see what my nephews are up to. They're probably having a couple of beers on the sly."

Chilled, Callie wrapped herself in a towel. Marc would say this woman was coming on to her, but she thought maybe Victoria was just looking for someone to do things with. After all, teenage boys were notoriously immature.

Upstairs, she warmed the sub sandwich she'd picked up on the way, popped a cork on a bottle of merlot and ate with only a candle for light. The warm night trembled outside. A buzzing June bug joined moths as they battered their wings against the screens. Cicadas sang from the trees and tiny gnats gathered around the candle.

After eating, she went back down the hill using a flashlight. She carried a kayak out of the boathouse and paddled onto the lake. A huge red orb rose over the trees along the eastern shore as the kayak gently rocked. The mosquitoes buzzing annoyingly around her head disappeared as bats zigzagged near, some so close she instinctively ducked. When moonlight drenched the water, tears slid down her cheeks.

She was spending a week at what used to be the family cottage. When her grandparents died and left it to their four children, all of whom had children of their own, dividing vacation times became complicated. Too many people with conflicting schedules trying to share one small space. The cottage was put on the market, and Callie hadn't the money to buy it. Her parents needed the cash for retirement, they said. They wanted to travel. Her sister lived in Seattle and wasn't interested. Of all her cousins only the one who lived the farthest away could afford to buy the place. He rented it out by the week. To him, it was an investment. To her, it was as if someone had cut out a piece of her heart.

Tired out by sun and wind and drink, she fell asleep only to awake in the night sweating from a dream she immediately forgot. Heart pounding, she watched the moon ride over the lake. When her pulse quieted, she turned on a light next to her porch bed and picked up her book—*The Tortilla Curtain*. With every turned page the characters headed toward disaster. She badly needed distraction at this time of night when all her mistakes revisited her. In the morning, the book lay face down on her chest.

Before she went down to the lake, she took a good look in the mirror. She'd showered before going to bed and now her hair lay flattened by sleep. She stuck her head under the faucet and dried her hair into a semblance of order. Auburn in color, it was thick and short with a slight wave. She saw a few gray strands here and there and thought that thirty-eight was a bit young, but it was probably in the genes. She washed the sleep out of the corners of her eyes and decided she looked presentable enough. After applying sunscreen, her only makeup, and brushing her teeth, she went outside into another cloudless slightly breezy day. She was waiting on the pier when the MasterCraft motored up, and she grabbed the boat before it bumped the post.

"Morning, Callie." Victoria patted the bucket seat next to her as the boat rocked on its backwash. "Sit next to me."

Victoria eased the boat away from the pier. "We'll take my nephews skiing. Then we can do whatever we like." She glanced at Callie over the top of her sunglasses.

Callie stared back, wondering what this woman wanted from her.

Victoria's eyes were hazel, her gaze penetrating. "How long are you going to be here?"

"A week."

"Guess we'll have to make the most of it."

Of what, Callie wondered.

Victoria pushed the throttle forward, pinning Callie to the seat. They sped to the far end of the lake and coasted up to a long pier with a Shore Lander. Victoria tied the boat to the dock and, stepping out, offered a hand to Callie.

"I'll wait here," she said.

"You sure? The boys are probably not even up."

But they were coming down the staircase, taking the steps two and three at a time. "Where you been, Aunt Vicki?" one of them complained. He had a boyish face on a young man's body. The kid with him was smaller and skinnier.

Vicki ignored the question. "Callie, these are my nephews, Bradford and Charles, known affectionately as Brady and Crawfish. Want to ski, boys?"

In answer, the boys jumped into the water.

Victoria threw out the towropes and started the engine. It muttered under its hood. "Do you have a last name?" she asked, sitting behind the wheel. "Mine is Browning."

Callie glanced at her. Nice profile—straight nose, long lashes, strong chin. "Callahan. My given name is Norah, but no one who knows me well calls me that." It had been her grandmother's name, Norah Lee.

"Ah," Victoria said as if she understood. "Do you have a phone and e-mail address?"

"Of course." Sunburn hid her flush.

"Why don't you write them down?" Leaning across Callie, she opened the dash compartment. She smelled of coconut oil and her breast brushed softly against Callie's arm. Callie pressed against the back of the seat, trying to escape the intimate touch. "Rummage in there. You'll find paper and pencil."

Not sure she wanted to share where she could be found, she nevertheless scribbled down the information and stuffed it in the small storage area.

"Will you be back?" Victoria guided the boat out onto the lake until the towropes stretched tautly.

"I don't know. Maybe." She kept her gaze on the boys as they yelled for Victoria to "Hit it." Rising out of the water in unison, they each dropped a ski and leaned against the ropes, going in opposite directions.

"Where is work?"

"I'm a partner in a small business that sells swimwear and related stuff." They were hanging on by their fingernails in a too-tight market. Marc wanted to expand into exercise equipment. She wanted to sell the place and get a job where somebody else took the risks. She'd fantasized when they moved into Marc's uncle's building that maybe she'd make enough money to buy back the cottage, but all the money had vanished into inventory and all her time had gone into working.

"Your own business. I'm impressed," Victoria said as one of the boys fell and the other released the rope, sinking into the lake.

"They're down," Callie said belatedly.

Pulling back the throttle, Victoria laughed and circled toward her nephews.

"Sorry." She'd been watching the skiers but seeing instead the store and the empty hours she spent there. Unimpressive was the right word.

"That's okay. I can usually feel it when they let go of the rope. Hey, what are you doing tonight?"

"Me?" she asked stupidly.

"Do you see anyone else?" Victoria said with a smile.

Brady and Crawfish grabbed the ropes that slid behind them, and the boat effortlessly pulled them to their feet.

"What I did last night. Swim, eat, kayak, read."

"Call me Vicki, by the way. Victoria is a mouthful."

"Okay," Callie said.

"Want some company?"

"Tonight?" The woman must think she was a dope, repeating everything.

Vicki glanced at her and smiled again. "I'm not good at being alone in the woods."

What woods, Callie thought wryly. One or two trees don't make a forest. All she'd seen were a well-groomed lawn and expensive buildings. They passed Vicki's pier twice before the boys tossed the towropes and sank into the water.

Vicki circled and eased up to the dock. "Hey, guys, I'm going over to Callie's. You can have the boat when I get there. Okay?" Without waiting for an answer, she turned to Callie. "Stay right there. I'll be back in a flash." She galloped up the small hill to the sprawling log house at the top.

The boys splashed each other with a fierceness that ended in Brady dunking Crawfish. "Give up, give up," he said whenever he allowed his skinnier brother to catch his breath.

"Hey, don't drown him," Callie said, "not in front of me anyway."

They looked at her with interest. "Where you from?" Brady asked.

"About forty-five miles from here. Where are you from?" She lived outside the Fox Cities on a creek in an old farmhouse with mice that ran around with impunity. The cat spent hours crouched by the baseboards, trying to catch them. When he did corner one, if it was still alive, she'd take it outside and turn it loose. Her daughter loved the place because there was room for a horse, which Marc was taking care of right now. Callie would have brought her old dog with her, but she'd had to have him put out of his misery a couple of weeks ago. Renal disease. She couldn't think of it without crying.

"Illinois."

No surprise. Probably half the lake property owners were from Illinois.

Vicki walked out on the pier carrying a cooler. "Had to pack a few things. You guys can ski over there."

"You want us to come get you later?" Brady asked as he and Crawfish put the skis back on.

"I'll let you know if I do." Vicki winked at Callie, who responded with an uncertain smile. She felt as if she'd lost all control.

Brady lifted the cooler onto Callie's pier after the two women climbed out. "Take it easy with the boat, boys," Vicki cautioned.

Dripping water, the two brothers got into the craft. "We will, Auntie." Brady gave a mock salute and pushed the throttle. The boat surged forward in response.

"Hey," Vicki yelled. "Slow down!"

"What's in the cooler?" Callie asked, nudging it with her bare foot.

"Beer, wine, snacks, even clothes." She dropped her sunglasses down her nose and eyed Callie. "This is serious business."

Callie decided to ignore the comment. It would only be as serious as she let it be. She had come here to make some decisions. Vicki wasn't one of them. She was a distraction. "Want to put the perishables in the fridge?"

"I'll put the cooler in the boathouse if that's okay." The boathouse was built into the hill.

"How long are you staying?" she asked.

"Till my brother and his wife turn up, or one week, whichever comes first. They're working out the terms of their divorce."

It made Callie think of her divorce eight years ago. She'd ached for her daughter who had desperately tried to keep her parents together. No wonder, she thought. For eight years her daughter and son, Lucy and Tony, had been shuttled back and forth between her and their father. Tim got them most weekends. She had them during the week, which never seemed fair. Their weekends were always more fun, because she worked during the week and they had homework and after-school activities. She'd spent much of their growing up years driving them back and forth to soccer and basketball, volleyball and 4-H. A year ago, Tony had lost all interest in sports. He'd always been a bench sitter, allowed to play only when the team was winning. Now both were on vacation with their dad and his second wife. When they returned, they'd have a couple weeks with her before school started.

She'd planned this vacation for the three of them. It was the first time she'd been back since the place was sold three years ago. Now she was glad she was alone. What would her kids make of Vicki? They'd probably think the boat was great fun, but maybe

Vicki wouldn't be hanging around if the kids were here.

Vicki relaxed in one of the beach chairs. "This is a piece of luck—sitting in the sun by a lake with a pretty woman." She shaded her eyes and smiled at Callie. "Something's troubling you, isn't it?"

"You," Callie said. "I've never met anyone so determined to be…my friend." Was it only friendship Vicki wanted? Nah, what else would it be? She looked at Vicki's short fingernails and put the thought away where she stored everything else she didn't want to think about.

"Teenage boys aren't exactly stimulating company."

Callie laughed. "I don't mind being alone." Actually, she was used to being alone. As the kids grew, she became more and more solitary. Sometimes she thought it was making her strange, especially when she talked to herself. "I like to read. I need to do some thinking."

"Ah, tell me about the thinking. Maybe I can help."

She hated talking about the store, because it made her feel like a failure. "I don't think so, but thanks for offering. I have to decide this myself."

"Does it involve a woman?"

She gave a startled laugh. Where had she been mentally that she'd misinterpreted Vicki's interest? "No, it's not about a woman."

"Now I am intrigued. Would you like to meet a couple friends of mine? We can walk there. It's down the beach that-a-way." She pointed east.

"Sure, why not?"

They made their way down the lake in the water, climbing over or swimming around piers. The property was near the east curve of the lake—a sandy beach, a wood pier and a white house at the top of a rise with a red barn behind it. She had often noticed this place set back behind tall Norway pines. The two women sitting in chairs under a willow tree looked up from the books they were reading. A large dog ambled over and nosed Callie in the crotch. She reached to pat him and was reminded of her dog.

It had been selfish to keep him alive when he was suffering. She blinked back tears.

"Junior, stop that. Come here," one of the women ordered. The dog obeyed, stretching out at the woman's feet, panting, its tail beating the sand.

"Hey, how are you two?" Vicki asked with a slow smile. "Callie, this is Kate and Pat and Arthur Junior."

Callie thought she saw recognition in the blue-green eyes looking out from under Kate's visor. The other woman's gaze was open and friendly. Kate said, "I've seen you around here."

"Yes. We used to own a cottage just down the beach." She pointed. Her smile felt tight as if the sun had shrunk it. "I'm Callie Callahan." She stretched out a hand.

The woman took it. "Kate Sweeney. This is Pat Thompson."

"Are you looking for a volleyball game, Vicki?" Pat asked. The net was set up in the water.

"A few volleys would be fun, don't you think?" Vicki threw a questioning look at Callie.

"As long as it's in the water, I'm game." Although she knew she'd be terrible at it.

Pat and Vicki did most of the volleying. Kate and Callie tried, but the ball slipped through their hands or seemed to be just out of reach. The dog cavorted around them excitedly. Callie and Kate were sopping wet when they quit. Laughing, they staggered to the chairs on the beach.

"I always liked your place," Callie said.

"I knew your family from a distance. Sometimes Bobby would walk the shore, casting. His little sister usually tagged along." Callie's cousin Bobby was six years her senior. His younger sister, Jacqui, was four years older, insurmountable age gaps when Callie was a child.

"Bobby bought the place. He lives in California and rents it out to the rest of us."

"That must have been a bitter pill."

"Yes." This wasn't something she could talk about without emotion. The volleyball blurred as it rose and fell across the net.

Vicki and Pat appeared to be evenly matched. The dog lay down in the shallows and drank.

Kate said, "I'm very sorry."

"Thanks. Me too. Do you spend summers here?"

"Yes. My kids, who aren't kids anymore, come for a few weeks or weekends. Otherwise, Pat and I are here alone. How long are you staying?"

"Till Saturday. Have you known Vicki long?"

"A few years."

"I met her yesterday when she nearly ran me over with her boat. It seems like forever."

"Are you serious? Did that really happen?"

"Oh, yes." She told the story. "She's hung around ever since. I think she's trying to make up for nearly killing me. I hope you didn't meet her that way."

Kate laughed. "Nothing like that. Her brother built a place on the lake about three years ago."

"Looks like a hotel," she said.

"That seems to be the trend."

"What do you do here all summer?" Callie asked, truly curious, hoping it didn't sound prying.

"I write an advice column, which I can do anywhere. Pat teaches and has the summers off. We met on this lake. I was putting in my pier and she helped me."

"Really? If I wrote a letter, would you answer it?" She could hardly believe she'd said that. What would she write about? There was no advice to help her. She'd lost the cottage and she was going to lose the store.

"Of course. The local paper carries me," she said with a smile.

"Just kidding." Callie'd picked up the weekly paper when she stopped in town on her way. She'd have to look at the advice column.

Vicki and Pat were splashing through the water toward them, Pat balancing the volleyball in one hand. Water droplets glistened on the curly ends of her short sandy hair. Callie stood, ready to go.

"When I see the boys, I'll flag them down and come get you," Vicki said before turning to Kate and Callie. "Pat wants to ski."

"Good. Well, nice meeting you both." Callie started wading toward the cottage.

Vicki caught up with her. "What's the rush?"

"I'm expecting a call." She wasn't, of course. It was one of those convenient white lies that got her out of social situations when she wanted to leave.

"Did Kate tell you she's an advice columnist? I thought maybe she could help you."

"I don't think so."

Vicki pulled her into deeper water. "Cool off, girl. Life is too short to be so uptight."

Callie shook free and began swimming toward the cottage. As a kid, she swam across the lake regularly, but now after less than a hundred feet, she stopped to tread water. "I'm out of shape."

"Skiing will get you fit really fast."

Vicki was like a burr. She was less than a foot away, in Callie's face. Callie took a deep breath and went under. When her feet touched the bottom, she felt Vicki's mouth on hers. Her eyes popped open in shock and she pushed her away, rising to the surface in a stew of bubbles. Vicki broke the water at the same time.

"Just getting a sample," Vicki said with a grin.

Disoriented, Callie began to swim away. Vicki kept up with her. "Did I ask for that?" Callie said, heading for shore. She would wade the rest of the way.

"I guess I got the wrong vibes."

"What vibes did I give off to make you think I wanted that to happen?"

"Well, you came with me today."

"That means I want to kiss you? Where do you get off?"

"I'll wave the boys down if they come by. You'll just have to put up with me till then. I can't carry the cooler home."

"Why don't you go back to Kate's place and pick up your

cooler later?"

"Really? You want to get rid of me that badly?"

"I do." They had reached Callie's beach, and she threw herself in one of the chairs.

Vicki strutted to the boathouse and carried the cooler out. "I'll take it with me."

That would make her look callous to Kate and Pat. Did she care? She did. Besides, she wasn't angry anymore. It was just a kiss. Vicki had misread her, was all. "Oh, just wait with it till your nephews come by." She picked up her book and pretended to read.

Vicki took a beer out and sat on the cooler at the end of the pier. "Do you want one?" she asked.

"I don't like beer."

They sat in separate silence in the hot afternoon sun for what seemed an hour to Callie but was probably only ten minutes. "Look. I'll give you a ride home."

"No, thanks. I'll wait for the boys. I thought you had to catch a phone call."

"I do. I better go up." She was now thoroughly annoyed. Going up was the last thing she wanted to do and, of course, there was no phone call unless she made it. She could mix a drink, though, and take her cell phone back down. Maybe Vicki would be gone and if she wasn't, it was Callie's beach. Why should she be driven upstairs?

She could see Vicki on the pier from the cottage. She was either nursing the same beer or had taken out another. She called the store number and Marc picked it up on the fourth ring. "I was with a customer. How's it going?"

"There's this woman who won't leave me alone." She told him what had happened so far.

"Why fight it?" he said, laughing. "Go with the flow. How long has it been since you had a date anyway?"

"You forget that I date men," she said coolly, and he guffawed.

"Use that rod up your ass for fishing, honey. Have some

fun."

"Are you selling anything?" she asked.

"A swimming suit here, goggles there. I had an order for team swimwear. I also talked to an exercise equipment dealer."

"Great. I'm not spending any more money on that place."

"Hey, I'll talk to you later," he said. "I've got to go. Another customer."

"Wait, wait. How is Tawny?" Lucy's horse.

"And don't forget Randy." The horse's companion goat. "They're fat and sassy. They scare the piss out of me when they come thundering across the field."

She laughed. "Stay on the other side of the fence. Are you keeping Randy away from the grain?"

"Sometimes I'm lucky and Tawny goes through the gate first. Sometimes I'm not."

Randy shared the horse's grain whenever he could, but even she had trouble slamming the gate between them. When Tawny went into the enclosure, the goat squeezed through with him. "Thanks for taking care of the animals. I know it's not something you want to do."

"You should rename the cat Killer. He's disposed of at least fifty mice." Marc tended toward exaggeration.

"I suppose he's eating them." She feared he might get sick. He sat on her lap at night while she read or watched TV. He was good company. His name when she got him from the local humane association was Yellow Belly, which she'd shortened to Bell and then Bill.

"He never eats the whole carcass. He leaves certain parts lying around the house," he said dryly.

She hung up, wondering if he was right about the rod. Was she really such a stick-in-the-mud? She mixed herself a vodka and tonic and sat on the bench out front, waiting for Vicki to leave and thinking about how little she had dated since the divorce.

Dating had been an ordeal in itself, the getting to know someone all over again. What had made it intolerable were her kids, who had proved to be forbidding judges. Maybe she should try the Internet, but any date she made would still have to stand up to teenage scrutiny. It was easier to stay home or go out with friends.

Vicki's nephews picked her up, finally. From her beach chair Callie noticed a woman crossing the MasterCraft's wake on one ski. She was engulfed in a spray of water shot through with sunlight.

"Hi. I hope I'm not interrupting anything."

Startled, she looked up to see Kate and the dog. "Not at all. Sit down. Is that Pat skiing out there?" Junior bounded over to Callie and licked her face.

Kate called him to her side. "Sorry about that. He likes you. It is Pat. She and Vicki are such athletes. They put me to shame."

"Me too. Don't worry about Junior. I like dogs. I lost mine a couple of weeks ago."

Kate sat in the other chair and gave Callie a sympathetic look. "I lost Junior's predecessor, Arthur, a few years ago. Then this one showed up. Someone dumped him on our doorstep. Never found out who." Her eyes scanned Callie's face as if inviting her to talk. A short silence followed, till Kate glanced at her reading material. "How's the book?"

"*The Tortilla Curtain*? It's not an upper, but it's a good read."

"Someone who read it said just when you think nothing else can go wrong, it does."

"That's pretty much true. It's fueled by fear and desperation—the story of a yuppie couple and a pair of illegal immigrants."

"Don't tell me anymore," Kate said. "I want to read it. Are you here alone this week?"

"My kids are vacationing with my ex and his wife."

"Did they grow up on the lake too?"

"Until the cottage was sold. I may come back with them for a week before school starts."

Kate nodded. "And what do you do?" A fair question since Callie had asked the same about her.

"Well, nothing as glamorous as giving advice. I own a swim

shop with a friend in the Fox Cities." Mortgaged to the hilt, she could have added.

"I'll have to come look. I need a new swimsuit. We have a condo in the Fox Cities for the winter months. About that advice, it's not always so good. Just last week someone's wife found out her husband is gay and wanted to know what to do. They have three kids."

"What did you tell her?" she asked, fascinated.

"That he was unlikely to change. I suggested counseling for all of them. Of course, that won't alter the facts. It's sort of a cop-out."

"Talk about being caught between a rock and a hard place. Do you get many letters like that?"

"Where there is no good solution? Yes. Actually, I'm thinking about retiring."

She had a lovely smile, Callie thought, smiling back. "I bought a paper when I was in town." She fumbled in her lap for it. "I'm glad I did now."

Kate laughed. The lines etched on her face by the sun deepened. "Don't expect too much." Then she added, "Writing a column like this keeps me humble and grateful. Humble because people want my advice and grateful that I don't have some of their problems."

"I can't wait to read it." Flattered that Kate had confided in her, she asked, "Did Vicki tell you I asked her to leave?"

Kate nodded. "She's a little forward, which can be off-putting, but she's lots of fun."

A hint? Like Marc telling her to take some risks? But she'd looked forward to the quiet kind of entertainment—reading, swimming, sailing. "Actually, I need to make a decision." Why had she let Marc talk her into going into business with him? She'd had a perfectly good job with the county in child protection, albeit a heartbreaking one. She'd worked more hours than she'd wanted, which was really difficult when the kids were younger. No more hours than she put in now, though, for less money and bare benefits. She heaved a sigh. "I guess fun means something different to me. My business partner, Marc, told me to lighten up." You had to specify what kind of partner you were talking about these days.

"Well, I'll let you get back to your book." Kate got to her feet, and the dog sprang up beside her. She put a hand on his head.

"Would you like a drink? A vodka and tonic or something?" She didn't want her to go. She had this feeling that Kate could help her.

"Thanks, but we're eating out tonight and I'm driving."

"Thank you for coming over. I wish you'd stay." She liked this woman. She felt comfortable with her.

"You know that Vicki will put in here if I hang around. You might not be able to get rid of her this time. Besides, I have a few things to do before we go out."

"Of course you do. Maybe I'll see you before the week is over." She stood too, feeling for some reason that she should.

"You will."

She watched her go, guessing that Kate and Pat were life partners and wondering how that worked. With kids, with parents, with finances? Who do you leave the cottage to, for instance? That she cared surprised her.

She opened the paper and read the advice column. There was a letter from a guy who couldn't get a second date, even though he said he was nice looking, if a little short, and fun to be with. He had a good job and was in his mid-thirties. Kate told him to join some groups. She said there were a lot of women out there who never got asked out because they were a little heavy or tall or weren't considered good looking. Behind the face and figure there might be a very interesting and fun person. He should keep trying.

Callie thought of her friend, Sandy Clark, who was overweight. There were several men who confided in her, who went out to lunch with her to talk about their women troubles, who golfed with her, but who never asked her out on a real date—including Scott Trudeau. Sandy had introduced Callie to Scott.

He had been her last real date—a better than average looking guy, well-mannered and kind. Marc even liked him, and the kids treated him better than they treated any other man she'd dated. She went out with him for two months but when he began to get serious, she backed off. She still went out with him occasionally, usually for Friday night fish. Sometimes Sandy joined them.

She climbed into bed that night half in the bag. The sun, the wind and the drink again sent her spinning off into sleep. Vicki had not returned. Maybe she had gone out to eat with Kate and Pat. Regret that she hadn't been invited was her last thought.

The next morning she slept late, waking to the sound of motors. The sun slanted through the trees and into the windows, giving off a dusty light. She looked at her watch with disbelief. Nine forty. She'd missed the best part of the day, the quiet hours. No-wake hours were over.

When she went down to the lake half an hour later, she noticed the MasterCraft floating in the deeper water about a hundred feet west of the pier. Vicki stood between the seats, casting toward shore. She waved.

Callie lifted a hand. She set her book bag down, pushed the kayak into the lake and, hugging the shore, paddled in the opposite direction. No one was on the beach at Kate and Pat's place. She continued around half the lake and cut across when there was a lull between motorboats, returning along the shore. If she'd been up earlier, she might have seen a heron or egret. Now only the gulls hung around, taking to the air when a boat came too close.

Despite her reservations, she was glad to see that Vicki hadn't left. "Catch anything?" she asked.

"Yep. Catch and release. Do you fish?"

"Nope." She placed the paddle across the kayak and considered the things she didn't do that Vicki did—fish and water ski and drink beer.

"Do you eat fish?"

"Sure."

"How about dinner tonight at my place? Kate and Pat will be

there. Salmon on the grill."

"What time?"

"I'll come get you around five. I'm picking them up too."

"What can I bring?"

"Just yourself."

Wine, she thought. It was all she had to offer.

The day went by too quickly. Sunbaked and water soaked, she went upstairs to shower and change around four. All day she'd watched Vicki's boat and others circle the lake, towing skiers or tubers behind them. Annoyed because the noise and props drove away wildlife and churned up the water, she felt like shooting holes into their hulls. What a waste of gas.

She was swinging her bare feet in the water when Vicki pulled up to the pier at five. Callie handed her the bottle of wine and got into the boat.

Vicki held the chilled chardonnay up to the light and read the label—Chateau Ste. Michelle, the best Callie had. "Hey, thanks. How was your day?"

She put on her sandals as she thought about her day, although it was no doubt a rhetorical question. "Good. Can I ask you something?"

"Sure. Anything." Vicki eyed her over the tops of her sunglasses.

"Don't you get bored driving mindlessly around the lake all day?"

"A little. It would have been nice to have had you in the boat with me." Vicki backed away from the pier and idled forward toward the east end of the lake. "I have something to say to you."

Callie waited.

"I want to apologize for yesterday, kissing you like that. It was impulsive. Can we put it behind us and spend some time together?"

"Sure." She felt like a prude, the kind of person she detested. "What do you do for a living?" she asked, thinking she should find out more about her.

"Marketing." They were coming up to the pier where Kate and Pat waited. "I work for CBF Papers."

"I thought you lived in Illinois," she said, surprised.

"The boys do, not me." Vicki stood and reached for a pier post, but Pat beat her to it. "Hop in."

"Are we drinking already?" Pat asked, spying the wine. She held up a six-pack of beer. "It's cold."

"Let's wait till we at least get to Vicki's," Kate said.

Vicki eased the boat out on the lake and pushed the throttle partway. Callie welcomed the breeze the speed generated and the noise of the engine, which discouraged conversation. She had little to say. However, she'd brought along *The Tortilla Curtain*, which she'd read that afternoon. She fished it out of her bag and handed it to Kate.

"Thanks." Kate turned it over and read the jacket copy. "I promise to finish it before you leave."

"No hurry," Callie said.

The boys were splashing in the water, throwing a ball back and forth with a couple of other guys. "Mom and Dad are coming tomorrow," Brady said as Vicki drove onto the Shore Lander and turned off the engine.

"Yeah?" Vicki climbed on the pier and offered a hand to the others. Kate was the only one who took it. "What did they say?"

"Just that they'll be here in the afternoon. We're going out to eat tomorrow night." He leaped to catch the tennis ball.

Vicki nodded. She led the others up the stairs to the log house. A porch wrapped around the main floor. "Grab a seat while I get the food and drink."

Callie sat in a green wicker chair and pitched her voice low as Kate took the one next to hers and Pat went to help. "I remember when there were only a few places on the lake, when cottages had one bathroom, no garage, no big boats."

"I know. We considered ourselves lucky to have running water," Kate said quietly.

"We swam during the day and played games like hide-and-seek or cards at night. I still swim and play cards. And read. There was no TV."

"Sometimes on rainy days I think it's nice to watch a movie," Kate said.

The screen door slapped and Pat and Vicki emerged, carrying trays with drinks and a plate of appetizers. "Vodka and tonic for you two, beer for Pat and me. And snacks." They set the trays on the glass-topped wicker table.

"Want to see the place, Callie?" Vicki asked.

"Now?" Thirsty, she tried not to gulp. The Mexican roll-up she sampled went down easy. So did the chips with guacamole.

"When you finish your drink, I'll take you around."

The boys bounded up the hill and stood dripping on the porch, eating the food. "Hey, there's more in the kitchen. Eat that." Vicki followed them inside and came out when they did. They headed back down to the lake.

"If I don't watch them, they'll eat everything."

The drink was lulling Callie to sleep. She blinked and sat up straighter.

"Come on. I'll show you the house." Vicki took her hand and led her inside.

The living room and dining area and kitchen were one huge room, separated by counters and a table. Rustic furniture and a massive fireplace defined the living area. A hall led to a bathroom and two bedrooms, one with its own bath. Upstairs was an open loft with two more bedrooms and a bathroom off it. Skylights lightened the wood interior.

"This is my room." Vicki threw open the last door and walked inside. It looked like the other rooms—rustic double bed and dresser, one chair, huge walk-in closet.

"Nice," she said.

"You don't like the place, do you?" Vicki smiled wryly.

Startled, Callie met her keen gaze. "It took a lot of trees to make this house." For some reason, she wanted to laugh.

"I know. It's kind of tasteless, isn't it?"

"I didn't say that." She would never be so rude. Then she lost control and burst out laughing. Immediately contrite, she said,

"I'm sorry."

"What's so funny?" Vicki looked stricken.

"Nothing. I don't know. Sometimes when I drink I laugh at stupid things."

"Well, maybe you should have another drink. I like to hear you laugh. Come on." Vicki put a hand on her shoulder and steered her downstairs.

By the time they sat down to eat in the huge room at the immense table, Callie was doing a lot of laughing. Vicki drained the pasta and set it on the table with the grilled salmon. Pat put salad in their bowls and poured the bottle of wine Callie had brought.

Kate raised a glass. "To the cook."

The lights on the boat glowed like fireflies when Vicki took them home after eleven. Callie's memory of the rest of the evening after dinner was sketchy. They'd sat on the porch and then on the beach, talking, with a glass of wine at everyone's elbow, except Kate's. And everyone but Kate seemed a little fuzzy around the edges. Even though Callie tried very hard to enunciate each word, the consonants came out slurred.

Vicki dropped off Kate and Pat first. Kate steadied Pat as she stepped on the pier, and Callie got the feeling that Kate wasn't happy with the drinking. She'd stuck with water after the first glass of wine. Callie told herself that she would do the same from now on or not even take that first drink, but even as she vowed not to, she knew she would.

When they returned to Callie's pier, Vicki turned off the engine and tied the boat to a post. "Don't you want to sit here and look at the sky?" The moon was up, its light blotting out a lot of stars. "It's so nice out."

The air brushed her skin like feathers, but even so, Callie longed to dive into bed. "Thanks for the great evening, but I've had too much sun, too much alcohol. What I need is sleep."

"Let me walk you up the hill."

"Hey, I'm as steady as you are. I'd have to walk you back

down."

"We could walk up and down all night. Wouldn't that be fun? I've got the flashlight, though," Vicki said, clinching her offer.

Even with the flashlight, they stumbled. At the door, Callie said, "I'll turn on the outside light for you."

Vicki followed her inside. "Now thish ish how a cottage should look," she said.

"Thanks for everything, but it's time to go home, Vicki."

"Let me stay."

"Remember the boys." Callie closed the door and Vicki turned and stumbled into the night, her flashlight wavering.

However, she only went as far as the bench out front where she lay down and pointed the flashlight at the sky.

When Callie woke up in the morning, Vicki was still there, flat on her back with her arms across her chest. She stared at Vicki for a moment before hurrying to the bathroom to relieve herself. After, she stepped out of her clothes and got into the shower.

The pounding on the door reached her ears through the falling water. She pulled aside the shower curtain and yelled the obvious. "I'm taking a shower."

"I have to pee," Vicki called back. "Let me in. I won't look."

"Find a tree," she shouted and closed the curtain. There were woods around the cottage. No manicured lawn, just tall grass and ferns and bunches of wildflowers.

Vicki was gone when she came out. She ate breakfast and went down to the lake with another book, *World Without End*, Ken Follett's sequel to *The Pillars of the Earth*. It was over a thousand pages long. She was in no danger of finishing it before the end of the week.

Friday evening Kate sat on the pier next to Callie and handed her *The Tortilla Curtain*. "You described it perfectly. The ending was a nice touch, wasn't it? It brought everything full circle."

Callie knew her face glowed with sun and pleasure. She hadn't talked to anyone since Vicki had pounded on the bathroom door.

"It did. Good to see you." It would have been good to see anyone. "I subscribed to the weekly newspaper, the one with your advice column in it."

A slow smile stretched across Kate's face. "Did you? Do you want to go out for fish with us tonight?"

"Vicki, too?"

"I heard she spent a night on the bench outside your cottage."

"Yes. I didn't know she was still there till morning. I feel kind of bad about it." She hadn't seen Vicki since. "I guess I was at a loss as to how to deal with her. I haven't seen her on the lake either."

"She went home the next day. I think she's probably in Europe right now."

"Europe!" she repeated. "Is she vacationing there now?"

"She travels all over the world. It's part of her job. She was only here to keep an eye on the boys. So, want to go out for fish around five? We'll pick you up." Kate smiled.

"Yes, I'd like that." She was trying to picture Vicki at work, thinking she must present a very different persona. She didn't realize she was frowning.

"Is something wrong?" Kate asked.

"Why didn't she tell me she was leaving?" But she had, she recalled. She'd said she'd be at the lake till her brother and his wife arrived.

"I had the impression you didn't want her around," Kate said softly.

"I didn't, not all the time, not always in my space." She looked at Kate for understanding.

"I know. You'll see her again, I'm sure. She lives in the Fox Cities too."

Of course, she does, she thought. That's where CBF was located. "If you talk to her, tell her I said hello." How dumb. It was a wonder Vicki had hung around at all. She must have been desperate for companionship or determined to make up for the near accident.

The Moose Inn was smoke-filled and crammed shoulder-to-shoulder with people waiting for a table. Callie and Kate and Pat edged up to the bar and sat when a couple abandoned their stools. They ordered drinks and ate the popcorn the bartenders put in front of them and talked over the din of voices.

"The food must be really good," Callie said loudly, "if all these people are willing to wait so long for it."

"The popcorn is good, too," Pat said, signaling for another beer. "Want one?" she asked Callie.

"I'll buy. You drove." She felt torn. A smoky bar was not where she wanted to spend her last night here. She longed to be out on the lake in the kayak, but she'd been lonely when Kate stopped by and was still curious about the two of them. Right now, though, she couldn't think of a question that didn't sound nosy.

When Pat's name was called, they followed the hostess into the dining room. It was quieter in the corner where they sat to eat. "I saw you sailing today," Kate said. "You're brave to be out there with the speedboats after what happened."

"It was my last day." She felt enormously sad about having to leave the next morning.

"I remember how I hated leaving. I rented a cabin down the lake before I met Kate." Pat gave Kate a smile, which Kate returned.

This had been Callie's lake, her cottage. It was far more difficult to give up what once was yours than to give up what you never owned, she thought. "You're a lucky one."

Pat and Kate exchanged smiles again. If they saw her envy, they gave no sign of it. "What's the name of your store?"

"Aquatics, Inc." Marc had wanted to incorporate. He'd thought they might be sued if someone drowned with their goggles on or their fins carried them too far.

"We'll come see you there," Kate said as the waitress put their food down.

When they dropped her off at the cottage, Callie walked down the hill. She heard a dog bark when she stretched out on the pier. Probably Junior, she thought. A whippoorwill called repetitively from across the lake, and a dazzling array of stars hung in the dark sky. The moon came up late now that it was on the wane. Bats flitted across the water ignoring the mosquitoes that circled her head and eventually drove her upstairs.

Chapter 2

The house was quiet. No kids to greet her. Only the cat twining around her legs, meowing. She stopped to pick up mouse parts with a paper towel and throw them outside, then continued to the bedroom with her bag. On her way back to the kitchen, she turned on public radio and picked up the cat. His ear twitched as she crooned to him, telling him how handsome he was and how much she'd missed him.

She'd dreaded coming home. This is how the place would feel when the kids left for college in a few years. Maybe she should take in a renter. She'd had this idea before. The whole upstairs was empty. Nicky, the previous owner, had turned the area into a small apartment, equipping one of the three rooms with kitchen appliances and carving from the other two a bathroom. But what if Callie disliked whoever moved in? The kids might not want someone in their house. They sure hadn't liked her choice of men. She'd had this argument, too.

Through the window, she saw Tawny in the field with Randy glued to his side, heads down, eating the life out of the pasture. She'd go out in a bit and give Tawny some grain. He wasn't much bigger than a pony, a sun-bleached palomino. Lucy showed him in 4-H.

The cat lay sprawled on her lap, purring loudly. "They never should have named you Yellow Belly," she said. "I suppose someone thought it was funny. You're no coward, are you?" He wasn't even afraid of dogs. He'd swatted her old dog whenever he came near.

Another dog? There was a thought, but she didn't want to walk a dog in below zero weather or even twenty above. She'd have to take a dog to the store too, and she couldn't leave one alone overnight. Nope. A dog was out of the picture right now. The dog they'd lost a few weeks ago had spent his days sleeping. A younger animal would be more demanding.

"Oh well," she said to the cat, "I've got to go." She gave him a treat, filled his bowls with fresh food and water and slipped out the back door while he was eating.

She walked toward the fence, calling Tawny. The palomino's head jerked up like a giraffe. He turned to see her better and galloped toward her with Randy hot on his tail.

Dan, the neighboring farmer who owned the goat, also owned the barn that had once been part of the property. He used it for storing machinery and hay. Sometimes she went inside just to smell the hay.

She'd bought the house and five acres from Nicky Hennessey, a photographer and, she suspected, a lesbian. Nicky had purchased a condo with Beth Forrester, a local attorney. She'd seen Nicky's work on the walls of banks, in restaurants and galleries. If she had a little spare cash, there was a watercolor she'd love to buy of the lilac bushes blooming next to the shed out in the field.

She just managed to slam the gate behind Tawny before Randy got there. The goat's hooves clanged against the steel bars of the barrier. More than once she'd turned around to find him rearing up, his pointy, bearded face level with hers. It still scared the shit out of her. She put grain in Tawny's feed tub and threw a handful of oats to the goat.

It began to rain as she drove into town. Mist hovered above

the road where the drops cooled the blacktop. The humidity made her hair even more unruly, so that sometimes she thought she looked like a madwoman. She pulled up in front of the swim shop and drew a deep breath to ward off the suffocating effect the place had on her. There was another car parked out front in addition to hers and Marc's.

The door jangled as she went inside. Marc looked up from a catalog and grinned when he saw her. "Home from the hinterland."

She noticed no one else in the store. He gestured toward the dressing rooms when he saw her looking. "Your friend, Sandy Clark."

She smiled, and then her eye caught the lineup of exercise equipment at the back of the shop. "How much did that cost?" she asked quietly.

"Nothing. It's on consignment." He came around the counter. A lean man with dark hair and eyes, he smiled widely, showing large white teeth. When she first met him, she'd thought he looked a little predatory. "What do you think?"

"How will anyone know we've got this stuff?" They couldn't sell it if no one came looking.

"Oh, ye of little faith," he said.

Callie's head jerked toward the noise outside the front window. She thought the truck was coming through the glass at them, just like the speedboat had borne down on her, and let out a little shriek.

Marc hurried to the door, calling back over his shoulder. "It's the sign company."

She sat on the bench near the counter, watching, until Sandy came out of the dressing room area. "Find anything you like?"

"Hey, is that really you, girlfriend?" Sandy carried several suits over her arm. "How was vacation?"

"Great. How is work?"

"Not so great." Sandy's expressive face beamed at her. "You know, I usually look like a whale in a swimming suit, but this"—she held up a black one-piece—"actually is not too bad. I look more like a manatee." She laughed.

She suppressed a laugh and went behind the counter. "Come on, Sandy. Don't put yourself down."

Sandy handed her the suit and continued conversationally, "I've joined a water aerobics class at the Y."

"Good for you." Callie wrote up the sale and took Sandy's charge card.

"What's all that noise out there?"

"They're putting up a new sign."

"I saw the ad in the paper—ten percent off everything. I'd buy one of those exercise bikes, but there's not much room in my apartment. Besides, how would I get it home?"

"Marc would deliver it free of charge."

"I'll come back and try one out. I have to go to work now."

She followed Sandy to the door, curious about the sign, belatedly thinking that she'd better find out how much it cost. Marc stood near the truck, talking to the man on the ground. Their necks craned upward toward the two men in the box guiding the sign into place. How had this all gotten done during the one week she was gone, she wondered. She watched with arms crossed as the two men fastened the sign to its base. It read *Aquatics, Inc.* and under that *Swimwear And Exercise Equipment.*

When the truck left, she and Marc stared at the sign. "Well, what do you think?" he asked. "Colorful, isn't it?"

"How much?" she asked.

"Oh, don't worry about that. We have a third partner who is paying for it."

"How can you sell a partnership without my signature?" She followed him into the store.

"I didn't." He walked backward, hands in the air. There was a fluid grace about Marc in all his movements, even this one. He could be disarming, but she was having none of it.

"So what happened?"

He slipped behind the counter and snatched up the phone on the first ring, saying, "Aquatics, Inc. Swimwear and exercise equipment…Yes, she's here and she's mad as hell. You explain."

His eyebrows shot up as he thrust the phone at Callie. "Our third partner."

"Hey, Callie. How's it going?" Vicki said.

"You're the third partner?" she asked incredulously.

"Yes. I went in to see the place and decided to invest. You've got a nice little shop there, Callie."

"We've got a nearly bankrupt little shop here." Would she never get rid of this woman, who had somehow insidiously invaded her life? Should she be grateful? "I thought you were in Europe."

"Who told you that?"

"Kate."

"Nope, but I'm going next week."

When she hung up, she threw a bleak look at Marc. "How did this happen?"

He told her that Vicki had come into the store asking questions and offering solutions while Callie was gone. She had a lot of contacts. "That's how the sign went up so fast." The exercise equipment he had already ordered.

"I leave for one week and come back to all these changes I never authorized. We're already wallowing in debt. Now we'll be swallowed up by it." She stomped around in a little circle.

"We're saved," he said. "Look on the bright side for once, Cal." He hesitated before continuing. "We're going to have classes here for those interested in buying the exercise equipment. See those five bikes?" He pointed toward them. "They're for cycling classes. I thought maybe you could teach, since you've taken spinning classes at the Y."

She stared at him, nonplussed. "What? Who am I going to teach?"

"Oh, there are at least eight people interested, including your friend Sandy. I figured Thursday evening would be a good time since we're open late anyway. The class would be from six to six thirty. The Saturday class would be from ten to ten thirty." He gave her a rueful smile and lifted his shoulders, spreading his hands in a why not gesture. "What do you think? Those who sign up get fifteen percent off any piece of equipment and free delivery."

She stared at him, open-mouthed before laughing a little in disbelief. "You've already signed these people up, haven't you?"

He nodded, looking a little nervous. "This way they're committed. Otherwise, they'll blow it off."

That was how she found herself in a noon cycling class at the Y. She was still a member and occasionally swam laps or took yoga or aerobic classes. The instructor was trying to kill them, she decided, as she hovered over the seat, straightened, and hovered again, turning the resistance up every minute or less. They were now on the highest level. Her calves burned.

"Grab a drink, back off on the tension and sit down. We'll take a heart check and then we're going to sprint—thirty seconds on and thirty seconds off," the instructor said.

Sitting often proved more painful than standing. Callie pushed herself to the back of the narrow seat, trying to take the pressure off her crotch that even padded biking shorts failed to protect. Had she been so sensitive as a kid when she rode a bike everywhere? She put fingers to her neck. Her heart rate was still on the chart. She slugged back some water and grasped the handlebars, ready when the instructor said, "Go!"

Fifteen minutes into the class and she was already watching the clock. Little puddles of sweat lay on the floor under the two men in the first row. In front of her, a woman's butt bounced as she sprinted. Callie closed her eyes and willed the hands on the clock to move.

After class, she walked slowly down the stairs. One of the guys clattered past her. "Good workout, huh? You okay?"

"Oh, yes." She forced a smile. "Just a little stiff." Her knees ached, and she wasn't nearly as old as him.

"The more you ride, the easier it gets," he said reassuringly, disappearing into the men's locker room.

As she reached for the door to the women's locker room, it flew open, bumping her shoulder.

"Oh, I'm so sorry. Are you all right? Callie, is that you?"

Her gaze flew to the woman's face. "You have an uncanny knack for running into me."

"Don't I, though." Vicki followed her into the locker room. "I've never seen you here before. Were you cycling?"

"Yes."

"You can cycle at the shop."

"I was brushing up on my skills, so that I can teach a class at the shop," she said with a wry smile. "Now if you'll excuse me, I have to shower and get back to work."

Vicki bit her lower lip, a gleam in her eyes. "Hey, I'll see you on Thursday. I'm taking the class."

"Don't you cycle here?"

"Yeah, but I'd like to have a machine at home."

"Great," Callie said with irony she knew would be missed.

She parked in front of the shop next to another vehicle. The door was locked. It crossed her mind that Marc might be in danger. Someone could be robbing the store—hardly worth the bother—or in the process of murdering him. Marc had a penchant for drawing trouble to himself. Not long ago he'd been beaten up outside the gay bar for fooling around with another man's lover. Marc denied he'd done any such thing, but he had a history of not being able to resist a challenge.

She drove around to the alley behind the store and opened the door with her key. Marc came hurrying out of the dressing room straightening his hair. "Callie! Back already?"

"Yep." She sat on the bench near the dressing room, waiting for someone else to come out.

When the man did emerge, carrying several swimsuits and cycling shorts, he smiled innocently at her, said, "Hello," and turned to Marc. "I'll take these two."

"Callie, this is Ronnie Schwartz. He signed up for a cycling class. Callie is my partner. She's teaching those classes."

"Great idea. I'm buying these cycling shorts to protect my butt." He held them up to show her and gave Marc his charge card. "Think I'll need them?"

"I don't know since I'm not a man. I need them."

Both men laughed a little. She'd decided to scream at Marc after Ronnie left. Marc ran the charge and bagged the clothes. "See you on Saturday," he said.

"Hold a bike for me." Ronnie waved a hand and Marc ran after him. She couldn't hear what they said to each other when Marc unlocked the door.

"I, um, know Ronnie from way back when." Marc walked toward her, smiling nervously.

"I see." Instead of accusing him of locking the door during business hours, a laugh burbled out of her. "You know him well. Next time put a sign on the door saying you're out to lunch and when you'll be back. I thought maybe you'd been murdered."

He sat next to her and gave her a guileless grin. "Quite the opposite." And they both laughed.

"I'm putting an ad in the paper for a boarder. The whole upstairs is empty." She needed to stop drawing on the divorce settlement. Tim's insurance covered the kids but not her. She had a major medical policy through the store. He paid support and that helped with food and clothing.

"Yeah?"

"I'll ask for a female boarder. The kids never liked the men I dated. They only tolerated Scott, and even you liked him."

"The kids don't want another father. When are they coming home anyway?"

"A couple weeks before school starts."

He eyed her seriously. "You need to get a life, Callie."

"Well, I can always proposition a customer." She burst into laughter and only stopped when he slapped her on the back.

"It wasn't that funny," he said. "Ronnie and I used to be lovers."

Thursday at the shop, she checked her e-mail and found a reply to her ad. A woman named Meg Klein. She shot a message back, giving directions and her cell number, suggesting Friday or Saturday after six or Sunday morning around ten. The afternoon dragged by. A few customers came in, mostly older women trying on swimsuits.

It seemed weeks had passed since she'd been at the lake, not days. Around five, Marc breezed through the door with a sub and fries for her dinner. "I figured you needed sustenance before this class." Their agreement had been that she would work at the shop for a small salary while he kept his job at The Print Shop. Neither made much money.

By six, four people were on the bikes. Sandy Clark was on one, Ronnie on another, her old boyfriend, Scott, was on a third, and Vicki rode the fourth. Callie nervously faced them on bike number five. Others in the store stood by watching, talking with Marc and each other. She'd never seen so many people in the place at one time.

Glancing at Vicki in her biking shorts and shoes, she thought she was probably the one who should be teaching the class. Callie was torn between working Vicki hard and going easy because of Sandy. Already her crotch hurt. If she did much of this, maybe she'd develop calluses.

She said, "Go at your own pace. That's what they tell us at the Y. If you don't want to stand, sit. If you don't want to increase the resistance, don't. If you don't feel up to sprinting, go slower. It's up to you. Turn the resistance to three on the knob and warm up for a couple of minutes."

She took them through all the paces she'd been put through by the instructors at the Y—standing, climbing hills by putting on resistance, sprinting, doing jumps by alternately sitting and standing. Sweat poured off Sandy and Scott, pooling at their feet. The back of Callie's shirt clung to her, while Vicki and Ronnie chatted as they pedaled effortlessly. Her inability to wear them down annoyed her, and she called for a standing sprint. "If this is your first time, don't try it." She couldn't sustain it, though. Twenty seconds later, she told them to sit and started the cool down. Sandy Clark's face was beet red, and Callie wondered if her friend would ever want to ride again, much less buy one of the bikes.

After stretching exercises, she walked over to Sandy. "My legs are wobbly. How are yours?"

"Shaking, but that was a good workout. I'd like to buy a bike, but I'm afraid I won't ride it at home. I need a class like this to motivate me."

Callie was about to tell her she could take cycling at the Y when Marc came over. "We can do this once a week on Thursday nights. We'll have to charge, though. Are you interested?"

"Are you sure we don't need a license or something?" Callie asked.

"I'll look into it," he said smoothly, "but let's schedule Sandy in on Thursdays. We'll go forty-five minutes. Make it worthwhile."

Callie gave him a searing look. This was supposed to be a two-time thing.

Scott stood nearby, wiping off his bike as Callie had instructed. "Hey, I'd come," he said. "How are the kids, Callie?"

"They're on vacation with their dad."

"Ah," he said. "You're a free woman."

"Yeah. Lucky me." She thought maybe he was going to ask her out, but he turned to talk to Sandy.

"Hey, lucky woman," Vicki said in her ear. "That was fun. Are we going to do it again?"

"You'll be in Europe," Callie said, thinking her life had gone from boring to hectic.

"I'll be back. Want to go out? Have a drink? Eat dinner?" Vicki asked.

"I ate dinner. What I want to do is go home and take care of the animals."

"It's okay," Marc said. "You can go." He was taking down names for next Thursday's class. "We might have to have two classes."

"Are you sure we should be using these bikes like this?" she whispered in his ear. "They aren't ours." She felt he had taken over not only the shop but her as well.

"It'll be fine," he assured her and waved her off.

"What animals do you have?" Vicki asked as Callie picked up

the backpack she used as a carryall.

"A cat, a horse and a goat."

"Wow," she said.

"I live about eight miles out of town." If she meant to discourage Vicki, this wasn't the way to do it.

"My car is outside."

"I have to get up early tomorrow."

"So do I."

She looked into Vicki's gold-flecked eyes and thought, why not? "Okay. Come see the cat and horse and goat." Maybe Randy would put his hooves on her shoulders and scare her away or maybe he would lower his head and butt her.

Vicki held her ground as the horse and goat galloped toward her. She was supposed to close the gate behind Tawny as directed. When she slammed it shut and turned around, she found herself face-to-face with the bearded goat. Rigid with fear, she shrieked and shrieked as Randy danced on his hind legs, his pointed face in hers.

Callie laughed out loud, even though she could have been looking at herself. Randy scared her silly, too. She pulled Vicki backward toward the other gate, and the goat's front hooves came down on the metal rungs of the panel that separated him from Tawny.

"You set me up," Vicki said in a mildly accusing voice. She was shaking.

Still laughing, Callie put her hands on her knees, trying to catch her breath. Finally, she managed to say, "I know. I'm sorry."

"You're not sorry. You wouldn't be laughing." But then hysteria set in and they both leaned against the fence, howling, doubled over almost in pain.

Callie was the first to sober. "We have to open the gate and let Tawny out on pasture."

"Not me," Vicki said. "I don't have to do anything."

Callie entered the pen where Tawny was pressed against the

gate nosing the goat. The animals were making snuffling noises. She pushed the horse away and pulled the gate inward so that he could thunder out onto pasture. "I can't wait till Lucy comes home. This is her horse."

"Her goat, too?"

"No, he belongs to Dan who owns the barn. Horses are herd animals. Tawny would be lonely without Randy."

"Aptly named. I thought he was trying to mount me." Which set Callie laughing again. When Vicki said, "Hey, it wasn't that funny," Callie recalled Marc saying the same thing about Ronnie. It only made her laugh harder.

If Vicki was hoping something would come of the evening, she must have been disappointed, Callie thought as she lay in bed that night. Still stricken by occasional bouts of laughter, her insides hurt.

Meg Klein gave her a call on Saturday. "I'll be there right around six. Is that okay?"

"Do you think you can find it?" She was at the store. The morning customers who had come to watch the cycling class had stayed on for another, scheduled on the spot by Marc because of all the interest. But it was Callie who instructed both classes, and her calves were cramping.

"Oh, yes, I've been there before."

"Really?"

"I boarded a horse with Nicky Hennessey when she owned the place. You bought the property from Nicky, didn't you?"

She had, of course. There'd been no horses at the time, just the fenced-in field and pen next to the barn. "My daughter has a horse. Right now he has a goat for a companion. I wish it were a horse."

Meg chuckled. "You don't like goats?"

"I don't like him jumping on me."

Another laugh. "A male goat?"

"He's been altered."

"Sometimes it doesn't make much difference. I'll see you

later. Looking forward."

"Me, too."

The cycling classes went well. The participants were all Marc's friends, and although she rode them hard, she saw no puddles on the floor, no one wiping off excessive sweat with the towels provided. Instead, they chattered like girls. If you're really working hard, you don't have the breath for idle prattle, she thought, and she ended the class with a series of standing sprints. She figured she wore herself out, not them.

When she left, young men surrounded Marc who, with clipboard in hand, was holding forth on the benefits of exercise. He waved her off. "Go, sweetie. I've got everything under control."

She stepped outside into the humid heat of the afternoon. The next thing she knew she was in her driveway, having completely spaced the ride home. From a distance, she heard a tractor chugging and guessed Dan was cutting hay. Sometimes she and the kids helped him load the bales on a wagon and put them in the barn. He never charged her for the hay she used.

After changing clothes, she got the riding mower out of the garage, checked the oil and gas and climbed on. This was Tony's chore, and she'd let it slide, hoping it would wait till he came home. It took close to an hour to mow the front, side and back lawns. She bounced across the rough ground over the endless tunnels the moles had dug, creeping along in low gear. If she mowed any faster, the long grass killed the engine. She figured she'd get done just before Meg arrived.

She'd spent her Friday evening cleaning the upstairs. It looked plain and poor to her, the furnished rooms small and boxy. The rough plank flooring squeaked underfoot, and the faded flowered wallpaper smelled of age. She'd dusted the furniture and wood floors. The problem would be explaining to Tony, who at fifteen wanted to live upstairs and have his private space. She was afraid he might move in with his dad if she took this away from him.

With Tony on her mind, she paid little attention to what she was mowing, and on her last swath a cloud of yellow jackets stormed out of the ground under the mower. The first sting alerted her. It burned into her leg like an electric shock, causing her to shriek. She batted the insects off her legs and arms and jammed the Simplicity into high gear. When it was away from the nest, she threw the machine into neutral, jumped off and ran, still screaming, still swatting. Her heart hammered long after the wasps ceased their pursuit. Yellow jackets had been known to kill those they attacked. Tonight when it was dark and they'd all returned to their hole, she'd spray it with wasp and hornet killer.

From a distance she waited for the yellow jackets hovering around the mower to leave. Only then did she put the machine away in the garage. The mowed grass, gone to seed, lay in clumps across the expanse of yard. Callie wasn't into raking. She didn't care about a manicured lawn. She liked the occasional bunches of wildflowers that popped up, like daisies, and the ever present dandelions.

She went into the old farmhouse, took off her clothes and stepped into the shower. Angry looking welts were popping out on her arms and legs. A yellow jacket doesn't die when it stings, like a honeybee does. It continues to attack. When she turned off the shower, she thought she heard a car and quickly pulled on shorts and a T-shirt. Running fingers through her hair, she hurried outside.

A woman with long, enviable legs was climbing out of an old F-250 truck that shone with care. Wisps of blond hair had escaped a high ponytail and framed her face. When she smiled, her gray eyes lit up. She wore short shorts and a T-shirt with a picture of a horse on the front and the words Buy American under it. When she turned, the back read American Quarter Horse Association.

Callie stared at her admiringly for a moment before holding out a hand. "You're Meg? I just got out of the shower. A band of yellow jackets attacked me when I was mowing." She gestured at the yard.

"Mean as sin, aren't they?" Meg's gaze traveled over her and

Callie grew hot. She wanted to cover the unsightly welts. Meg shaded her eyes and turned toward the field where Tawny and Randy stood in the open-sided shed that protected them from the weather. "The horse and goat?"

"Tawny and Randy. It's like they're stuck together with invisible glue."

"They hate being alone. Horses do anyway. I wouldn't like being shut in a pasture without any company. Would you?"

Callie laughed a little too hard. "Hadn't thought about it, actually. Want to see the upstairs?"

"Sure. Nicky's younger sister lived up there."

"How well did you know Nicky?" she asked as they walked toward the old house.

"Pretty well. We're still good friends."

The cat met them in the kitchen and wound himself around Callie's legs. She bent to pick him up. "This is Yellow Belly. We call him Bill."

Meg laughed, a throaty sound. "Is he a yellow belly?"

"Not really. He came already named." She gave the cat a treat and he hunched over his bowl. In the middle of the floor lay the innards of some poor mouse. "Oh, Bill," she said as if this were a rare occurrence. Embarrassed, she picked up the body parts with a plastic bag and put them in the garbage. "I hope you're not scared of mice."

"Actually, the only place I don't want to see mice is in my bed."

The comment endeared her to Callie. "I've never had one in mine, but I can't make any promises."

They climbed the enclosed stairs to the second floor. Already Callie wanted her to move in. She thought even the kids would like her. She sighed, though, when she reached the top step and looked around. She stood aside to let Meg into the kitchenette that branched off into the two smaller bedrooms and bath. "This is it. You know, I could take the wallpaper off and paint the walls." It was a feeble offer, one she hoped Meg wouldn't take her up on.

Meg walked through the rooms and returned to where Callie stood. "Don't bother. It'll do as is. The price is right." At two hundred fifty a month, it was a bargain. "There's one more thing, though. I still have a horse. We're a package deal."

At this point, she would have considered reducing the rent to induce Meg to stay. Instead, she forced herself to say, "For a hundred more, he can move in too. That doesn't include grain and hay, though." Maybe her money worries were over.

Meg gave her a beautiful smile and closed the deal. "Brittle will be happy here."

Callie stared at the smile as the corners of her mouth jerked upward. "Maybe I can give Randy back to Dan." That would be a bright spot, she thought, not caring if she'd charged enough.

Downstairs, Callie wrote a receipt for the check Meg gave her.

"Is it okay if I get my horse now?"

"Sure."

"Great."

Callie watched her walk to her truck, envying her long, tanned legs and the blond hair that shone in the sun.

That night after dinner she took her wine out to the front porch and watched evening fall. Lightning bugs flickered in the grass. Disturbing images of Meg ran through her mind—the sensual mouth, the wide eyes.

Sunday morning she awoke to a vehicle rumbling down the gravel driveway. She glanced at the clock, surprised to see it was close to nine, then leaned over enough to raise the blind. The motor home parked out by the garage meant her parents were back from their travels. She jumped out of bed and pulled on shorts as her mother unlocked the door and called her name.

"Hi, sweetie, we're back. I'll make the coffee."

Yawning, she walked barefoot into the kitchen. "Hey, Mom. How was the trip?" She'd gotten a postcard from every stop, it seemed. "Haven't you been home yet?" Her mother looked like she'd just gotten out of bed, too. Her dyed reddish brown hair was flattened on one side as if she'd pressed up against the window.

Her mom pointed toward the open door. Through the screen they could see the RV. "That's home."

"Where's Dad?" The smell of coffee filled the room.

"Out looking at the horses. Did you buy another one? Give me a hug, honey."

She moved into her mother's embrace, smelling the familiar odor of her cologne, Chanel No. 5. Even with her eyes shut, she'd know it was her mom, soft and cushiony. "Nope. I've taken in a boarder. It's her horse."

"What a good idea," her mom said, pouring the coffee. That's how it was with her mother. She sort of took over, and Callie let her do it. "How's the business going?"

"Well, we've got a line of exercise equipment now. I'm giving cycling lessons to help sell the bikes and bring people into the store." She sat at the table, put her bare feet on another chair and took a sip of the coffee. A warm breeze wafted through the screen, bringing with it the smell of cut grass.

"What are all those welts, honey? Have you got bedbugs?"

"No, Mom. Yellow jackets. I killed them all last night, I think." She drank a little coffee and studied her mother, who seemed about the same. Once in a while she wondered what she would do when her parents died. Fine wrinkles creased her mother's cheeks, encircled her mouth and fanned out from her eyes. She had beautiful eyes, a sapphire blue, and brows that arched expressively over them.

"You're so self-sufficient. If there's no one new in your life, that's probably why." Her mom sat across from her.

"There are two new people in my life. One I can't get rid of and my renter. Both women."

Her mom said, "Well, at least you won't be alone," which surprised her.

"I'm not alone. Remember Lucy and Tony, your grandchildren?"

"They're with their dad and soon they'll be off to college."

"In a few years." She drank the hot black coffee contentedly.

The screen door opened and her dad bounded up the few steps into the kitchen. "Hey, sweet thing. How's my baby girl?"

She gave him a hug. "Your baby girl is good, Dad. You look great. Both of you," she hastened to say. "Tan and happy. Isn't that what we all we want?" If we can't be rich, she thought.

She gazed at her father, the love of her life. White hair fringed his freckled balding head, and he looked back at her out of pale blue eyes with sagging eyelids. But he was still flat bellied and broad shouldered and when she leaned into him, she felt safe. He would always be on her side. "What bit you, honey?"

She told him about the yellow jackets.

"They're mean, not a bit like honeybees. Don't ever kill a bunch of honeybees. Did you know they're disappearing?"

"I heard, Dad. No one knows why."

"It's probably chemicals or something like that," he said.

"Are you on your way home?" she asked.

"We just couldn't wait to see you. Your sister said to say hello."

"Yeah, how is she anyway?"

"You should take the kids and go out and visit," her mom said. "Want some breakfast? Have you got pancake mix and syrup and bacon?"

"Sure." She jumped up to get everything, hungry already. "Want some help?"

"No. You just talk to me and your dad."

Meg drove in while her mom was frying pancakes. "That's my renter."

They all looked through the screen at Meg striding toward the house, a backpack over one shoulder, a duffel bag over the other. Callie's dad quickly rose and started toward the door. She followed.

"This is my dad, Meg. Is there more stuff in the truck that needs carrying in?"

"You can call me Cal," her dad said, taking the backpack and duffel from Meg.

"Hey, thanks. That must be confusing, having practically the same name."

"Not really. No worse than being a junior. Then you're both John or one's Johnny or Junior," he said with a quick grin and a wink.

"There's more stuff in the truck and horse trailer. Am I interrupting something here?"

"No. You're just in time for breakfast." Callie walked with Meg to the rig and took a heavy box to lug upstairs.

"Books. Maybe you should wait for your dad."

"No. I'm good." She hefted the box, hardly feeling its weight, wondering only why she kept smiling.

"Great." Meg grabbed a huge suitcase and rolled it toward the door. They'd left a TV on the front seat and a DVD player in the back. A bookcase and some other stuff lay in the bed of the truck. More must be in the trailer. Were these all of Meg's possessions? She was sure Meg had a few years on her. Maybe she didn't accumulate things.

She introduced Meg to her mother on the way through the kitchen. At the top of the stairs, she set the box down and stood for a moment with Meg.

Meg took a deep breath. "Never thought I'd be back here."

Callie resisted asking why. There was an aura about Meg at that moment that she couldn't decipher—a sort of sadness that she hesitated to tap into—and then it evaporated when Meg smiled.

Callie's dad appeared behind them, the TV in his arms. "Where do you want this?"

When everything from the truck and trailer was moved upstairs, Meg begged off breakfast and went outside to take care of the horses. She would feed Tawny, too, she said. She was going to put her horse in the barn when she fed.

"Pretty woman," Callie's mom said, cutting up a pancake.

More than pretty, Callie thought, eating hungrily. When alone, she fixed herself quick, easy meals, like frozen pizzas and boxed macaroni and cheese. If her mother hadn't made breakfast, she'd have settled for a piece of toast.

Her mom looked at her dad. "By her age, though, you'd think she'd own a house or condo or live in an apartment."

"Maybe she wants to be near her horse," Callie said.

"Not everyone wants to own a house or condo, Laura. There's a real convenience attached to renting. No taxes, no maintenance. You can walk away whenever you want to," her dad added.

Her mother said nothing more, but Callie thought she saw questions in her eyes.

When her parents left, Callie walked over to the fenced-in area. Tawny and Randy were pushing against the closed gate, while Meg brushed her horse inside the pen. A sorrel with a strip of white between his eyes, Brittle dwarfed Tawny. Dust motes danced in the cloud of sunlight that surrounded Meg and the horse. The two of them stamped at the flies hanging around their legs. Abruptly, Meg reached into the feed tub for a spray bottle and doused herself and Brittle. The flies made their way to Tawny and Randy, tormenting them instead.

Callie never heard the car in the driveway, nor did she know that Vicki was there till she spoke.

"Hey, what's happening?"

"I thought you were on your way to Europe tomorrow morning."

"I am. I'm packed and ready to go. Thought I'd come out and say goodbye before I left." She nodded at Meg, who walked over to the fence.

Meg wore the same shorts she'd had on the day before along with a sleeveless athletic shirt. Watching her, Callie realized the word that best defined her was sexy.

"You just moved in, I hear," Vicki said, eyeing the tall sorrel twisting his long neck toward Tawny and the goat. Tawny whinnied and the goat made a bleating sound. Brittle pawed the ground. "Nice horse."

"His back sags and his coat is rough, but he was a great show horse in his day." Despite the dust, Meg's hair shone in the sun. Fine wrinkles fanned out from her eyes and mouth. "We're growing old together." She smiled at Callie.

Callie turned hot. She mumbled she had to do something and walked away. Ran away was more like it, she thought disgustedly and wondered why. She went to see if any yellow jackets were hanging around the hole she'd sprayed the night before, but then she forgot to look. Instead, she sat on the mower in the garage till Vicki came seeking her.

"What a stunning woman," Vicki said. "Why did you go away?"

"I remembered something I forgot to do."

"Do you want to hang out?"

"You sound like one of my kids." She envisioned Tony with his unruly hair and inscrutable eyes, still awkward in his developing body. A boy-man of few words, he spent most of his time on the computer. Lucy was impossibly slender with long, wavy hair and soft brown eyes like her father. She chattered endlessly but mostly to her friends, walking around with the cell phone her dad gave her pressed to her ear.

Vicki opened a lawn chair and sat down. "Tell me about your kids."

"You'll meet them soon enough if you're still around when they get back."

"How old are they?"

"They're teenagers. Well, Lucy will be thirteen this year. Do you remember being a teen?"

"Yeah. Miserable age. I did nothing but fight with my parents and brother. Want a beer? We could pretend we're back at the lake, sitting on the beach."

"Kind of early, don't you think?"

"Nope. Maybe Meg would like one."

"I don't have any beer. Remember? I don't drink it."

"I have some in a cooler in the trunk of my car."

Callie watched her fetch a beer from her Audi with a touch of envy, certain that Vicki never had to worry about money. She stood and stretched and went into the house. She wanted a drink herself now that Vicki had one, but she had this rule that she wouldn't consume any liquor till five o'clock, and it was barely afternoon. Looking out the window, she saw Vicki talking to Meg. They were walking toward the house.

She ran to the bathroom and gazed at her image—red face, wild hair, welts on her forehead and cheeks. She was brushing her hair when she heard the screen slap shut.

With feigned casualness, she returned to the kitchen where Meg told her she'd fed the two horses and put them out on pasture. "Think I'll go upstairs and unpack a few things."

Callie nodded and Vicki asked, "Want to go out to dinner with us tonight?"

"Thanks, but I'm meeting a friend later." Meg climbed the stairs, closing the door behind her.

"I don't remember you asking me if I wanted to go out to eat," Callie said.

"Didn't I?" Vicki looked guileless. "Do you?"

"I guess." There was nothing in the fridge except eggs and bacon. Another breakfast would be okay, but then there would be nothing for Monday night unless she grocery shopped. She and Vicki moved outside under the maple, where Callie opened the newspaper and read Kate's column.

"She's good at this. Her answers are on track and to the point."

"She's retiring. Maybe you could take her place."

"Think so?" Would she be good at it?

"Sure, why not? You could do sort of an internship with Kate. Why don't you ask her?"

"I don't know her that well." She was thinking as she said it that maybe Vicki might suggest her to Kate. It would be the sort of thing that Vicki would do.

Meg left when she and Vicki went inside to change clothes for dinner. Apparently, Vicki carried attire for every occasion as well as a cooler of beer in her car. Callie heard the screen door shut and looked out the window as Meg's truck bounced down the driveway.

"I'm driving," she said when Vicki came out of the bathroom

in tailored jeans and a tight fitting V-neck top.

"Hey, you look great. I've never seen you dressed up." Callie wore a pair of summer slacks and a silk blouse. It wasn't her idea of "dressed up."

Downtown was crowded, as usual. They grabbed two stools at Casablanca when a couple abandoned them for a table. Vicki ordered a Corona and guacamole with chips. Callie asked for a margarita.

When the waiter put the food and drink in front of them, Vicki said, "Help me eat. Everything is a la carte here."

The place buzzed with people. "I know." She'd eaten here with Scott on their first date. "You're going to be tired tomorrow."

Vicki, who had been slumping over the bar, straightened her spine. "We'll eat and leave." Her capacity for beer amazed Callie. She'd seem inebriated one moment and sober the next. Right now she was running a hand up Callie's back.

Callie squirmed under the touch. "Don't," she said quietly.

"Doesn't it feel good?" Vicki leaned toward Callie, her breath beery.

"Not here." Her face suffused with color.

"Are you hot?"

"I'm embarrassed. Please stop."

Vicki dropped her hand and put both elbows on the bar. "Let's order."

They had left Vicki's Audi at Callie's. On the drive back, Vicki put her hand on Callie's thigh. "I should stay the night at your place, you know. Otherwise, I risk getting stopped."

True, Callie thought with a sigh. "What about your luggage and ticket? You'll have to be at the airport by five at the latest."

"I've got everything with me."

Meg's truck was still gone. The two women went inside. Callie turned on the kitchen light as Bill purred around her legs and dropped a live mouse on her feet. She bent over and picked the rodent up by the tail. It appeared to be unhurt, so she took it outside and turned it loose under a bush. The sky was lit with stars, and for a moment she stood with her head thrown back, breathing in the smell of cut hay and sweet clover.

Inside, she showed Vicki the small guest bedroom, which they also used for storage. Boxes were stacked on one side of the bed. There were a dresser and a bedside table with a lamp, but nothing was warm or inviting about the small space.

"I'll see you when I get back." Vicki tossed her bag on the floor. She looked exhausted. "Thanks for letting me crash."

The next morning Callie awoke to the sound of Meg's truck. Meg had apparently been out all night. Vicki was already gone. She'd heard her leave earlier. While making coffee, she watched Meg let the two horses into the smaller pen and stiff-arm the goat as he lowered his head threateningly. When he reared, Meg slammed the gate. After separating the horses, she scattered a handful of grain on the ground for the goat before turning on the hose and filling the water tank next to the gate. By then, the horses had finished eating, and she released them—first Tawny, then Brittle. That's how she would do it if she had to, Callie thought with a wavering courage.

She showered and ate breakfast without ever seeing Meg, who must have gone upstairs while she was in the bathroom. She put her lunch in her backpack and slung it over her shoulder. Before she got into her car, she took a deep breath to carry with her to town.

At noon Sandy came through the door. Callie had seen no one all morning. "Hey, girlfriend. Thought you might like some company for lunch."

"God, do I ever." She and Sandy had worked together in Child Protection Services for the county. Sandy still did. "What a fool I was to give up my job for this." She made a sweeping gesture.

"You don't want to come back," Sandy said, popping the tab on a soda. "Have you forgotten how hard it is to protect kids? They never want to be relocated, even if they're scared. They lie or maybe they just don't know they're being abused because it seems so frighteningly normal."

"Had a bad morning?" Callie asked, taking a bite of her sandwich. The bread clung to the roof of her mouth.

"Yeah." Sandy sighed. "Another case where the mother would rather keep the boyfriend than protect her kid. What is the matter with these women? How can you go to bed with someone who abuses your child?"

"Maybe she needs his paycheck?"

"Not this guy. He's the unemployed live-in who sometimes babysits."

Callie remained silent for a few moments. She was remembering why she'd wanted to leave child protection. "Why do you stay?"

Sandy shrugged. "It's easier to stay than go. You have to have something to go to, like this store you started with Marc."

"That was the biggest mistake I ever made, bigger than marrying Tim."

"C'mon. Tim isn't so bad. He's a good father." She bit into her sandwich and chewed quietly. "I've been thinking. Being a kid sucks. It's all about what parents you get."

"That's not exactly profound, Sandy."

Sandy brightened. "I'm not profound. Being an adult isn't always so hot either, but at least you have some control over your life."

"Hey, I've got a roomer living on the second floor and another horse in the field. I think she was looking for a place to stay where she could board her horse. Otherwise, why would she want to live in my upstairs? She takes care of the horses, too."

"She's not scared of Randy?"

"I don't think she's afraid of anything." Meg came to mind—hair bright in the sunlight, eyes like rain clouds, long, slender legs. She mentally stopped herself and, for some reason, thought of Vicki. "You met Vicki Browning at the cycling class. Do you remember?"

"She wanted to go out with you."

"I didn't tell you how I met her, did I?" She watched Sandy's reaction as she brought her up to date.

"She's a lesbian," Sandy said mildly.

"I think so. Why does she hang around me?"

"Did you tell her you're not interested?"

"It doesn't seem to make any difference. We could be friends if she'd just back off."

"Uh-huh." Sandy took her upper lip between her teeth. She looked deep in thought.

"What?" Callie asked impatiently.

Her forehead smoothed. "Nothing. It's okay to be a lesbian, and she's an attractive woman."

"I know that, but I'm not attracted to her or to any woman."

Sandy looked unconvinced, and Callie pictured Meg stiff-arming Randy. She was lying and she knew it.

The phone rang, startling them both. Callie went to answer, and Sandy gathered her things and waved goodbye.

She drove home slowly, enjoying the July afternoon, hot and thick with unshed rain. The irrigation systems moved slowly across the cornfields, the water evaporating in rainbows. When she navigated the potholes in her gravel driveway, dust enveloped the Saturn. She'd rolled up her window in advance. The car had air, but the house did not. Trees shaded the roof, and the surrounding fields offered no barrier to the hot summer winds that blew across them. This day, however, there was no movement of air.

She stepped out into a breathless world. The two horses and the goat stood inside the shed, tails swishing each other's heads. The flies were biting. In a flash of recall, she pictured the horsefly chasing her over the side of the sailboat.

She'd left most of the windows open in the house. The cat lay on the kitchen floor, panting. "Poor little guy," she said, wetting a rag with cold water and washing him. He raised his head and licked her hand. She turned on the overhead fan and felt the hot air move.

After changing into shorts and an undershirt, she checked herself out in the bedroom mirror. Not too slender, nor too tall, kind of curvy and short, actually. Five foot three, one hundred twenty-eight pounds. Her hair frizzed in the high humidity. Her dark blue eyes gazed back at her, their pupils nearly the same color, and her nose and cheeks glowed red.

Back in the kitchen, she fried an egg and bacon sandwich and took it out to the porch. When her phone vibrated in her pocket, she fished it out and read Tony's name and number in the display. She'd called her kids once a week since their departure. Sometimes she just left a message. "Nothing exciting going on here. Tawny is fine. Bill's good. I'm great. Have a marvelous time. Hello to Tim and Shirley. Love you madly." She missed their presence in her life, the physical assurance that they were well, the noise factor they added, their young faces and voices. Sometimes she even missed the squabbling.

"Hey there," she said brightly.

"Hey, Mom. We're ready to come home." Tony's voice startled her as it slid down the scale. "Can you send us tickets? Dad won't buy them."

"Where are you and what happened?"

"We had a huge fight, Mom," Tony said sullenly.

She could hear Lucy in the background. "Let me talk to Mom."

Tony said, "Call her on your own phone."

"Who had a fight?" Callie asked. "It's hotter than hell here. No air, remember? You're better off wherever you are."

"Shirley is always telling us what to do." His voice rose as he imitated his stepmother. "Pack up the tents. Roll up the sleeping bags. Clean the fish." His tone returned to normal. "I think they brought us along to be their slaves."

She stifled a laugh "You have to help. You can't be deadweight."

"We're not, Mom. Shirley said you spoiled us."

Callie shifted in a pool of sweat. She caught herself before saying something nasty about Shirley, knowing her son was not above manipulation. "Where are you anyway?"

"In Colorado. Will you send us tickets so we can fly home?

We can hitch a ride to Denver."

"Wait a minute. No hitchhiking. You both could get killed. Let me talk to your father."

There was a long empty space before Tim came on the phone. "They're playing the parent card, you against me. Shirley just wants some respect. Lucy is okay. It's Tony who mouths off at her." He paused. "I lost my temper and slapped him. He called her a bitch. I don't think she heard, but I did."

It was the most Tim had confided to her in years. "I see," she said. Tony would think he was wronged, of course, but he couldn't call Shirley a bitch even if she was one. "So, what is your solution? Tony wants to come home."

"Well, he can't," Tim said flatly. "He'll get over it."

She bit her tongue. There was no point in saying something she'd regret. "Let me talk to him again."

Tony said sullenly, "I suppose he made it look like I deserved being hit."

"Did you call Shirley a bitch?"

"She's not like you, Mom. She's always bossing me and Lucy around, and Dad always takes her side."

"Look, son, you can't bad-mouth your stepmother in front of your dad. Would you sock someone who called me a bitch?"

"Yeah, but you're my mother."

"It's no different. Your dad's sorry. Now you be sorry, too. This is a great opportunity to see the country. I can't afford to take you on such a trip." Of course, at his age he probably wanted to be home with his friends.

No answer.

"Tony? Be big about this. Okay?"

"Okay, Mom," he said, sounding surly. "I still want to come home."

"That's nice. I miss you. I love you. Now put your sister on the phone."

"It's my phone."

"Yeah, well your dad pays the monthly bill for it. Remember that."

"Hey, Mom," Lucy whispered. "Dad was really mad at Tony."

"I know. How are you, sweetie? I miss you."

"Me too, but we're doing all kinds of cool things. We're going to the Grand Canyon tomorrow. Dad says we can ride mules down to the river. I don't think Shirley wants to, though. She's kind of a sissy."

"It's a good thing you're whispering. I'm a sissy, too. I'm afraid of Randy."

"Aw, he's okay. He looks so funny when he puts his hooves on my shoulders."

"Well, you're a brave girl."

"He's only a goat, Mom. He just wants some grain. I'm gonna miss the county fair."

"The county fair is tame compared to what you're doing. You can go next year. Tawny's coat is dull and he has a belly anyway. He's not in show condition. We have another horse here." She told Lucy about Meg and Brittle.

"Cool," Lucy said. "Love you, Mom."

"I know. I love you too."

Chapter 3

The night was nearly as hot as the day. Lightning bugs flashed in the grass and trees. A few early crickets chirped loudly. Moths battered against the screen. Callie sat on the porch with Bill stretched out on her lap, his head hanging off her knees. The screened-in porch was as close as the cat would get to being outdoors.

The porch light was just strong enough for her to read, and she was deep into *A Thousand Splendid Suns* when the screen door slapped shut. Meg stood in the pale aura of light. She wore shorts and an undershirt. Her hair was drawn off her neck in that high ponytail.

"Thought I'd get some air," she said.

"I'm sorry we don't have air-conditioning."

"I'd rather be hot." Meg bent forward and ran a hand over Bill's back. Droplets of sweat glistened between her breasts.

Bill purred loudly and Callie stared at the long, slender fingers nearly brushing her belly. Her heart knocked loudly as she breathed in the smell of Meg's hair, her skin—the odors of shampoo and lotion—fresh from a shower.

Meg took the chair next to hers and asked about the book, and Callie turned it over so she could read the title. "It's about two women in Afghanistan, married to the same brutal man, but first it takes you through their childhoods and Afghanistan's recent history, before and through the Soviet invasion to the Taliban years, and how it affects the two women." Probably more than Meg wanted to hear, she thought.

"Sounds sad. I never understood why men want to keep women tied to a stove and a bunch of kids. Well, not all men, but too many."

"It's got to do with being able to, don't you think? A lot of men don't believe women are their equals." She looked away. It wasn't just the heat that kept her from catching her breath. It was the proximity of Meg. "What do you do for a living?" she asked, thinking she should have asked that question before she rented the upper floor to Meg.

"I'm a medical technician. It's a good job because you can do it anywhere."

"Are you thinking of moving?"

"No, but it's nice to know that I could if I wanted to. And you?" Meg turned toward Callie.

She returned the look, wondering what was the matter with her? Why did this woman make her feel so vulnerable? "I used to work for the county in child protection. Now I own a swimwear and exercise equipment store with someone else."

"Really? You want a beer?"

"No. I wouldn't turn down a glass of wine, though. There's an open bottle in the kitchen." Starting to get up, she said, "I'll get it."

"Stay there. I'll do it."

The cat jumped off her lap as Callie stood to switch off the porch light. Out of the darkness, trees and shrubs and movement began to emerge. Bats swooped and darted just as they had at the lake. Under a ragged pine she noticed a possum making its slow way across the yard toward Dan's field of corn.

Meg returned a few minutes later with a bottle of Blue Moon and a glass of merlot.

"Thanks," Callie said, taking the wine as Meg slipped into the chair next to her again.

"How do you like it here?" Meg asked, her voice sultry as the night.

"It's okay. I didn't really think about the isolation when I moved in. My daughter wanted a horse. I thought I wanted a horse, but I didn't. Not really." Truth told, she was a little afraid of the horse but too ashamed to say so.

"That's all I ever wanted. A horse of my own." Meg tilted the bottle back and drank. "This is nice with the lights out."

The thick, humid air enveloped them.

"Your daughter is horse crazy? How old is she?"

"She loves Tawny, but she loves the cat and the dog that died. She probably loves the mice."

Meg threw back her head and laughed, a throaty, musical sound, and Callie was inordinately pleased that she'd amused her.

"I also have a fifteen-year-old son who is a computer nut. Both kids are at the Grand Canyon with their dad and his wife."

"You must miss them," Meg said, glancing at her.

"Yes," she said, but right now she missed no one. Glad for the dark because it hid her confusion, Callie was forced to recognize her attraction to Meg. Where had it come from? It scared her. Could you suddenly turn into a lesbian? She'd have to ask Marc. "I'm used to being alone," she added.

"Yeah, me too." Meg spoke quietly. "Me and Brittle. Think I'll go to bed. Thanks for the company."

After she was gone, Callie stared out at the night for a few minutes—seeing Meg, hearing Meg—before going inside. In bed, she ran a hand over herself, imagining another's touch, and her fingers slid between her legs.

When Marc showed up at three thirty on Tuesday, she put her book down behind the counter. There had been a slow but steady flow of customers. She told him she'd sold two swimsuits, a pair of goggles, a set of water dumbbells and a knee length bodysuit.

He clapped appreciatively.

Knowing he would laugh at her, she stumbled over the words. "I just wondered if it's possible for someone who's straight to be attracted to someone who isn't."

He looked confused for a moment, his dark brows drawing together. "Are we talking about you?"

"A friend of mine," she lied.

"Vicki is really good-looking, and she's smart and rich. What more could you want?" He leaned on the counter and looked into her eyes. "So, honey, you're falling for a woman."

She turned away. Was she?

"Look, Cal, you've been divorced for ten years."

"Eight."

"Okay, eight years, and you haven't found a man. You're not even looking. Along comes an attractive woman, and you finally realize who you are."

She laughed. "You're so full of shit. I haven't fallen for Vicki."

"Did you fall for a man in all these years?"

She had married Tim because she was pregnant with his child. She liked him. He was a good father, but then he met Shirley and dumped Callie. Callie's pride hadn't let her forgive him. However, she'd never considered a woman and said so.

"You wouldn't let yourself. Now along comes Vicki and you find out why you haven't been dating any men."

She whooped with laughter. "Vicki drives me up the wall."

He looked hurt. "Well, who is it then?"

Her laughter turned to a wheeze. She felt dizzy and put a hand on the counter. "God, I think I'm going to puke." Running to the john, she barely made it. The remains of her lunch floated in the toilet bowl.

He stood in the doorway. "You better go home, sweetie."

Flushing the toilet, she protested. "But I was fine a few

minutes ago."

"It's the flu. It hits you like that. You're well one minute, the next you're sick."

"Who will watch the store tomorrow?"

"You'll probably be fine."

She drove home with the windows closed and the air on. Meg's truck was gone. The horses stood nose first in the shed, hiding from another boiling hot day. She grabbed a pail in the mudroom and took it to her room where she lay gingerly on the bed. As she drifted into a feverish sleep, the cat jumped up and lay on her feet. She awoke twice and rolled to the edge of the bed, where she barfed in the pail. Curling into a fetal ball, she willed herself to sleep, hoping that when she awoke again she'd be well.

Darkness was falling when she next opened her eyes. Lifting her head a few inches off the pillow caused another dizzy episode. She desperately had to pee and was consumed by thirst. She got up slowly and grabbed the pail's handle, then realized it was empty. She'd never heard anyone in the room. Not Meg, she hoped. There was a glass of ice water that had miraculously appeared on the bedside table. She sucked the melting cubes, afraid to drink too much.

She staggered to the bathroom, closed the door and sat on the pot, head in hands, the pail at her feet—just in case. Where had this come from? It was like the gay thing, striking her out of nowhere. After rinsing her face and brushing her teeth, she returned to her room and undressed. With only an undershirt and panties on, she slid between the sheets. All set for the rest of the night, she thought, except she hadn't fed the cat. When Bill was hungry, he wouldn't leave her alone, and Bill was no longer on the bed. Maybe Meg had fed him. She could only hope.

Sometime in the night, the bedroom door opened. Pretending sleep, she cracked open an eyelid and saw Meg. She shivered despite the heat and reached for a cover, which Meg pulled over her.

"I fed the cat and the horses," Meg said, putting a cool hand on her forehead.

"Thanks." Eyes closed, she shivered again at the touch.

The next morning when she got up and went to the bathroom, the dizziness was gone, leaving her weak and hungry. She stripped and stepped into the shower as Bill sat nearby, waiting to lick the shower floor after her. It was like any morning, except she was grateful to be on the mend. She guessed you had to be ill to appreciate being well. Her cell was ringing when she went back to the bedroom to dress.

"How are you, sweetie?" Marc asked.

"Better. I'll be at the store on time."

"Sure you shouldn't just stay home and rest?"

"And who is going to take my place?"

"Maybe we should hire somebody else."

"We can't make a profit as it is. How can we do that?"

"If you go back to work, we could."

"Yeah, I thought of that myself. See you later." Filled with wonder that Meg had covered her in the night, had felt her forehead for fever, had brought her ice and dumped the puke in the pail, Callie still cringed at that thought—she who had taken care of sick kids, who had changed hundreds of diapers.

Meg came down the stairs as Callie put bread in the toaster. "Hey, thanks for helping last night."

"No problem. You were pretty sick. There's a short-lived virulent flu going around." Meg wore a white pantsuit.

Callie thought she looked angelic in a sort of sensual way. "I guess. It came on so fast it was incredible. I was literally well one minute and vomiting the next."

"It can happen that quick. I've got to run. I'll take care of the horses tonight. I'll take care of them every day unless I can't and then I'll tell you. That all right?"

"Hugely helpful," she said.

Meg laughed. "Take it easy today. You don't want to relapse."

"I will." If she got really sick, maybe Meg would wash her

fever away with a cool cloth or climb into bed with her to keep her warm. Then she remembered how she'd felt last night and scotched those thoughts. Where had they come from anyway?

At the store she called Sandy to ask if her position had been filled. She knew there'd been no rush to replace her because of a budget crunch.

"No. Have you looked on the Web to see if they're hiring?"

"Yeah. Nothing. We're treading water here."

"Will it help if I buy a bike?"

"No, absolutely not. I'm looking for ideas, not a bailout."

"Why don't we do lunch? I'll come there." As if it were a choice. Callie would have to close up in order to leave.

When Sandy arrived, flushed from the sun, lunch in hand, she said, "I've got an idea. What's the difference if you board two or twenty horses? You could easily make a thousand a month."

Shaking her head, she said, "Who would take care of them?" She imagined a thundering herd rushing across the field toward her and shuddered. "I don't have shelter or room. Two horses and a goat eat all the grass. It would be a muddy mess."

"It was just an idea." Sandy looked deflated.

"A good one, Sandy, but not very feasible. I don't own enough land."

"You could sell the land and make a bundle." Sandy had stopped for a sub, and Callie eyed it hungrily. "Want to trade?"

"You're too generous, Sandy. You'd give away your birthright."

"What the hell does that mean?"

"Not sure." She bit into her dry turkey sandwich. "Your inheritance maybe. And I don't think I want to sell the land." It wouldn't be enough to buy the cottage back, and where would she put Lucy's horse, or Meg's? Besides, did she want to live with bulldozers and construction crews?

"Guidance counselor," Sandy said suddenly. "They're looking for one at Brook Middle School."

"How do you know that?"

"A client's mother. Remember the guy who was accused of

sexually abusing students in March? He was canned and I'm not sure they replaced him. Let's look it up."

The computer brought up the job site and there it was. "I can fax your qualifications over from work."

"I don't have them with me. I'll have to write a letter, too."

"Do that after work and e-mail them to me. I'll do the rest. You should be a shoo-in with your work record. You even have your masters in social work." In Sandy's eyes, Callie already had the job.

With the cat on her lap, Callie spent two hours writing an introductory letter, telling of her enthusiasm for helping young people, her past performance as a social worker in the county's child protection services, her references. The difficult part was squeezing it onto one page. She e-mailed the letter to Sandy, along with her resume.

Sandy responded immediately. "Got it all. Looks good. I'll send it tomorrow from work. Keep your eyes crossed."

She smiled. She'd never been able to cross her eyes. With a glass of wine in hand, she went out on the porch with the cat. Meg gave her a start, sitting quietly in the dark. Callie thought she was upstairs. "I didn't hear you come out here."

"I tried not to disturb you. You looked like you had some serious work to do." Meg threw her a smile and Callie's physical reaction caught her by surprise. Her heart jumped and blood rushed to her face. She took a drink of wine, hoping to calm herself, and noticed her hand was shaking. What the hell was wrong with her anyway?

"You must feel all right."

"You mean the wine. That's probably stupid." She dumped the contents out the door onto the grass.

Thunder rumbled and lightning zigzagged in the distance. As they watched, the wind picked up, the rumbling became booming and lightning eerily lit up the yard. Rain began to fall—at first, a soft pattering on leaves and roof and then a deluge. The air turned cool.

"Think I'll go to bed." Meg raised her voice over the sound.

"Me too," Callie said, suddenly cold and tired. She was only hanging around because Meg was there.

Curled up at the end of the bed, Bill raised his head as she changed her clothes. It was a lonely bed, she thought, climbing into it. She'd always liked sleeping alone, though, reading late into the night. Sometimes waking up in the wee hours and turning on the light to read some more. The rain brought the temperatures down into the seventies. It felt cold.

The next evening as she was shuffling around the kitchen, cutting up peppers and onions, Meg came through the door.

"Hi," she said, heading toward the stairs.

"Want part of a pizza?" Callie asked on impulse. "And a salad?"

"Sounds good, but I have to feed the horses first."

"I can wait."

When Meg came downstairs, she set a six-pack on the table. "Want to share?"

"I've got wine. Want some help out there?" she asked, sure that Meg would decline her offer.

"Nah. I'll be done in half an hour, tops." She wore jeans and a sweatshirt, her hair tied back as usual. "What a change in temperature, huh? The horses will be happy." The thermometer had dropped fifteen degrees.

Callie watched from the window, gauging the right time to pop the pizza in the oven. The salads were already made, and she had a glass of wine at her elbow.

Meg took off her boots in the mudroom, slipping on tennis shoes. "There. Can I help?"

"Nothing to help with." Callie took the pizza out of the oven. "It doesn't even have to rest. The beer is in the fridge."

They were eating their salads when Meg told Callie that she and Brittle would be gone next weekend.

"Are you going to a show?" Callie asked, knowing she would miss her.

Meg gave a little laugh. "No. I retired Brittle from the show ring. I'd have to keep him slick and fit if I wanted to show. We go on trail rides now. I have friends who own eighty acres in Portage County. They've cut trails through the land that hook up with the Tomorrow River Trail. There's a campsite for horses and people. It's fun. Want to go with?"

Her first piece of pizza was partway to her mouth. It hung from her fingers, forgotten. "Go with you?" she repeated stupidly.

Meg's eyes bore into hers as if trying to understand her. "Have you got plans for that weekend?"

"I work on Saturday. I teach a cycling class." Her brain froze at the prospect of spending a weekend with Meg. She would have to ride Tawny, and she never rode Tawny.

"Well, I guess you can't go then."

But she wanted to go, to spend two days with Meg, to sleep in a tent with her. Her body literally tingled at the thought. "We can cancel the class or Marc can teach it."

"There you go." Meg smiled, her teeth white against her tan.

"I've never gone camping with a horse." It had been twenty years since she'd gone camping at all. "What do I take?"

"Pack clothes for riding and sleeping, a canister for water, wine if you want it, and a sleeping bag. I'll take care of the rest."

The call on Monday for an interview caught her off-guard. She hadn't given much thought to what she would say, nor did she expect to hear from the middle school so soon.

"Can you come in tomorrow at three?" the principal, Alan something-or-other, asked. The last name escaped her.

"Of course," she said. She'd call Marc and ask if he knew anyone who could take her place at the shop. Otherwise, she'd close for however long it took.

Marc suggested Ronnie Schwartz, the guy who had been in the dressing room with him. "He's unemployed. We can slip him a few bucks and if you get this job, maybe he can work at the store."

"Maybe," she said. They'd have to find someone to take her

place.

She'd never been one to talk much about herself, and she went to the interview fearing she'd not have good answers to their questions.

The principal, Alan Tomlinson, fortunately introduced himself again. The superintendent and the president of the school board sat in on the interview, along with the librarian who would be her mentor if she got the job.

She told them she had worked with troubled children and difficult parents, that she knew how to test and was looking forward to steering students toward the right courses. Later, she wondered if her answers had been wordy enough, if she'd shown the proper enthusiasm, if she had conveyed confidence. The school board member had asked her where she expected to be ten years from now. She'd said on a beach in Hawaii—ha, ha. No, seriously, she hoped they'd give her a chance to prove herself.

The week sped by. Callie had little time to worry about the coming weekend trail ride, but when she did think about it, she wondered what had gotten into her. She wouldn't be able to walk after a day on Tawny. A night on the ground would surely finish her off. Meg might even have to give her a leg up on the horse. When she told Marc about her plans for the weekend, he looked at her with disbelief and then asked for a lesson plan for cycling.

Sandy showed up for group cycling Thursday evening. When they were cleaning up their bikes afterward, Sandy asked if she wanted to go to the City Art Fair on Sunday.

"Wish I could, but I'm going on a trail ride this weekend."

"Biking?" Sandy asked.

"No, horseback riding."

"I thought you didn't like horses." A disbelieving frown appeared between Sandy's brows.

"I don't dislike horses. I just haven't had much of a chance to ride," she said, forgetting how well Sandy knew her.

Sandy snorted. "You could ride every day. Hey, but that's okay. Have I met this person you're going with?"

"My roomie? No, but you will if you ever come out."

"I can't wait."

When Callie came home Friday, Meg was packing the trailer. "I'll change and help you."

Outside again, she threw a bale of hay down from the loft in the barn and carried it to the trailer. The stems poked through her jeans.

"We might need two," Meg said, picking it up and flinging it into the bed of the truck. She wore shorts, her long legs disappearing into cowboy boots. On some people this might have looked funny. On her, Callie thought it sexy.

Callie's gaze strayed to the worn T-shirt covered with sweat and bits of hay that clung to Meg's body. When she raised her eyes to Meg's face and saw the ironic smile there, she cleared her throat and said, "I'll get another bale."

Together they loaded the trailer with buckets for feed and water, enough grain for two days, grooming equipment, bridles, pads and saddles and fly spray. In the bed of the truck were camp chairs, a box with cooking supplies, along with the hay. Meg put her sleeping bag and clothes in the front compartment, which she called a dressing room. There was a cushion the size of a double bed over the gooseneck part of the trailer.

"Is that where we're going to sleep?" Callie asked, throwing her sleeping bag and backpack in the compartment.

"Yep." She grinned and lightly slapped Callie on the back. "Are you ready for this?"

It was the question Callie was asking herself, and she jumped a little at the touch. "Sure. What time are we leaving tomorrow?"

"Early. It's warming up again. How about six thirty? We just have to eat breakfast and load the horses."

"Sounds good." She felt like a kid again in awe of an older cheerleader. She followed Meg's gaze to the car crunching down the driveway.

"Hey, you two." Vicki leaned out the window of her Audi. She parked in front of the garage and walked over to where Callie stood with Meg. "What's happening?"

"We're going on a trail ride tomorrow."

"You're going to ride Tawny?" Vicki sounded amazed and amused.

"I am," Callie said, trying to look in control.

"I got the idea that wasn't your thing. What about cycling class on Saturday?"

"Marc is handling that."

"I think I'll feed the horses and go upstairs. Nice to see you, Vicki." Meg winked at Vicki.

Callie watched Meg walk away, wondering what the wink meant, wishing it had been directed at her.

"I couldn't wait to get home to see you," Vicki said. "Are you going to be gone all weekend?"

"I think so." The exciting prospect of spending a weekend with Meg was seriously compromised by the fact that she'd be riding Tawny.

"Well, let's go out to dinner. I'll buy."

"Why don't we just eat here? We can have sandwiches and chips."

"I missed you." Vicki followed her into the house.

"You already said that. How was your trip?"

"Busy. If you go with me someday, I'll find time to sightsee." Vicki picked up the cat, which struggled to be free.

"Oh, sure. Your company would be thrilled if I tagged along."

Vicki set Bill on his feet. "Has he caught any mice lately?"

"A few. So, what did you do?"

"Went to a couple of wineries. I've got a bottle from the Loire Valley for us to share. It's chilling in my cooler."

They ate on the porch. Vicki poured the wine into their glasses. "Kate and Pat invited us to spend next weekend with them."

"Us?" she asked, surprised.

"Yes. How do you like the wine?"

"It's very good. Thanks." She was no connoisseur of wine, even though she drank a lot of it, but this stuff was light and tasty.

"Thank you for the sandwich and potato salad," Vicki said. "Well, will you go with me next weekend?"

"Sure. What time?" She liked Kate very much and had saved her columns, although she didn't know why. Her interest in giving advice had fizzled. However, she'd be giving advice if she got the guidance counselor job.

"Friday whenever you can get away. We'll all go out for fish when we get there."

She was surprised at how pleased she was by the invitation. But she thought it would be odd to be at the lake staying at somebody else's place.

The next day, she took her coffee outside into the cool morning. Dew glistened on the grass and clung to the spider webs that quivered between the bushes. She felt badly when she accidentally broke one. It had been so carefully wrought.

Meg handed her Tawny's lead rope. The small horse craned his neck toward the fence where the bleating goat was trying to climb the gate. She nearly dropped the lead rope when Tawny whinnied loudly. "Don't step on me," she said to the horse as he pawed the gravel.

Meg led Brittle to the trailer, tossed the lead rope over his long neck and he jumped into the dark, narrow space. She hooked the tail chain behind him and went to the little window in the front to fasten his head.

Then she took Tawny's lead rope from Callie and pointed him toward the empty side of the trailer. Tawny balked and Meg clucked a couple times, smacking him lightly on the rump until he jumped in. When the chain was behind his tail and his head fastened, Meg closed the trailer's tailgate.

The goat bleated louder, renewing his attempts to climb the fence, and Tawny neighed in answer.

"I think you better call Dan and tell him the goat is going to be alone. He might hurt himself."

Callie pulled her cell out of her pocket. "Hey, Dan. Yeah,

I'm up early. Look, we're taking the horses on a trail ride and Randy is trying to climb the fence. Yeah. Thanks." She snapped the phone shut. "He's on his way."

Dan drove in as they were pulling out of the driveway. Meg braked and talked to him through the open window. "It's been a long time."

"Are you here to stay, Meg?"

"As long as I stay anywhere."

"I've got a friend for Randy." He reached across the truck seat and put a smaller goat on his lap—a pointed hairy face with floppy ears and wide set eyes peered at them. It bleated in answer to Randy's desperate calls. Tawny began pawing and whinnying. The trailer rocked.

"We better get going. See you later."

"How far?" Callie asked as they turned north out of the driveway, wondering how long before Meg found a better place to live and keep her horse.

"An hour, maybe less." Meg glanced at her, eyes bright. "Are you excited?"

"Yes." She was, so much so that it alarmed her. Her guts were tied in knots but mostly from worry. "How long are the trails?"

"Long. We'll be out all day." Meg grinned in a way that left Callie wondering if she was laughing at her. "Vicki must be a good friend of yours."

"We had a rocky beginning."

"How so?"

She told the story, and Meg threw back her head and howled. "That is too good to keep quiet."

"And now she hangs around. I think maybe she's trying to make up for almost killing me."

Meg laughed again. "You're serious, aren't you? She hangs around because she likes you. She's a cool chick."

"She's a lesbian," Callie said as if she were revealing a secret.

Meg laughed so hard this time that Callie worried she might go off the side of the road. "No shit," she said when she could talk.

Callie turned crimson and stared out the passenger window. The young corn shone in the morning sun. In the ditches, spiderwort and daylilies and chicory bloomed. Everything looked brighter now that the heat had been washed away. She felt foolish. Of course, Meg knew. Meg touched her arm and she jumped.

"Hey, it's okay, Callie." Out of the corner of her eye, Callie saw Meg's smile. "We're going to have fun."

Much too soon, they turned onto a long narrow, sandy driveway. Meg parked in a field next to another truck and trailer, near a long stable. She waved at a woman walking toward them through the rough grass.

"You couldn't have planned better weather, Liz," Meg said as the woman neared.

Short gray hair fitted the older woman's head like a cap, separating around small ears. If only she could wear her hair like that, Callie thought, looking into the woman's pale blue eyes. She stretched out a hand. "Hi. Nice place." What she'd seen was nice. The field, the side of the stable, the ranch-style house in the distance.

"C'mon. I'll show you the barn. Once she gets on her horse, Meg won't get off."

They traipsed through the grass to the stable. Only two horses stood in the stalls. The others were mares with foals in another field, Liz said. "You can put your horses in here tonight."

"Thanks," Meg said. "Are you going with us?"

"Of course." Liz clapped Meg on the shoulder. "I'll saddle up in here."

"Okay. Let's unload, Callie."

Callie's heart took off at a trot. She could do this, she told herself, wondering why she was. She glanced at Meg, who strode toward the trailer slightly ahead of her, obviously eager to get going. Callie dragged her heels, hoping to slow things down.

Meg unhooked Brittle's head and opened the tailgate. He backed calmly out, pausing for Meg to take his lead rope and tie him to the trailer. She then unlatched Tawny and he shot backward so fast he nearly sat down in the grass. Meg tied him to the other side of the trailer, where he started to paw, hitting the trailer tire with his hoof. He whinnied loudly, looking around him as if he'd never been anywhere.

"Brush and saddle him and let's go."

Callie approached Tawny warily. She curried him as he continued to paw and look around. His whinnies turned to fluttering nostrils. Meg came around the trailer, leading her saddled and bridled horse.

"You don't do this often, do you? Hold Brittle and I'll saddle Tawny." Meg held the saddle pad in place with one hand while she threw the saddle over Tawny's back as he skittered sideways. "Whoa!" she said, straightening the saddle and fastening the girth. She undid the halter and slid it over Tawny's short neck before slipping the bit in his mouth and the bridle over his ears in one smooth motion. She tightened the girth again and exchanged horses with Callie. "Need a leg up?" she asked, looking a little grim.

"Thanks, no. I could have saddled him myself," Callie said, while Meg watched her put a foot in the stirrup and attempt to throw a leg over Tawny while the little horse moved away. Meg reached for the reins and held him still.

"Does anyone ride Tawny?" Meg asked, putting two halters and lead ropes on her saddle horn before swinging effortlessly in the saddle.

"My daughter, but she's been gone most of the summer."

Meg studied Callie for a moment. Liz was riding across the field toward them on a long legged bay. Callie felt dwarfed next to the other two horses. Tawny pulled the reins through her fingers, trying to snatch a bite of grass.

"You lead, Liz. I'll bring up the rear," Meg said, her face unreadable.

As Liz moved away on the bay, Tawny followed, still trying to get a mouthful of grass. Callie clucked and the little horse broke into a rough trot. Hanging on to the saddle horn, she tightened the reins and bounced precariously, like a hard rubber ball, until Tawny caught up with Liz's horse and slowed to a walk. Only then did she relax a little.

When they reached an opening where a stream ran through, Callie tensed. Her butt and thighs were already sore. Why hadn't she just told Meg the truth? She wasn't a horse person. This was not her idea of fun.

Liz crossed the stream. Tawny balked, then took a giant leap. She grabbed for the horn too late. Left behind, she landed on her rump in the soft moss on the edge of the stream. Only then did she realize she'd been the one screaming.

Liz caught the loose reins as Meg bent over her. "Are you all right?" Meg asked, lifting Callie up by the armpits and steadying her against her body. "Anything broken?"

"I don't think so," she said shakily, sure that Meg was concealing a smile. "Just my pride."

"Let's change horses." Without waiting for an answer, she grabbed Callie's ankle and boosted her up on the sorrel's back. Brittle stood perfectly still. "Never could get Nicky to ride him," Meg muttered. "She was a lot like you that way."

Meg jumped the creek and, shortening one rein, threw a leg over the palomino. She held the reins taut, till the horse stood still. "Okay. Let's go. I'll follow."

The bay moved off, and Brittle followed like a gentleman. She didn't have to pull on the reins or hang on to the saddle horn. All she had to do was sit quietly. Straddling him stretched her legs, though. Brittle was a much bigger horse than Tawny. When she'd hit the ground, she'd jarred her back.

She soon forgot about her discomfort as she looked around and saw the birds—noisy chickadees, muttering nuthatches, a flicker pounding away at a tree. Liz pointed out a doe and her fawn. She turned, intending to show them to Meg, and saw a lathered Tawny quietly bringing up the rear. Meg's long legs brushed plants along the side of the path. Her feet hung close to the ground.

When they stopped for lunch, which Meg and Liz had packed behind their saddles, Callie nearly fell while dismounting. Meg caught her before she hit the ground and helped her to her feet.

"Sorry," Callie muttered, ashamed of her lack of control. Her muscles refused to obey her commands. They quivered uncontrollably.

Meg put halters on both horses, let them drink from the stream that had looped back, and tied them to branches. Callie lowered herself gingerly onto one of the stumps circling a fire pit. She still felt Meg's body against hers, embarrassed that she had to be caught. Meg must be wondering why she was here. She was unable to explain it herself.

Other horses and riders began sifting into the area. Some stopped to join them. Callie forgot their names as soon as they introduced themselves, but Meg seemed to know everyone. The air smelled of horses and leather. Callie washed down a sandwich and a bag of chips with warm water and tried to look as if she was having fun.

The afternoon seemed endless. She was again riding Tawny, which was an easier stretch for her legs. He hung his head and walked quietly, only breaking into a trot when the others did. When he did, pain rippled through her back and thighs. If she got through the day, she promised never to do this again.

Eventually, they somehow circled back and emerged from the woods into the grassy field where they'd started, which was now half full of trucks and trailers. She dismounted, hanging onto the saddle until she could stand on her own. Meg put Tawny's halter back on and tied him to the trailer. Callie pulled the saddle off and nearly fell under its weight. She tried not to stagger as they led the two horses to the stable where they fed and watered them.

"Are you okay?" Meg asked as they exited the barn.

"A little tired. I'm not used to riding." She watched where she stepped, afraid she might slip on a pile of manure. Her legs trembled.

Meg laughed and patted her on the back as if she were a kid. "I never would have guessed. You're a good sport, though."

"Nicky didn't ride either?" She looked up at Meg and wished she hadn't, because she tripped. Again, Meg caught her.

"Whoa, woman. No, Nicky didn't ride. She took wonderful pictures, though, and went to the shows with me." Her smile twisted as if with regret. "Are you hungry?"

"Famished." She was more exhausted than hungry, as if she'd biked a marathon.

The smell of brats grilling over the fire made her feel queasy. She sat carefully on one of the lawn chairs from the back of the truck, and Meg put a glass of wine in her hand. That was all she remembered. She woke up, lying fully dressed on the mattress in the gooseneck part of the trailer. Meg lay sprawled next to her, asleep.

Consumed by thirst and unable to find her shoes, she hobbled outside barefoot in search of water. The sky had clouded over, and she prayed for rain. There was no sign of anyone awake. The horse tied to the nearest trailer slept standing up, one hind leg cocked. The roaring fire had burned to embers. The muscles in her thighs quivered with each step. She made her way through the dew-wet grass toward a gravity pump at the end of the stable. She stuck her head under the spout and drank, then straightened and wiped her mouth. With a hand on the small of her back, she stumbled to the trailer.

Meg turned toward her as she climbed onto the mattress. "Are you all right?" she muttered.

"I'm okay," she lied, sure she'd never survive another day on horseback.

Meg scooted nearer and Callie breathed in her smell, a mix of horse and fresh air and some other scent. She wanted to bury her fingers in Meg's hair, but that was unthinkable.

"Come here," Meg said, lazily throwing an arm around Callie and pulling her close. "You're cute, do you know that?" Callie's heart galloped around her chest. Her excitement must have been apparent, because Meg said, "Hey, calm down. Take a deep breath. I'm not planning mayhem here."

Callie was in the middle of telling Meg she was beautiful, when Meg kissed her sleepily. "Mmm," she said, pressing herself full length against Callie. "You taste good, woman," she murmured into Callie's mouth.

By now Callie was speechless, lost in the kissing, the gentle probing of Meg's tongue and the feel of Meg's long, lithe body against her own. She buried her fingers in Meg's hair and kissed her back. The rest was a blur of feeling, of touching and being touched. Meg slowly drew her toward climax, an ache so exquisite that it edged on painful and eclipsed every other sensation. To stave off orgasm, she reached for Meg and mimicked her movements.

When it was over, Meg rolled away. "That was nice. Let's get some sleep now." Her breathing quickly evened out.

Callie lay very still, reliving what had just happened with near disbelief. When she finally slept, it was from exhaustion and she only woke up when Meg brought her coffee. Watching Meg's face instead of the coffee, she nearly dropped the cup. What did she expect to see? Approval? Desire?

Meg kissed her on the mouth. "There, is that better?"

Flushing, Callie burned her lips on the coffee. "Damn, that's hot."

"Ready to ride? Come out and grab a bite. You must be starved."

She was. She'd eaten nothing last night. "What happened after the wine?"

"We carried you to bed. You passed out." Meg smiled and ducked out of the trailer.

Callie brushed her hair into a semblance of order while peering at her image in a tiny mirror stuck on the wall. After cleaning her teeth, worrying that her breath might have smelled sour last night, she put on her shoes and went out into a morning full of sunlight. The clouds of the night were gone. She would have to ride.

When they left late afternoon, Callie thought that her thighs were permanently and unnaturally stretched. Her muscles trembled when she walked and ached if she tried to cross one leg over the other. Meg said little on the drive home, and Callie spoke even less.

Randy and his new friend bleated and clambered at the gate as Meg and Callie unloaded the horses. Tawny neighed, his nostrils dilated, his upper lip fluttering. It was a noisy homecoming. Meg took the lead ropes and Callie opened the gate. Brittle and Tawny galloped off, tails and heads high.

Meg stood with hands on hips as the horses dropped to their knees and rolled. She had fed the animals in the trailer. "I'll unload. You go inside and take a hot bath."

"No," Callie said flatly. She would not be patronized. "I'll help."

"Okay, but you look like everything hurts."

"If I had Nicky's good sense, I'd have stayed home." But then she would have missed last night.

Meg laughed. "That's true, but Nicky had Beth. Has Beth." She turned away, her smile gone.

She loves Nicky, Callie thought, picturing Nicky as she remembered her from their two meetings—taller than Callie, more slender, with dark hair and piercing blue eyes. She was close to crying and, roughly pulling Lucy's saddle out of the tack compartment, she sat down with it on the sparse gravel.

Meg started toward her, to pick her up no doubt, but she got to her feet and carried the saddle to the former milk room in the barn where Lucy kept it. It felt like it weighed as much as she did when she set it on the sawhorse. She turned and walked into Meg, who grabbed her by the arms.

"Hey, little woman, go take that bath. Let me take care of this stuff."

Blindly, she stormed toward the house, not understanding why she was mad or at whom. She fed the cat before she turned on the shower. After washing her hair, she filled the tub and gingerly lowered herself into the hot water. She was crying when she leaned against the porcelain. Closing her eyes, she covered them with a wet washcloth.

"Want your back washed?"

She jumped, startled out of half-sleep. She thought she'd

locked the door. Quickly covering her breasts with the washcloth, she sat up.

Meg was leaning against the doorframe, arms crossed. She held a screwdriver in one hand.

"You unlocked the door."

"I was worried you might pass out again." Her eyes flickered to the washcloth. "No need to cover yourself, not from me." She crossed the room in two strides, took the cloth from Callie and washed Callie's back. "If there was more room, I'd climb in with you."

Callie didn't think she could stand that. Where would she look? The whole weekend seemed unreal. The memory of the previous night washed over her like the tide, sucking her under. Had it really happened the way she remembered?

"Listen. I apologize for last night. I was half asleep and wasn't thinking." Wringing out the washcloth, Meg gently placed it over Callie's breasts. She left the bathroom, closing the door quietly behind her.

Stunned, Callie settled lower into the tub. Turning on the hot water faucet with a toe, she wondered if she'd just been blown off. Callie had never experienced sex that consumed her, and it sounded like she never would again. How unfair. Why show her what she'd been missing all these years just to take it away? Maybe it was better, though. The kids would be home soon.

When she heard voices, she drained the water and climbed out of the tub. The room spun and she leaned against the door, listening. Meg was telling Vicki something, but she was unable to make out the words. She didn't want either one to find her naked and vulnerable. She pulled on clean shorts and a T-shirt and padded barefoot out of the room.

Both pairs of eyes turned toward her. The two women stood in the kitchen in a pool of light. She looked from one to the other and sat in the nearest chair.

Meg asked, "Are you all right?"

"Water," she said, her voice sounding far away.

"You don't look so good." Vicki filled a glass and put a hand on Callie's forehead. "You're warm."

"It was the hot bath. I think I'll go to bed, though."

"Good idea. I'll stop by the store tomorrow," Vicki said.

Vicki's thick hair—blond at the tips, darker underneath—framed her tan face. She had high cheekbones, curly eyelashes, small ears and a wide mouth. Her neck was strong, her chest deep and her body athletic. Callie's ears rang as she drained the glass and assessed the two women.

Meg was slender, agile and fair. With blond hair piled high, her long neck exposed, she looked deceptively frail. Her wide, smoky eyes and sensuous mouth drew Callie's gaze, and she found it hard to tear her eyes away. The memory of last night's romp in the trailer washed over her again.

"See you tomorrow," she said at last, getting up and tottering toward her bedroom.

Chapter 4

In the morning she found the note her mother had left near the coffeemaker the previous day. Her parents were heading north to a campsite on the Wisconsin River flowage. Why, she wondered for the umpteenth time, hadn't they bought the cottage instead of a motor home?

After dropping two pieces of bread in the toaster, she leaned on the counter, dressed in summer slacks and a sleeveless shirt. Tapping one sandaled foot on the floor, she looked through the open window. The smell of some sweet flowering plant hung in the air. Meg was out there feeding the horses. Callie ate her toast and drank her coffee standing. She was brushing her teeth when Meg came inside and went upstairs.

She'd half expected Meg to come to her room last night, but she'd slept alone. Only her aching body reminded her that the weekend had really happened. On the way to the store, she tried to make sense of her feelings, but they spiraled out of reach, just like Meg. She wasn't used to not being in control of herself.

She parked behind the shop and walked slowly, painfully to unlock the front door. A short woman with dyed blond hair stood outside. No one had ever been waiting for her to open. The woman made a beeline to the swimsuits and was sorting through them when Callie asked, "Can I help you find something?"

"I saw your commercial on the news last night. I didn't know you were here. I've been ordering online, but I have to guess at size. It's better to try things on, don't you think?"

"What news?" she asked, sure the woman was wrong, that it was some other place's ad.

"The late news on Channel Three." She took four suits off the rack. "I'll just try these on. Where are the dressing rooms?"

Callie pointed. When the woman was out of earshot, she called Marc. "Were we on the late news last night?"

"I meant to tell you about that."

"Who paid for it?"

"Our silent partner. She's in the commercial. She's pretty good, too. She said she always wanted to be on TV."

"How come I'm always the last person to know what's going on?"

"You were gone."

"I don't believe they made this commercial over the weekend."

"Hey, be happy. It will bring in customers."

"I've got one now. Are you coming over after work?"

"I can't wait to hear about the trail ride."

"I think I'm permanently bowlegged." The woman came out of the dressing room. Callie hung up and pasted on a smile. "Did you find one you like?"

"Oh, yes. I'll take this." She placed a black Speedo with thin white stripes on the counter. "I want a couple of dumbbells, too, the kind you use in the water. Have you got any of those?"

"You bet." The door jangled as two women entered. Three customers and they'd been open less than a half hour.

The morning was busy. During a break around twelve thirty,

she unwrapped her sandwich. The phone rang and she sighed, the food halfway to her mouth. It was Alan Tomlinson, telling her that the job as guidance counselor was hers if she wanted it. They had checked her references last week.

It took her a few moments to place him and ground herself before she said, "I do want it. When do I start?"

"The Wednesday before Labor Day weekend. We have an in-service that day. The kids won't start until the following Tuesday."

"I'll be there. Thanks."

"See you then." And he was gone.

Wow, she thought, and called Sandy to tell her.

"I knew it! That's just great."

"Thanks to you. You're a good friend, Sandy."

"Glad I can help. I'll see you on Thursday. You can tell me all about the trail ride."

She moaned. "I can hardly walk or sit."

Sandy laughed and Callie looked up to see Vicki, holding a Subway bag. "I'll bet these are tastier than that."

"Vicki's here. Talk to you later." Callie rewrapped her sandwich. "Yeah, I'll bet they are too."

Vicki handed Callie a sub and sat down on the bench next to her. "Tell me about the trail ride."

Callie took a bite. "Mm, good. Thanks." An image of Meg sprawled on the trailer bed flashed behind her eyes. She longed to talk to someone about what had happened, but there was no one except maybe Marc, and he would make light of it. She wouldn't be able to bear it if he laughed. "Everything hurts. That's the sum of it." The muscles in her thighs still quivered whenever she moved.

Vicki laughed and patted Callie's knee. "I wondered how you would fare."

She looked Vicki in the eyes and said, "I hear you're in a commercial on the ten o'clock news."

Vicki briefly met her gaze. "Just a short one. It's great fun. Want to be in on it, too? Marc does."

"Why am I the last person to know about these things? I'm a partner in the store, too."

"I apologize. I thought Marc told you." Vicki smiled unconvincingly.

Callie thought she'd rather lose the shop than be beholden to someone who wasn't going to benefit from its success. "Vicki, look at me." The gold flecked, hazel eyes honed in on her. "I can't let you foot the bills for these things."

"What if I bought into the store?"

"Why would you want to? It's not a good investment, Vicki. In fact, it's a bad one."

"Let me be the judge of that, Callie. Eat your sub while it's warm."

"It's not warm anymore. Don't throw your money away."

The door opened and they both looked at the two women coming through it.

"Hey, what are you doing in town?" Vicki asked.

"We're interrupting your lunch," Kate said. "Don't get up. We want to look around."

Callie got up anyway and finished her sub standing, while Vicki stuffed the remainder of her bun in her mouth and went over to the rack. "I'll help."

Kate turned to Callie. "You're coming with Vicki this weekend, aren't you?"

"I wouldn't miss it. Thanks for asking me." She smiled, wondering if Kate was someone she could talk to. Kate was fond of Vicki. She might not want to hear about Callie's confusion over Meg. Anyway, Callie had no idea how to phrase her feelings.

They all left at the same time—Vicki to return to work, Kate and Pat to grocery shop. Before Kate and Pat went out the door, they each bought a swimsuit. Kate also purchased aqua shoes. It felt lonely when they were gone.

Callie and Marc and Vicki signed new partnership papers on Thursday in the attorney's office. Callie felt as if she'd been run over by an unstoppable force. She watched the commercial that night. Meg, who came home shortly before ten, watched with her. They sat side by side on the old sofa in the living room. Callie had made a big bowl of popcorn. Her nerves jumped whenever her hand touched Meg's as they scooped the popcorn out.

During the commercial Vicki walked around the store, pointing out the swimwear and exercise equipment. She looked young and tan and fit and sounded enthusiastic. "Hey, come in and choose a swimsuit and accessories for the beach. Join a cycling class and get fifteen percent off any piece of equipment plus free delivery. Or just look around." She ended the commercial by mounting a bike, dressed in a cute pair of biking shorts and a tight fitting tank top.

"I'd buy from that woman," Meg said with a grin as Callie turned off the TV. "Why is she doing your commercials?"

Even with popcorn between her teeth, Meg looked good. Whenever Callie talked to Meg, their one sexual encounter rushed at her, leaving her nearly speechless. She wanted to ask why there hadn't been another. Why didn't Meg come downstairs and climb into bed with her at night? Instead she said, "She likes being on TV, and she bought into the place."

"Really? It makes sense then. I didn't know the place was up for sale."

"I think it was a hostile takeover."

Meg laughed. "You're a funny woman, Callie. Brittle and I'll be gone over the weekend. Another trail ride. Want to come along?" Only kernels were left in the bowl.

Cracking one with her teeth, she said with a mix of regret and relief, "I can't. I'm going to a friend's lake home."

"That sounds like fun. See you tomorrow. I'm going to bed."

"Yeah, me too." She hid her longing with a casual stretch. Should she ask? But nothing came out when she opened her mouth to speak. How could she say, "Why don't you sleep with me?"

Vicki drove, speeding west on US 10 before turning off

onto State Road 49. The Audi had all the amenities money buys, including a GPS system.

"Nice car," Callie said, running a hand over the leather seat that Vicki had adjusted to her frame.

"I love it. It gobbles gas, though. I'd buy a Prius, but they don't have enough room for all the stuff I carry around in the trunk."

"I didn't think gas efficiency would be something you'd worry about."

"Everyone should worry about it."

She realized she'd never had a serious conversation with Vicki about anything. "I agree."

They'd been lucky with the weather. The forecast predicted temperatures in the eighties and no rain till at least Monday. As they turned off the highway onto a county road, Callie fought the familiar excitement that crept over her. She'd be on someone else's agenda.

What she didn't expect was the other couple, which meant she had to share a bedroom with Vicki. They dropped their overnight bags on the twin beds in a room Kate's daughters had shared while growing up. The open windows looked over the lake. Callie breathed deeply the smells of lake and pines.

Vicki came to stand beside her. "Nice, huh?"

Callie stepped away. "Yes." She wanted to put on her suit and walk into the water.

"How about a swim?" Vicki asked, as if reading her mind.

"I'd love one, but I don't want to be rude."

"That's the first thing I always do when I come here." Vicki started shedding her clothes.

Callie got her suit out of her bag and, turning her back, quickly put it on.

Vicki was standing with hands on hips, waiting for her. "Let's go see if we can get anyone else to go in."

They were early. The other couple hadn't arrived yet. Pat and Kate were on the beach with Junior. The water was warm and inviting, and Callie walked in without hesitation. Treading water, she looked down the shore toward the cottage of her youth. There were empty chairs on the beach, and the sailboat floated on its anchor. A speedboat was fastened to the pier between two posts. Envy stabbed her, even though she'd steeled herself to expect this. The people might be her cousins.

"Do you know who's at our old place?" she asked Kate, who was swimming nearby.

"No one I recognize. We could walk down there tomorrow."

"I probably should. I might be related to them." She smiled then. "This is so nice. Thanks for thinking of me."

"I think of you every time I see someone at your cottage. And I'm very glad you came. I thought we'd go out for fish when Cory and Beth arrive. Beth's my oldest. Cory is her husband. You'll like them."

"I know I will," Callie said, sure only that she would be slightly envious of anyone with close ties to Kate.

Vicki and Pat were volleying a ball over the net, while Junior splashed around them excitedly. "Shush, Junior. No barking," Kate said and, miraculously, the dog shut up before rushing to greet the couple walking down the hill. "Here they are now."

They looked young to Callie, although they couldn't have been more than ten years younger than she was. Beth was tall and fair and slender. Her husband was taller, leaner and dark—hair, eyes, skin He had huge hands and nearly pulled Kate off her feet into an embrace.

Kate introduced Callie and Vicki as friends who were already on the guest list when Beth called to say she was coming. "Would you like to go out to eat? Those were our plans."

"Love to, Mum." Beth linked arms with her mother and walked toward the house with her.

Callie watched them together, knowing without being told that Beth was pregnant. She smiled when Kate let out a whoop and hugged her daughter. Cory grinned and lifted dark eyebrows. In looks, he reminded Callie of Marc.

"A baby on the way," he said proudly.

Pat joined Kate and Beth in a round of hugs and Cory put

long arms around Vicki and Callie as if to draw them into the general joy. "Is this Kate's first grandchild?" Callie asked.

"Yes, and we're happy to be the carriers." His smile warmed her.

"What's with the 'we' stuff, Cory?" Beth smiled sweetly.

When she and Vicki went to their room to change, Callie said, "I feel sort of like an intruder."

"We're not, though. We're the expected company."

"But they're not company. They're family and this is a special occasion."

"Well, we can't leave tonight. That would be too rude." Vicki stood in her bra and panties watching Callie pull on slacks and a shirt.

"Get dressed," Callie said irritably, refusing to look.

Downstairs they took two cars to the Moose Inn. Pat rode with Callie and Vicki, and Callie put the question to her. Should they leave?

"No, of course not. Beth and Cory are staying the week. Beth will have plenty of alone time with her mom." Pat was sitting up front at Callie's insistence.

Callie wondered if this made Pat a grandmother, too. Did she consider herself a stepmother to Kate's kids? She thought of Meg, unable to imagine her in that position. But she could envision Vicki in Pat's place.

Whenever Meg came to mind, so did sex. She would not be able to talk to Kate about Meg now. As if she would have anyway, she mocked herself. Kate's attention would be focused on her daughter. She wished Beth hadn't chosen this weekend.

The Moose Inn was crowded and smoky and noisy as it had been the last night of Callie's vacation. This time, though, they left and went to another restaurant halfway back to the lake. There they sat outside, looking up at a small ski hill, its chair lifts unmoving, the cleared slopes empty. Crickets sang in the early evening. The fish fry was greasy and good. Callie drank a vodka and tonic followed by a glass of some horrendous red wine. They toasted Beth's unborn baby, due in late March.

And then Vicki raised a glass to Callie's new job.

"That's wonderful, but why didn't you say anything?" Kate asked.

She hadn't wanted to horn in on Cory and Beth's news with her own. Actually, she hadn't told anyone except Marc and Sandy. Marc must have spilled the news to Vicki. "I would have gotten around to it. It's nothing compared to having a baby."

When Callie and Vicki climbed into their beds separated by several feet of floor, Callie turned her head toward the open window. The stars and a half moon floated in the dark sky. Saddened by the loss of her cottage, so near yet so inaccessible, she told herself she would wander down the beach to see who was there tomorrow, with or without Kate.

Vicki's voice floated across the room. "You're a secretive one, Callie. Did you tell Meg about the new job?"

"No. I will."

"You never said much about the trail ride. Did you sleep in a tent?"

"There's a double bed in the gooseneck. We slept there." A plane winked across the sky, appearing to travel among the stars. "Do you wish you were at your lake home?"

"It's not my place. It's my brother's. I use it as mine, though. But, no, I'm happy to be here. It's lonesome there alone. It's lonely over here, too. Can I join you?"

"Not a good idea." She wondered briefly how it would be with Vicki and quickly pushed the thought away. "How do you suppose Pat feels about this baby?"

"I think she's pleased. Why wouldn't she be?"

"What is their relationship anyway? Kate and Pat? I know they're together, but how much together? Like a married couple?"

"They've been with each other about ten years. I don't know how they work everything out. The kids will probably get the lake home, since it's a family place. Is that what you mean?"

"I guess."

"When you're married, legally you share everything unless

you write up a prenuptial agreement. If you're gay, you have to have powers of attorney for everything."

They'd never discussed being gay. It had hung in the air between them. "Were you ever married?"

"Not me. It was a big disappointment to my mom, since I was the only girl in the family. What was it like for you? Being married?"

The night air carried the odors of water and pine and flowering plants, like sweet Joe-pye Weed. "Not very successful. I got two nice kids out of it, though."

"When do I get to meet them?" Vicki lay with her arms under her head, her face turned toward Callie, whose eyes had adjusted to the dark.

"Soon." The house would be full of sound again. She heard their voices in her head—laughing, fighting and talking—their feet slapping the floors. There was nothing quiet about her kids.

She drifted into sleep, into a world that made no sense.

The next day she and Kate walked down the beach while the others skied behind Vicki's boat. Vicki had driven to her brother's lake home and taken the MasterCraft. As Callie and Kate waded through the shallows, climbing over the piers and swimming around them as she had done with Vicki when she first met Kate, Callie told her that Vicki had bought into the store.

"How do you feel about that?" Kate asked.

Asked like a therapist, Callie thought. Maybe it came from writing an advice column. "I don't honestly know. She's turning things around with her money. We've had a lot more traffic since she appeared on TV. I don't understand her motives."

Kate laughed. She was laughing a lot this morning, probably a spillover of elation at Beth's news. "I don't think Vicki would make a foolish investment, even though she really likes you."

"That's encouraging, I guess. I took in a roomer."

"I know. Vicki told me about her."

Callie was curious. "What did she say?"

"That she's attractive and that she's sort of a mystery, she and her horse."

They were standing on the beach at Callie's former cottage. A man and woman were coming down the steps. Neither was related to her. "Let's go," she whispered to Kate. "I don't know these people."

"Nice day." Kate waved a hello.

"Sure is." They smiled and the man said, "We need a spotter. Do either one of you ski or tube?"

"The ones who do are out there right now." Kate pointed toward the MasterCraft. "I'll ask one of them."

"Thanks."

Cory drove for the couple and skied behind their boat. No one else wanted to. He lifted an arm whenever he came into view. Callie and Kate spent most of the day in the water, while Beth rode in the MasterCraft with Pat and Vicki.

"So, how's the column going?" Callie asked. The sun was a furnace, the wind its blower. She wore a visor and lots of sun lotion.

"Actually, I'm kind of tired of it. I've been doing this for too many years."

"It must feel good to make a positive difference, though."

Kate laughed happily. "I'd like to think that. What if I give the wrong advice? Sometimes I don't know what to say to the more bizarre letters."

The MasterCraft and the speedboat Cory was driving rocketed by. Huge waves rolled toward them. "My letter might sound that way," Callie said, blurting the words out before she could change her mind.

"Did you write one?" Kate asked. "Let's go sit on the beach a while. I feel like a prune."

"Me too." Gravity made her heavy as she waded out. She put on her sun shirt and settled in the beach chair.

They sat quietly for a few moments, watching the water. "I am so happy today," Kate said, and Callie decided she wouldn't spoil Kate's joy with her problems. Why would Kate want to hear? But then Kate asked, "Is it about Meg?"

"Yes," she said. When only silence followed, she continued. "We went on this trail ride and something happened. It hasn't happened again, but I can't get her out of my mind."

"Do you want it to happen again?" Kate turned a friendly smile on her, which Callie couldn't meet. It was like having a conversation where the subject wasn't identified. What was *it*? What *happened*? She was certain Kate knew what she was alluding to, though.

"It's so hard to talk about this, and I don't know anyone else that I can tell. I never thought about women this way until I met Meg." Meg exuded sex, at least to Callie. "I don't know what to do."

"Well, can you talk to her about it?"

"Not really. I think maybe she didn't mean for it to happen, that she just woke up and I was there." She'd convinced herself that this was true. She'd been convenient. It had been a friendly sexual encounter, a one-night stand. "I think she's in love with Nicky Hennessey. I bought my house from Nicky."

"Ah," Kate said. "This is one of those I don't know what to tell you things. I'd say follow your gut instinct, which is usually pretty accurate."

"Does this happen a lot? Does someone like me suddenly have feelings for another woman?" She had searched her memory for such emotions and found none. Had she been in denial all these years?

"I think it happens more than you or I would guess. Sometimes you like or admire someone so much that you love them. Maybe this is one of those things?"

She admired Meg. She liked her certainly, but she hardly knew her. "I think I'm in awe of her. She's so comfortable with herself. At least, it seems that way. Does that make sense?" Her face burned, even her eyes were hot, but Kate would attribute the redness to the sun.

The MasterCraft and the other speedboat were coming in, rolling on their wakes. Cory jumped into the water at waist-level and waved to the couple in the other motorboat as they drove slowly toward their rental cottage. Vicki cut the engine and she and Cory fastened the MasterCraft to the dock. The three women dove into the lake. Junior splashed after them and then flopped down in the shallows, lapping water.

"Thanks," Callie said quietly.

"I don't think I was much help, but anytime you want to talk, I'll listen. That's what friends are for. Right?" Kate flashed another smile at Callie. "I'm going back in."

The remark about being friends made Callie feel really good. She took off the sun shirt and followed Kate into the lake. They played volleyball. She and Kate and Cory on one side, the other three across the net. Cory couldn't do everything, though, and Callie's side lost.

When they took a breather, Pat sat next to Callie. "How's it going?" she asked.

"Okay." She felt as if she hardly knew Pat. "And you?"

"I'm happy for Beth and Kate and Cory. I love kids. I hear you have two."

"I do. I've rented my old cottage for another week." The one before she had to start her new job. "I'm hoping they'll want to come. You never know with teenagers, though. They'll probably want to stay home and be with their friends." She would make them come.

"You'll have to bring them over."

"I will."

"Vicki said she bought into the shop."

"She did."

"She's all excited about it."

"Well, I'm glad someone is," Callie said dryly.

Pat leaned forward and looked into Callie's eyes. "Vicki is full of good ideas and has lots of energy. She'll make a difference."

Callie sighed. "I'm sure she will. She probably saved the store, just when I was thinking about selling my share. But would you want someone to make decisions for you?"

"She can't help it. She thinks she's the fix-it woman." A small smile appeared. It reached the soft brown eyes.

Callie smiled in return. She knew she'd been invited because of Vicki. "I want to do my own bailing. What about you?"

"I guess I'd feel the same way." Pat leaned back and turned her face to the hot sun. "Want to play another game of volleyball? You and Cory and me on one side and Kate and Beth and Vicki on the other?"

"Sure."

Callie slept most of the way home on Sunday, even though she strove to stay awake. She would have hated for the weekend to end if she hadn't known Meg would be coming home, too.

"Wake up, sleepyhead," Vicki said as the Audi bounced down the driveway. "You slept nearly all the way."

Callie's eyes popped open. "Sorry." The horse trailer was parked out by the barn. She tried to hide the excitement she felt as she pulled her bag out of the backseat.

"I'm going to say hello," Vicki said, striding toward Meg who was unloading the truck and trailer.

Callie dropped her bag and went with her. Meg looked up as they approached. She was carrying a cooler.

"Want some help?" Vicki asked.

"If you want to get the duffel bag, that'd be nice." She smiled as if preoccupied.

"How was the trail ride?" Callie asked.

"Not the same without you. Liz asked where you were." Meg walked on past.

Callie ran to get her overnight bag and carry it to the house. She took it to her bedroom as Meg and Vicki climbed the stairs to the second floor. She was feeding the cat when they came down.

"No mice?" Vicki asked, looking around the kitchen.

"Nope. Maybe he's caught them all." They stood in a threesome for a moment, till Meg said she had some things to do outside and left.

With hands on hips, Vicki looked after Meg. "She'd be a hard one to catch and keep."

"I wouldn't know," Callie said, as if she hadn't thought about

Meg every day and night since last weekend.

"Did you see how those jeans fit and that tight T-shirt? What a great body."

"Vicki, come on." She wasn't about to admit that she, too, had noticed the worn jeans that curved around Meg's small behind and the sweat under and between her breasts.

Vicki looked her up and down. "You look pretty good yourself."

"I look like I've had two kids." Thin red lines tracked her legs. She had a little belly she tried hard to suck in, and her breasts drooped a bit.

"Is it bad to look womanly?" Vicki winked at her.

"Give it a rest," she said, trying to hide a smile.

Doors slammed outside. Callie turned an ear toward the familiar voices. The kids were home. Early. She felt a small twinge of regret, followed by guilt. Now Meg would never come to her bed. She hurried outside, calling back to Vicki. "Come out and meet my kids."

"Hey, take your stuff, Luce," Tony said.

"Mom, we're home." Lucy ran into Callie's embrace.

Callie buried her nose in Lucy's sweaty hair. Lucy had grown. She was now eye level. "I can't believe you're home."

"How's Tawny?"

"Go see for yourself."

Tony shuffled toward her as Lucy sped off. He was several inches taller than she was with large feet and hands. He looked more like his father than her side of the family. "Hi, guy," she said with a smile.

He gave her an awkward hug. She managed to kiss his cheek by standing on her toes. "Hey, Mom. What's happening?"

"Well, lots of things actually. Tell you later. This is Vicki Browning. Vicki, my son Tony and my ex, Tim."

Tony mumbled something to Vicki before asking about the chick out by the barn.

"She's not a chick, Tony. Her name is Meg and she's renting the second floor."

Tony eyed her as if she'd betrayed him. "I was going to live up there. You promised."

She sighed. "No, I did not promise, but we'll discuss that later also."

Tony threw his duffel bag over a shoulder and stormed toward the house.

She turned to her ex. "Hello, Tim. Did you have a good time with the kids?"

Tim's reddish hair flamed in a shaft of sunlight. "Yeah. I think we all had a good time."

"Where's Shirley?" She peered around him at the car, her arms crossed, her head high. It was her typical stance when she addressed Tim.

He leaned against the Lexus. Tim made good money. He looked tired and cross. "Home. How was your summer without the kids?"

"I missed them, of course." Not as much as she thought she would, though, but she'd never admit to that.

Lucy was running toward them, her long wispy hair flying. "Dad, come see the new horse. His name is Brittle." She grabbed his hand just as he was about to shake Vicki's.

"This is Vicki, Lucy," Callie said, intercepting Lucy. "Say hello."

"Hi." Lucy ducked her head. "Who is that lady out there?" She pointed toward the trailer.

"That's Meg," Vicki said. "You have such a pretty name, Lucy. It fits."

"Thanks." Lucy blushed.

Callie took a second look at Lucy. She was incredibly slender, in that delicate way girls her age sometimes were. She had lovely skin, not yet marred by hormonal changes, and large brown eyes. Her cinnamon colored hair was flyaway.

Vicki started walking toward the fence with Lucy and her dad.

Callie followed, arms still crossed. She glanced back once to look for Tony, but he was gone, swallowed up by the house, probably already on the computer.

"See the horse, Dad? Why have we got another horse, Mom?" They lined up along the fence with Meg at one end and Vicki at the other. "Can I ride him?"

"No, darling. He belongs to Meg here. Meg, meet Lucy and Tim."

"Hi," Meg said, turning toward Lucy, her lips stretching into a smile. "So you're the horsewoman of the family."

"Yep. I love horses." Lucy climbed the fence and walked toward Tawny, who moved away whenever she got close. It was Randy and the little goat that paid attention to her. Randy nipped at her pockets and she batted him away. His front legs lifted off the ground. Lucy looked small and vulnerable.

"Lucy, get out of there," Callie called.

"Aw, he won't hurt me." Randy turned away and Lucy stroked the little goat. "What's his name, Mom?"

"Don't know," Callie said.

"Pete. His name is Pete." Meg told her.

Lucy ran to the fence. "He's cute."

"Come back to the car with me, Lucy. I have to go, and you have to get your things. "Nice to meet you, Vicki. You too, Meg." Tim helped Lucy clamber over the fence.

Callie went with them. She asked why they were home early. Business, Tim said. His arm hung around Lucy's shoulder.

"I've rented our old cottage for a week."

"Sounds like fun."

"Can I ask a friend, Mom?" Lucy didn't walk. She danced or skipped or ran.

"We'll talk about that later." She really wanted time alone with her kids. Their father hadn't allowed them to take friends on his trip, but they'd see that as a reason for inviting friends on hers. They were adept at playing one parent against the other.

"Please, Mom. Please."

"Get your stuff out of the car, Lucy. I want to talk to your mom," Tim said.

When Lucy danced off, Tim said with a slight smile, "I was

getting you off the hook." His light brown eyes gleamed. "You're looking good, Callie. The summer must have agreed with you."

"Thanks." Sandy had once said that a person who feels defensive crosses his or her arms. She let hers fall to her side. "Did you have a good time with the kids? Did they?"

"We had our differences, especially with Tony. He's disrespectful to Shirley. She doesn't deserve it."

"Do you want me to talk to him about that?" she said, knowing it wouldn't do any good. She ran a hand over the fender of the dark vehicle. It looked washed and polished, not just back from a dusty trip. "Nice car."

He nodded. "Thanks. No, don't talk to him. That's not your job."

"Good mileage?"

"It's roomy and comfortable, which is what you want for a trip like the one we just took. I better go." They had little to say to each other anymore. The kids were the common thread.

"I'll keep the kids the next few weekends, at least till school starts. Okay?"

"Sure. Don't let them ride roughshod over you." He slid onto the leather driver's seat.

"I won't." She lifted a hand as he backed around and drove out. Rather than go inside, she went to the fence where Lucy was sandwiched between Meg and Vicki.

"Okay if Lucy rides Brittle?" Meg asked, winking at Callie.

Callie flushed with what? Pleasure? Confusion? She didn't know how to respond to a wink. Should she wink back? But by then the moment had passed, and she felt like a dope.

"It's okay, isn't it, Mom?" Lucy said eagerly.

"Of course. If I can ride him, anyone can." She laughed.

"You rode him, Mom? You never ride Tawny."

"I did ride Tawny. Didn't I, Meg? We went on a trail ride with Meg and Brittle."

"Can I go on a trail ride, Meg?"

"It's up to your mom." Meg went out in the field with Lucy on her heels, chattering about trail rides.

"I think I better go inside and see what there is to eat. I didn't expect the kids."

"I'll go get a couple of large pizzas. We can have a welcome home celebration."

Callie stared at her, amazed at her assumption that she was part of the family. She said, "If you let me pay for them."

"My idea, my treat."

It occurred to her that she should have a serious talk with Vicki about appropriate expectations. The more Vicki settled into her life, the less Callie resisted. Vicki made things easier for her. She also filled in the holes, the lonely times. She might even miss her if Vicki gave up the chase.

Later at the kitchen table, after Meg had gone out, Tony hunched over his plate, mumbling when spoken to. She didn't remember him as this withdrawn, this unpleasant. No wonder his father found him annoying. He'd just gotten home and already she was irritated with him. "Tell us about your trip, Tony," she said.

"Long." He inhaled a slice of pizza.

"Hey, the Grand Canyon was cool. So was Yellowstone. You said so yourself." Lucy challenged him from across the table. "You eat like a pig."

"Like you're Miss Manners," he shot back, his mouth full of red, doughy crust.

"Don't talk with your mouth full," Callie said, picking the pepperoni pieces off her slice with a fork.

"I'll eat them, Ma." Tony snatched the meat off her plate.

"Hey." Callie was protesting his manners, not the loss of the pepperoni. She shot an embarrassed glance at Vicki.

"You remind me of my nephews, Brady and Crawfish," Vicki said with a grin. "My brother stabs them with his fork when they do stuff like that."

"Yeah?" Tony looked at her with interest.

"Do you like to water ski, Tony?"

"Sure. Dad owns a Ski Nautique. Gets you out of the water just like that." He snapped his fingers.

"Well, my brother owns a MasterCraft. It gets you out of the water pretty fast, too. When you go to the lake, we can ski and tube."

"We're going to the lake?" Tony looked at her.

"Two weeks before school starts." She turned to Vicki. "I didn't know you were spending that time at your brother's place."

"I'll take vacation. We'll have fun."

"I'm asking Janie, Mom. Okay?" Lucy said.

"Will your nephews be there?" Tony stared at Vicki as if he'd just seen her.

"Afraid not. They play football, and they're from Illinois. Maybe next summer."

Tony no longer showed any interest in sports. Callie knew that joining any school activity would look good on a college application, but she never pushed.

"Shirley says Tony needs to untangle his legs and arms." Lucy giggled.

"That's not funny," Callie said, incensed.

"She hates me. I hate her." Tony stared at his plate, then reached for another piece of pizza.

"You just rub each other the wrong way." Callie wanted to rush to the nearest phone and yell at Tim, but just watching and listening to Tony made her realize how difficult it must have been for Shirley to deal with him.

Vicki left after supper. Callie walked out to her car with her and stood in the semi-dark as a skein of geese flew over, honking. How she hated it when winter forced her inside.

"I'll see you Thursday at cycling. I've got a conference in Madison Monday to Wednesday." Vicki smiled. One eyetooth was a little crooked, giving her smile some interest. Leaning forward, she kissed Callie on the cheek. "It was a fun weekend."

Surprised, Callie put her hand over the spot. "It was. Thanks for taking me."

"Hey, you were invited. Thanks for riding along."

"I wouldn't have been invited if it hadn't been for you."

Darkness fell imperceptibly, till they were swathed in it. "That's not true."

Callie watched the Audi's taillights until the car turned the corner. She had almost kissed Vicki back.

That night she fell asleep on the porch. She nearly shot out of the chair when Meg put a hand on her shoulder. "Go to bed, Callie."

Clearing her throat, she said, "I wasn't waiting up for you."

"Yes, you were." Meg's hair glowed, backlit by a lamp in the living room.

Maybe because she was still half asleep and had no time to think, she asked, "Am I wasting my time?"

"I don't want to hurt you."

She shifted in the chair to ease her back. "Why did you do what you did in the trailer that night?"

"Because you were there. Because I knew I could."

"I liked it," she said in a small voice, embarrassed by her need.

Meg took her hand and led her inside. Almost in a trance, Callie followed her to the bed where Meg covered her with her long body. As her mouth closed over Callie's, she said, "You're so willing."

Callie plunged her fingers into Meg's hair, loosening it from the ponytail until it fell in her face. As before, she got bogged down in the kissing. She never heard the door open, but she felt Meg stiffen.

"Mom, something's outside my window," Lucy said, "like a wolf. I saw it eating a rabbit. Mom? Who is that?"

Meg carefully rolled off Callie and slid to the floor where she crouched by the window as if she'd been there all along. "We heard something outside, too," she said in a calm voice. "Your mom called me in here to see what it was. Don't turn on the light."

"Go back to your room, honey. I'll be right there." Callie's heart fluttered with angst as she propelled Lucy toward the doorway, not allowing Lucy to look back, softly closing the door behind her. God, was she nuts or what? She could lose both her kids this way. But the feel of Meg's body against hers lingered.

There was no wolf outside Lucy's open window. A bush moved in the wind. A rabbit hunkered underneath it.

Chapter 5

Meg was gone when Callie left for the store the next morning. They had parted in the living room the night before, after convincing Lucy that there was no wolf, after Meg promised Lucy a ride on Brittle the next day. The only way Lucy would sleep was with her mother.

Callie unlocked the store and stepped inside. It smelled like the enclosed environment it was, artificially heated and cooled. She threw open the doors. She had spent the night wondering less about the consequences of getting caught in bed with Meg and more about whether she would ever get Meg in her bed again. Rubbing her thumb against her fingers, she imagined Meg's hair between them.

When Marc arrived late in the afternoon, his first words were, "You look like shit, sweetie."

"Thanks. You are so tactful."

"How was the weekend?"

"Great fun. Remember, I'm going to the cottage the second to last week of the month? Have you talked to Ronnie about working here?"

"It's about time you got a life. Ronnie is thrilled. He'll come in before then so that you can train him."

"Is he reliable?"

"He's a sweet man."

"How long have you known him?" She was hanging up clothes that had been left in the dressing rooms. The place had been a zoo all day. She still found it amazing that a commercial and a new sign could change the traffic so much.

"Forever."

"Tim brought the kids home yesterday afternoon." She had called them once late morning to tell Tony to mow the lawn. Lucy had phoned her twice, the first time wanting to know if she could ride Tawny and the second to argue why not. Callie had said she could ride when she got home.

"How are the little buggers? Why didn't you bring them with you?"

"They're not little anymore, and I'd have to drag them out of bed. Teenagers spend their mornings sleeping. Actually, Tony is a little difficult. He's so incommunicative, I worry about him."

"Want me to talk to him?" Marc offered.

"And what would you say?" In her opinion, well-meaning adults made matters worse. She could picture Tony rolling his eyes to Marc's advice.

"You're right. I'm no one to lecture." He grinned wolfishly. "You can go home now, you know."

"Good. I have to pick up some groceries."

At home, Tony was mowing, whizzing up and down the yard, leaving behind uncut swaths of grass. He was plugged into some music. Lucy and Meg were in the small pen with the two horses. After she put away the groceries, she went out to the barn.

"I rode Brittle, Mom. He's really cool. He does everything you ask him to. How did he get to be like that, Meg?"

"Somebody else trained him and then couldn't keep him. He was a show horse." Meg's eyes danced when her gaze lighted on Callie.

Callie felt a flush climb up her neck. Her head buzzed in the afternoon sun.

"Meg said I could go with her on a trail ride sometime if it's okay with you, Mom. I told her you wouldn't mind."

"Just for an afternoon." Meg put a hand on Lucy's shoulder. "She's a good little rider."

Lucy visibly puffed up. "Thanks." Lucy reached into her jeans pocket and pulled out her vibrating cell phone. She put it to her ear and danced away.

"Better her than me," Callie said and Meg laughed. "Want to eat with us? Hamburgers and frozen fries. It's the least I can do."

"I'm meeting a friend, but thanks."

Callie wanted to ask where she went night after night but, of course, she couldn't. "Another time. Thanks for being so good to Lucy."

"Hey, she's a great kid. Lots of potential there."

"For riding horses?" That wasn't what she had in mind for Lucy's future.

"It's a good hobby. Showing gives a kid poise."

"Well, the only show she goes to is 4-H Horse and Pony at the county fair, and she missed that one this year." Callie was thinking it was an expensive hobby.

"She'll be ready for next year." They were alone now. "Sorry about last night."

Sorry for what? That they hadn't finished what they started? But she found she couldn't ask that question either. "Me too."

The Saturday two weeks before Labor Day weekend, they drove to the cottage. Both kids wanted to stay home. Lucy's friend Jane was going somewhere with her family, and it was too late to ask anyone else. Callie threw Tony's clothes into a couple of paper sacks and promised him he could drive. He had his permit. That's the only way she got him into the car.

At the end of the driveway, the tires squealed as they hit pavement. Callie and Lucy were slammed against the backs of their seats. "Whoa," Callie said. "Take it easy. We're not late for anything. Let's get there in one piece."

Tony grunted something and grinned at her.

The smile transformed his face and startled her into saying, "You're handsome when you smile."

Of course, he didn't believe her. "Yeah, Mom, sure." He grinned into the rearview mirror. "Now the real truth. How do I look, Luce?"

Lucy was hooking up to her iPod. "Like a dope."

"Said like a true sister."

At least, he'd shed his surliness. "Do you remember how to get there?" Callie asked.

When they pulled into the sandy driveway that led to the cottage, Callie felt as if she was coming home. A sigh slipped from her. "Grab something to carry inside before running off."

The kids threw their clothes on the beds. Tony set the cooler down in front of the fridge. "Can I go now?"

"You bet." A warm breeze rushed in when she threw open the windows. She watched the kids hurry down to the lake. Lucy ran, but Tony was too cool for that. She saw the urgency in his step, though. On the pier, he grabbed Lucy's shoulders as if he was going to throw her in the water. She screamed and ran toward shore. Callie grinned. Everything seemed normal.

The warmth gave a false sense that summer would continue, even as the mellower rays and shorter days signaled its end. Callie put the groceries away and donned her swimsuit. She packed a book and sunscreen and a towel before joining the kids on the beach. Tony and Lucy were dragging things out of the boathouse, and she asked for a chair.

She would happily sit here all day, she thought, getting up only to swim or sail or go see Kate and Pat. She secretly hoped the two women would hear the commotion and come to visit her. Tony emerged from the boathouse with a fishing rod and started down the beach, wading and casting. Lucy splashed after him.

"You have to be quiet or you can't come," he said before they had gone far. How many years had it been since he'd let his sister follow him anywhere? Probably the last time they were here.

Callie settled deeper in the chair, burying herself in her book, glancing up every once in a while to see how far down the beach the kids had gone. She gazed appreciatively at the blue-green water and sniffed the soft breeze carrying scents from the lake—the smell of water and weeds and fish. Turtles lay in a line of largest to smallest on a log down the beach, some on top of each other.

The first speedboat appeared, followed quickly by a second and third. She looked up as Vicki's MasterCraft rocketed around the lake. The waves gently nudging the shore began to roll in, and the turtles scrambled off the log. That's when she saw the kids standing on the end of Kate's pier. She'd told them not to fish from people's docks, but someone was with them. Pat, she thought, who was waving down the MasterCraft.

The week turned into days of water skiing and tubing, playing volleyball, and sailing. On Wednesday, Callie sat with Kate on her beach. Everyone else, including the dog, was on the boat, except for Lucy and Tony who were tubing. Lucy's screams of terrorized joy echoed across the water.

"So how is Meg?" Kate asked.

Callie had phoned Meg the previous night to give her Marc's number in case she wanted to come to the cottage. Marc could take care of the horses and cat. She knew she hadn't forgotten to tell her before they left, but she wanted to hear Meg's voice, to know she was still there, to tell her again that she was welcome to join them at the lake. Sometimes she thought she'd dreamt the night in the trailer, but then she remembered Lucy catching her in bed with Meg. If one had happened, so had the other. "She's going to take Lucy on a trail ride. Lucy will love it. Until Meg came along, I was thinking about selling Lucy's horse. Horses are expensive hobbies."

"I'll bet."

"I still am thinking of selling him, actually. I haven't said anything to Lucy yet. She'll be back in school soon with even less time to ride. Got any good advice on this?"

"How attached is she to the horse?"

"She spends more time riding now that Meg is there, but lots of that time she's riding Meg's horse."

"Maybe Meg's horse will take the place of hers." Kate glanced at Callie. "I'm not good at giving advice to friends. Anyway, I gave notice. Someone else is taking over the column. It's a huge relief to be rid of it."

The MasterCraft sped past with Vicki skiing the last round. She let go of the towrope and coasted in, sinking when she neared shore. Pat pulled back the throttle and made a small circle with the boat as Tony reeled in the towrope and Lucy took off her life jacket. It was nearly five thirty.

"It's time for us to go back to the cottage." Callie stood and stretched. She was ready for a swim and a drink, in that order. The problem was the kids always wanted to be in the boat or riding behind it. Callie wished them to find their fun swimming, sailing and kayaking like she did.

"Want to drive the boat to your place, Tony?" Vicki asked.

"Yeah," he said enthusiastically.

"Want to swim with me, Lucy?" Callie asked.

"Is it okay if I ride, Mom?" Lucy said.

"I guess. Thanks for the company, Kate."

"Hey, anytime. See you tomorrow."

Callie stuffed her things in her beach bag and started down the shore. Her vacation with the kids was supposed to be a re-bonding of sorts, but when did that ever work? They would have been bored without Vicki's boat.

Tony stood behind the wheel, traversing the shoreline. Everything about him shouted, hey look at me! Callie fought off a jealous urge to snatch her son and daughter back from Vicki's grip. She paused and bent to look at a colorful stone, then sent it skipping across the water.

When she reached her beach, she stopped dead. Someone was sitting in one of the chairs. Her heart flipped as it always did when she recognized Meg.

"Didn't expect me to take you up on the invitation, did you?"

Slender and sexy in a two-piece bikini, Meg's golden skin was beaded with water. Her hair was pulled up in the high ponytail Callie always wanted to release.

Callie sucked in her breath. "I'm glad you did."

The boat bumped the pier, and Lucy jumped out and ran to greet Meg. "Vicki's here, too. That's her boat, Meg. Do you water ski?"

Meg smiled at the girl and lifted her gaze to Vicki and Tony and the boat. "I do. Do you?"

"I just learned how. Mom won't do it, though." Lucy flapped her elbows and clucked.

"I'm not scared. It was fun when I was a kid. I'd just rather do other things now," Callie said defensively.

"Mom would rather read a book. Boring…"

"Lucy, you're always reading books. So don't give me that boring stuff."

Meg laughed. "No fighting on vacation."

Callie felt foolish and was glad when Vicki joined them.

Vicki glanced from Callie to Meg. "I didn't know you were coming."

"I didn't either, but when Dan said he'd take care of the horses and the cat, I decided to take Callie up on her invitation at least for a couple of days. It's hot back home."

Especially on the second floor of the farmhouse, Callie thought, wondering if she had enough brats for dinner.

"Why don't you come over and eat at my place? It's kind of lonely there," Vicki said.

Tomorrow they'd have one more for volleyball, Callie thought. She became more and more superfluous, shoved to one side by the younger and more athletic.

The night ended with another ride in Vicki's boat. Callie's thoughts had gone ahead to the cottage and where everyone would sleep. No privacy there. She sat in the back with her kids, while Meg rode up front next to Vicki. She strained to hear their conversation, but the motor drowned it out.

The night was alive with the sounds of insects. She lay sweating on the sheets, listening. Vicki had gone home reluctantly, promising to be back at nine thirty on the dot when no-wake hours ended. Tony slept on the other side of the room, quietly snoring. Lucy was dead to the world in the rollout next to his. Meg's bed was only a few feet from hers, but Meg was turned away, facing the screen.

"There's something out there," she whispered.

"Like what?" Callie asked, galvanized out of a half-sleep.

"Whatever they are, they're fighting. Hear them?"

"Probably coons. I put out some bird seed." She listened to the squabbling. If she chased them away, they'd come back.

"They're rocking the pole," Meg said. "I'm going out there."

"Me too." She scrambled out of bed.

When they opened the door, the coons fled. The two women sat on the bench out front. Callie told Meg how Vicki had spent the night there, how she had locked her out. She felt Meg's gaze on her, her breath soft as the night on her cheek.

"What are you afraid of, Callie?" Meg drew her long legs up on the bench and wrapped her arms around them.

Callie looked at the stars. What was she afraid of? She spoke slowly. "That if I let her foot in the door, I won't be able to get rid of her."

"Maybe you won't want to get rid of her."

It was Meg she didn't want rid of, but she couldn't bring herself to say that. "Maybe. I went with this really nice guy, Scott, for a while, but I just didn't want to get involved. You know?" What did that have to do with anything?

Meg nodded. "Hey, some people don't want to tie up their lives. They like their options open."

"Like you?" The darkness made it easier to ask.

"Yes and no."

"Nicky," Callie said quietly.

"Let's go back to bed. We don't want to be tired tomorrow." Meg put a hand on her shoulder and steered her toward the door.

She had her answer, but Nicky wasn't available, was she?

Her gaze flew to Meg's empty bed when she awoke. Tony, too, was gone. Lucy slept on, her head covered by the sheet. Sunlight streaked through the windows. Tony's and Meg's covers were pulled up haphazardly. They had crept out while she and Lucy dozed on. Looking out the window, she spied Meg on the pier casting. Tony stood up to his shorts in water, also flinging his line into the depths. While she watched, Tony reeled in a fish, showed it to Meg and released it.

After putting on shorts and eating a piece of toast, she walked down to the lake. She'd go for a kayak ride before no-wake hours ended.

"Hey, Mom, I caught a big bass," Tony said as she carried the kayak to the water.

"I saw. How about you, Meg?" She looked up at Meg's tangled hair, sticking out of its ponytail like rays of sunlight.

Meg smiled, her eyes sleepy, happy. "He's got me beat, but I could do this all day and not care if I caught anything."

Callie paddled away, not really wanting to leave, but having put the kayak in the water, she felt she had to go. She was at the far end of the lake in the weeds where the water overflowed, watching a nervous heron stab at small creatures on the shoreline, when Vicki's boat eased her way.

Vicki killed the engine and picked up a rod. "The heron and I are fishing. Want to join us? I've got another pole." She held it up.

"I don't fish, remember?" She smiled up at Vicki, for some reason very happy.

"Gorgeous day, isn't it?"

"It is." The sky was a cloudless pale blue.

"Would you mind if I asked Meg out?"

"What?" She thought she'd heard wrong.

"You're not interested in me."

She felt slightly nauseous, the euphoria gone. The day hadn't changed, but she had.

"Are you?" Vicki's line sang toward the shore, ending in a plop as the lure dropped. The heron flapped its wings and squawked as it moved out of reach.

She stared at Vicki, and then looked away to hide her outrage. Fickle, she thought unfairly. "Go ahead," she said, unable to admit that she wanted things to stay as they were. It became perfectly clear to her in that moment that she liked Vicki's attention almost as much as she longed for a repeat of that night with Meg. She paddled toward the cottage blindly.

"Hey," Vicki called after her, firing up the engine. The MasterCraft drew abreast of the kayak. "I didn't think you cared."

"Why don't you tell the whole lake? Sound carries over water, you know."

"Sorry. I'll see you at nine thirty."

She paddled furiously, leaving Vicki behind. When she was far enough away, she splashed water on her face, surprised by angry tears.

Meg was still casting from the pier, but Tony was gone. "Hey, you okay?"

"Yeah. I'm just fine. Want some breakfast?" She beached the kayak.

"Nah. I brought some food. I already ate."

Callie stood on the shore, digging into the sand with her toes, miserable where only an hour ago she'd been content. She had to put on a good face. No one must know how she felt. She sat in a beach chair and watched Meg's rhythmic casts.

At nine thirty, she was still sitting watching Meg cast. She had no energy to go up the stairs, to put on her swimsuit or get her book or see what her kids were up to. By the time Vicki's MasterCraft barreled around the small point and headed toward the pier, Callie had gathered her feelings into a tight ball. This was for the best, she told herself. Let Vicki make up her mind for her. Damn Vicki anyway. No one had chased her like that, ever. Maybe it had scared her, but it had also given her a high.

She started up the steps before Vicki docked at the pier, passing the kids on their way down.

"Hey, Mom, where are you going? Vicki's here," Lucy said.

"I know. I'm just going to put my swimsuit on. I'll be down soon." She could hide upstairs. No one would know how fragile she felt, like she might shatter if someone said the wrong thing. They'd never miss her once they started skiing, nor would they expect her to participate.

It was Kate who found her, sitting in a chair in front of the cottage, a book in her lap, staring at the lake through the trees that marched down the hill. "So here you are. No one seemed to know."

Or care, she thought. "I just never made it downstairs."

Kate was looking at her with concern. "Is everything all right?"

She paused before taking the plunge. "Vicki wants to ask Meg out. She wanted to know if I minded. Why should I care?"

Kate sat in the chair next to Callie's. "But you do care."

She glanced at Kate, briefly meeting her gaze. "But why? I should be glad. It gets Vicki out of my face."

"I suppose you were flattered by her interest, and you are attracted to Meg. Right?"

"You won't tell anyone, will you?" She was vain enough to be humiliated.

"No, of course not. Can I help?"

"You already have. You're the only one I can talk to."

"My husband dumped me for a younger woman. I know what it feels like to be discarded. But you're not being dumped. You told Vicki you weren't interested. She'd be back in a minute if you gave her the word. Come on down. We need you for volleyball."

Callie laughed harshly. "Yeah, like a thorn in the foot. I'm a handicap."

"Well, so am I. I don't want to be the only one."

"Okay." She'd pretend she didn't mind Vicki's interest in Meg. It was a beautiful day. Why spoil it? But there it was, like a knife in the side. She felt betrayed, abandoned.

She and Kate walked down the beach to Kate's place where the others were already playing volleyball. She joined Kate and

Pat and Tony. They faced Meg and Vicki and Lucy. "Hey, why don't I sit this one out?" she said, but no one would hear of it.

The first ball flew past her head, and she nearly ducked. Fortunately, it went out of bounds. Then it was her turn to serve. Her overhand attempts had netted the ball so far, so she served underhand and the ball barely made it over the net. Meg slammed it across and Kate flung an arm out and missed. Pat managed to return it, only to have Vicki send it soaring again toward Callie. She put up her hands and it bounced off them and Tony popped it over the net where Pat fell face first in the water trying to return it.

They were all laughing, causing the dog to romp around, bumping into legs and splashing everyone. "Hey, big guy, you want to be on our side?" Meg said, patting him as he bounced off her.

Afterward, Kate asked Callie if she'd go with her to make sandwiches. "We can go home for lunch. You don't have to feed us," Callie protested.

Kate took her arm. "I want to. You're not going back there and hide. You've got no reason to do that."

Had it been obvious to anyone else? She had yet to meet Vicki's eyes or say anything to Meg. Instead, she watched them, wondering if Vicki had already made a move. It paralyzed her, this feeling of unimportance.

"I've got sliced ham. What do you think?" Kate said.

"Sounds good." Anything to have something to do, although she wanted to be outside making sure Meg hadn't gone off with Vicki. She wondered what right she had to be possessive about either of them?

They carried two trays of sandwiches and chips, iced tea and beer outside. After eating, the others went out in the boat while she and Kate cleaned up and then sat on the beach. She was calmer now, resigned, she thought.

She invited Kate and Pat and Vicki to dinner without having a clue as to what she'd fix. Refusing any help, she went back to the cottage early to make potato salad and slaw to go with hamburgers. When the others came, she fixed them drinks and they sat on the shore, while Lucy and Tony tossed a ball back and forth in the lake.

When it was time to go upstairs and start the grill, everyone except the kids offered to help, but Kate insisted on going with her. It was Kate who got the fire going, while Callie fixed herself another drink and made the patties.

By the time they sat down to eat, her head was swimming. She kept her mouth shut, hoping her kids wouldn't notice, and switched from liquor to water. The conversation flowed around her. She felt as dumb as a boulder in a stream.

The evening ended finally, allowing her to fall into bed. "You're drunk, Mom," Tony said.

Lucy defended her. "No, she's not."

"Go to bed," she told them with as much authority as she could muster. She wasn't sure when everyone left or where Meg was. Maybe she was spending the night at Vicki's place. She remembered Vicki saying how lonely it was there.

She awoke in the night when Meg tapped her on the shoulder. "Hey, the northern lights are putting on a show. Wake the kids up and come down to the pier. It's a no-miss."

The kids were groggy and unwilling, until Meg said, "You want to see this."

Lying on the pier, Callie watched the green sky pulse overhead. More people than they were watching. From around the lake came "Ohs" and "Ahs." Callie nearly laughed aloud, happy that Meg wanted to share this with her and the kids.

"Where is Vicki?" she asked.

"Out in the boat."

"We should have called Kate and Pat."

"They're on their pier."

"Mom, what makes it look like that?"

"I don't know, sweetie. Some atmospheric phenomena. It's called the Aurora Borealis. Wasn't this worth waking up to see?" She put an arm around Lucy and scooted close, basking in her warmth.

She fell asleep and again awoke when Meg touched her arm. "It's over. The kids are already on their way up. C'mon, woman."

Only regular stars glittered overhead. Callie wrapped her arms around Meg's neck and pulled her down. Meg's lips were cold and only briefly responsive. She put her hands on Callie's arms and freed herself.

"Don't forget the kids. It's dark, but we're not invisible." Her tone was kind. "Another time, Callie."

"Yeah. Right. Sorry." She got to her feet, stiff all over, glad that the night hid her expression.

Meg left the next morning. Lucy and Tony said their goodbyes and went down to the lake to wait for Vicki. Callie was unable to meet Meg's eyes.

Meg hooked a finger under her chin and lifted it. "Thanks for inviting me. It was great fun." She bent forward and kissed Callie full on the mouth.

Callie's eyes opened wide and Meg laughed. "You read like a book. You need to turn the page and get on with it."

"I will," she said, breathless.

"Don't come out. I'll be gone in a minute. See you at the house."

She watched Meg slip out the door, heard the truck start and leave. Determined to enjoy this last day, she put on her swimsuit and went down to the lake.

Chapter 6

Callie drove to Brook Middle School strung tight from too much coffee and not enough sleep. She hadn't begun a new job in fifteen years, not counting the store where she was her own boss.

The in-service took place in the cafeteria, where tables had been pushed back to the walls, leaving an open space. Everyone introduced him or herself. Her mentor, the librarian, Janice Gordon, stood next to her. Janice was a plump, pretty woman with a dazzling smile and good skin. The person doing the in-service had been brought in from outside. A bright, bird-like forty-some woman told them all to hold hands and close their eyes. She talked about how they were interdependent, that they needed to work as a team. Trust was the theme. That was just the beginning.

When it was over two hours later, Janice showed Callie to her office next to the library and closed the door before saying, "I don't know about you, but I could have put that time to better use."

Callie looked around the small room, at the window with a view of the parking lot, at the empty bookcase and bare walls with hooks where pictures had once hung. Taking up most of the desktop was a school calendar with dates for events like homecoming and parent-teacher conferences. Janice sat in one of the two chairs facing the desk. Callie took the one behind it. Her professional books wouldn't begin to fill the bookcase. She opened the desk drawers, empty except for pens and pencils and a legal pad.

"C'mon, I'll show you around," Janice said. "I'll bet you don't remember most of the names you heard this morning."

"None, except yours."

"You will learn them quickly enough."

In the library there were boxes of books stacked on top of each other. "Do you need help with these?"

"Most of them belong to teachers, who will pick them up soon enough. You haven't seen the staff lounge or the music room or the computer room or the gymnasium. We'll take a quick tour."

In less than an hour she was back at her office with names and faces swirling around her brain. "I'll go bring in my stuff now."

"Hey, Jim, have you got time to help Callie carry in her things?"

The tall man with a ring full of keys was locking a door down the hall. "You bet. Just lead the way."

"Thanks." Callie fell into step beside him. "I'm Callie Callahan, the new guidance counselor."

Her hand disappeared in his large grip. "I'm Jim Needham, the maintenance man. Anything you want, I can get. Almost." He smiled and winked at her.

"I'll remember that."

He hung around after setting her boxes down to give her advice. "Some of the kids are pretty lost. What they need is a pat on the back and a shove in the right direction. I think they're too rough on them these days, expelling them for some foolishness in the parking lot."

While he talked, she unpacked her things—putting her books on the shelves, her diplomas on the wall and a spider plant in the window. A vaguely familiar looking teacher stuck her head in the door and asked Jim for help. Callie was ready to be alone with her thoughts.

All staff met in the afternoon when school policy was discussed. Afterward, Callie went with Janice to the library and helped empty more boxes. Janice was married with two kids in college. She'd been teaching twenty-five years and expected to retire in five more.

Callie said little. She seldom talked about her work in child protection unless it was to Sandy. People failed to understand why they just didn't take the kids away from their parents or tell the mother to choose between the boyfriend and her children. No way could she make most people understand that legally that wasn't always possible and that kids seldom wanted to leave what they knew to go to someplace unknown. They preferred the familiar, even if it was a pattern of abuse. It depressed her to talk about those years.

"Do many kids ask to see a guidance counselor?" she asked.

"They ask or are sent for some reason or another. Some have scheduling problems. Those are the easy ones. Then there are the girls who are pregnant, the kids who are at risk for other reasons, the ones who need a little talk about hygiene."

It sounded a little like child protection. "Well, I guess I'll find out soon enough who shows up at my door. I thought there was a stigma attached to seeing a guidance counselor."

"There is, but the kids will be curious. You're new. That predator we had last year fooled even me."

"I remember reading about him."

A bell rang. Callie looked at the big clock above the door. Four o'clock.

"Time to go home," Janice said. "See you tomorrow."

She nodded. "Thanks for all the help."

At home, she stepped out of the car into the hot sun and stood there a minute, stretching her arms and back, shedding the past few hours. The school bus screeched to a halt at the end of the driveway and Lucy and Tony got out. Lucy ran toward her mother. Tony dragged his feet and looked at the ground.

"What do you see there, Tony?" she asked when he passed her on his way to the house.

"Nothing to see."

She remembered when he was young, eagerly telling her about his day.

"His fat friend ignored him." Lucy laughed. "Why do you want gross Peter for a friend?"

Tony lunged at her and she danced away. "He's a bully and a dope. They held him back a year."

"Okay, Lucy. That's enough."

"She's just a dummy. What does she know anyway?" he snarled and slumped into the house.

"Peter smokes and does drugs," she called after him.

Tony dropped his books and turned on his sister. "What do you know, you big baby? She cries if he talks to her."

"What does he say?" Callie asked.

"That she's a skinny, sexless, boring baby."

Callie put a protective arm around Lucy. "Does this Peter do drugs, Tony?"

Tony picked up his books and gave his mother and sister an angry look. "How would I know?" The door slammed behind him before Callie could question him further.

And this was only the first day of school, she thought. Her kids were in a different district from where she worked. "Go change, sweetie, and don't fight with your brother."

Callie went to her bedroom and threw herself on the bed. An incipient headache gathered behind her eyes. Was it better to be stressed or bored? The door pushed opened and Bill jumped on the bed. Purring loudly, he stretched out next to her. Stressed was definitely better, she thought, stroking the cat.

Fed up after a dinner where Tony snarled and Lucy tried to pick a fight with him, Callie told them to clean up the dishes and went outside. This weekend they would be at their dad's, no matter how they protested.

Meg was riding Brittle bareback in the field with Tawny and the two goats trailing after them. She rode up to the gate where Callie stood. "We could ride down the road a bit."

"Not even you can talk me into that," she said.

"Aw, c'mon. It's so nice out."

"Bareback? Are you out of your mind?"

"I'll put a saddle on the one you want to ride. You choose."

"Brittle, of course." She was nuts, she thought, but then she was nuts about Meg who was laughing at her.

Meg was giving her a leg up when Lucy raced outside. "Hey, I want to go."

"When we get back," Meg promised. "I have to talk to your mother."

"Did you finish the dishes?" Callie asked.

"I did them all by myself. Tony went back to his room."

"Good girl." She wriggled her feet into the stirrups as Meg moved off on a reluctant Tawny.

"You wanted to talk to me?" They rode in the wide ditch next to the road.

"Are you sure you want Vicki out of your life?"

It was strange to be looking down at Meg, her long legs tangling in the tall grasses. "She wants to go out with you."

"No, she doesn't. Not really," Meg said. "How was your first day at work?"

"Okay. Vicki told me she wanted to go out with you."

"Lucy is following us on her bike."

Callie hadn't noticed. Damn, she thought. "Where do you go every night?"

"Let it go, Callie," Meg said as Lucy caught up with them. The sudden appearance of the bike gave Tawny an excuse to jump around, but Meg calmed him down.

Callie changed horse for bike at the crossroads. She pedaled beside them for a while before turning toward home.

At the end of the first week of classes, Callie was exhausted.

She'd set up a group for the four pregnant freshmen girls, rearranging their study hours so that they could attend. She'd advised several kids on the courses they should be taking while they could still reschedule. She'd met with the vice principal about dealing with the tougher kids, the ones she couldn't handle. The job challenged her.

When Tim came for the kids Friday night, neither wanted to go. Callie knew he didn't want to make them either. "We just got home, Dad," Lucy whined.

He bristled. "My home is your home, too."

"Yeah, sure," Tony said in a surly voice, but he got into the car.

When they were gone, Callie went inside and fixed a drink. She carried it to the porch with a book. The cat curled up in her lap. He, at least, could never leave her. After sunset, she sat in the dark, knowing what it would be like when everyone was gone. Lonely. She awoke, cold and still alone without even Bill to warm her legs. He was lying on her bed when she climbed under the covers.

Meg came in and went upstairs. Another opportunity lost, she thought. Maybe she should go to Meg's bed. Would she send her away? She put on a robe and crept up the steps where she heard Meg talking on her cell.

"Forget it. I'm not here for your pleasure. You can't snap your fingers and expect me to come."

Callie turned and tiptoed back down the stairs. She started when Meg called her name.

"What are you doing? Eavesdropping?"

"I didn't mean to listen. I..." but she couldn't think what she was doing there on the stairs that made sense, other than the real reason, and finally said, "I wanted to make sure it was you."

Meg laughed harshly. "Yeah. Well, come on up and see."

Obediently, Callie climbed the steps and stood at the top, looking into Meg's stormy eyes. Her heart galloped around in her chest, making breathing difficult. "Look, I'm sorry. I won't do it again."

"Come closer. I don't bite. Well, sometimes I do." Meg's face cleared, the frown replaced with a knowing smile. She wriggled her fingers in a come-hither gesture.

Meg's bedroom walls were bare. Only a lamp and a book on the bedside table gave it any feeling of occupancy. Unpacked boxes were stacked in a corner.

Callie shivered as Meg lowered her on the bed, not even bothering to remove any clothing. She hadn't expected the bruising kisses, the abrupt and hurried sweep of Meg's hands. But as the minutes passed and Meg's body relaxed, her movements slowed. Callie was afraid she was going to give up and fall back on the bed. It was then that Callie felt the wetness on her face. She brushed Meg's tears away with the heels of her hands. "Don't stop," she whispered.

Meg's kisses turned gentle and her hands began a slow caress. Callie struggled out of her clothes and attempted to remove Meg's. Meg jerked her T-shirt over her head and wiggled out of her jeans. She started to move under Callie's touch. Callie, who was still learning, who was greedy to use all the means available to please Meg, was thrilled at the response.

Afterward, Callie burrowed into Meg's long frame. There were so many things she wanted to say, but they all seemed trite. She was still thinking about how to express her wonder when Meg fell asleep.

The next morning she awoke in a pool of warmth, alone. She threw the covers off, put on the sleep shirt and robe that lay in a heap on the floor next to her side of the bed and hurried downstairs.

Bill pressed against her legs, making it difficult to walk without tripping. She fed him and picked up the remains of a hapless mouse. It was fall. The rodents were looking for shelter again. Glancing out the window, she saw Meg in the pen, brushing Brittle, and felt suddenly shy.

After dressing, she went out with two cups of coffee. She carefully set Meg's cup on a fence post. Meg turned and smiled as if amused, and Callie's heart tumbled. Did Meg find humorous what Callie thought extraordinary? Her face flamed and Meg laughed.

Meg reached across the wire and lifted Callie's chin. "Hey, it was great. You're a fast learner. Thanks for the coffee. Grab a piece of toast. We'll go for a ride."

"I can't. I have to work at the store." She had promised Marc.

"Okay. I'll see you later." Meg went back to Brittle, who turned his long neck to look at Tawny and the two goats clustered at the gate. Tawny neighed and the goats bleated.

Callie lingered by the fence, drinking her coffee in the warm September sun and only went inside when the cup was empty.

Unlocking the back door of the shop, she felt the familiar inertia blanket her. What was it about the place that depressed her so? It was successful now, thanks to Vicki. She'd passed Vicki's Audi on the drive into town, not recognizing her soon enough to wave or honk. She supposed Vicki was on her way to see Meg. Maybe she would go down the road with Meg. Why did she mind when she didn't want to ride? But she did. Jealousy made her distrustful and desperate.

The shop was blissfully quiet for the first hour before it filled with bikers. Ronnie was teaching the spinning classes, and they were always well attended. Sandy cycled in the first class, as did Scott. The rest were Ronnie's friends. He now gave three classes on Saturdays.

While he yelled out commands, she stood behind the counter or helped customers. At the end of the second class, Vicki showed up. "Hey, how's it going?" She grinned at Callie, who grinned back. She was glad that Vicki was here, rather than with Meg. Meg didn't want to go out with Callie either, but she was willing to take her to bed.

"Okay. I passed you on the way into town."

"Yep. I talked to Meg a while. She went for a ride down the road. I came here."

She was about to ask what they talked about when Sandy

came over.

"You've gotten skinny," Callie said.

"I'm working on it. Scott is always exercising, so I do. I've had to buy all new clothes. Do you like the new me?" Sandy lifted her arms and let them drop.

"You look great, doesn't she, Vicki?"

"Absolutely. I better get on a bike. You coming, Callie?"

"I can't. I have to watch the cash register."

"I'll watch it," Sandy said.

Callie huffed through a brutal round of Ronnie's commands, which she began to think were aimed at her. Standing runs, standing hills, jumps and sprints. Or maybe she was just out of shape. She hadn't been at any cycling classes for a couple of weeks.

Marc came into the shop later, after she'd changed out of her biking pants and shoes. She said, "I'm leaving. Okay?"

Marc looked up from the cash register, and nodded. "Thanks for coming in. How's the new job?"

"Good so far."

"That's what I wanted to ask," Sandy said.

"I think I'll like it there. Thanks again for helping me get it."

"No problem. Talk to you soon." She linked arms with Scott and headed for the door.

"We helped that girl make some serious changes," Marc said.

"She's a good friend."

Vicki joined them. "Want some company, Callie?"

Marc smiled and winked. "You girls go on and have some fun."

Why not, she thought. The kids were at their dad's. Meg would probably go wherever it was she went, leaving her alone with only Bill for company.

Vicki followed her home. Meg's truck was gone, and it was only mid-afternoon. The horses and goats grazed side by side in the field. Inside, Bill meowed and rubbed against her legs. She gave him a treat and scanned the floor for dead mice. None.

"Where are the kids?" Vicki asked.

"At their dad's. Why didn't you go for a ride with Meg?"

"I don't have a horse. I couldn't steal yours."

"You can ride Tawny anytime. I don't mind. Neither will Lucy. Want something to eat? There's a pizza in the freezer."

"I have to have a beer with pizza." Vicki started toward the door.

"How do you keep your figure?" The question wasn't meant as a compliment. It was a commentary on all the beer Vicki drank.

Vicki gave her a slow smile. "I thought you'd never ask."

"Hey, I have to watch my weight. Not like you, apparently."

"I think you're perfect." Vicki almost looked shy as she turned to go out to her car.

When she came back in, Vicki said, "I have to tell you something."

"What's that?"

"That couple who were renting your cottage when we were at Kate and Pat's?"

"What about them?"

"They told Kate they were going to make an offer on the place."

Callie felt nauseous.

"I'm sorry," Vicki said.

It was as good as gone, she thought, mentally searching frantically and hopelessly for a way to keep it. Maybe Bobby wouldn't sell. There had to have been other offers. "Do you know more than that?"

"Pat said your cousin is considering the offer."

"How does she know?" she asked, suddenly angry.

"Because the couple told her so." Vicki attempted to look into her eyes.

She turned away, swallowing rapidly. Tears clogged her nose.

"Why don't you e-mail him or call him? Tell him you'd be

glad to manage the place for him. Maybe he thinks he's too far away to keep an eye on it."

If she opened her mouth, she knew she'd bawl, so she kept it shut.

Vicki put a hand on her arm. "Do you want anything? A drink?"

Like that'll solve anything, she thought. "Do you know how much they offered?"

"You'll have to ask your cousin. Don't just give up."

"I'll call him." She went to look for his number. Vicki went with her. When she found it, she called on her cell. The phone rang and rang. Bobby's message was terse. "Leave a name and number. I'll call you back." She did.

The afternoon and evening were spoiled. She'd thought when Bobby bought the cottage she'd lost the place, but now she realized losing it would happen when she no longer had access to it. She hung up. "He's not there."

"Call in the morning. Promise me. I'll stay here to make sure you do."

"What's your worse nightmare, Vicki?"

"It already happened," Vicki said.

"What?"

"My parents died in a car crash nearly two years ago."

"Oh." She hadn't been talking about people dying. "I'm sorry."

"Yeah. Me too, but it's true that time helps. It doesn't change anything. It's you that changes." Vicki shrugged. "You go on without them."

She was horrified. "Your brother is your only family?"

"Only immediate family." Vicki smiled but the glint was gone from her eyes.

"Are you close to him?"

"Pretty close," she said. "His kids are the children I never had."

"You must think I'm a whiner."

"I'd be whining too, but you can't just whine. You have to do something about it. Don't wait for him to call back."

"I won't, not that it'll do any good if he wants to sell."

"Hey, come on, you have to be positive. Attitude makes a difference." Vicki sat on the couch and patted the cushion next to her.

Earlier, Callie had hoped Vicki would leave before Meg came home, just in case Meg wanted to repeat last night. Now she didn't care.

"I'd like to stay," Vicki said.

"Why? I'm rotten company. I'm better off alone."

"That's why you need someone around."

"Meg will be home sooner or later."

As if conjured up by her name, Meg walked through the door. "Hey, girls, what's happening?"

Vicki told her. "Don't you think she should offer to manage the place for him? Maybe he won't sell it."

Meg glanced at the two of them, a little frown etched between her brows. She looked as if her thoughts were miles away. "Sure. What have you got to lose?"

Tears massed on Callie's eyelids, but she blinked them back and forced a smile. "Everything."

The next morning, Callie awoke to the smell of coffee. She pulled on sweatpants and a T-shirt before going to the kitchen. She immediately thought that Vicki had slept with Meg, that that was why she was still at the house, because it was clear she'd recently gotten out of bed. The thought outraged her. Fortunately, Vicki spoke first.

"I hope you don't mind. I slept in the guest room. I always carry a toothbrush and a change of undies."

"Why don't you just move in, Vicki?"

"Why don't you come to my house next weekend? You've never been there."

"I didn't know you had one." Callie poured herself a cup of coffee and plunked down in a chair. "What happened with you and Meg? I thought you were going to ask her out?"

Vicki's tan turned reddish. "She doesn't want to date. Those were her words. She was very nice about it. She said if she ever wanted to go out, you and I'd be the first to know." She slid into a chair across from Callie. "Do you love her, Callie?"

Callie dodged the question. "What is it about her?"

"She's goddamn sexy. I wonder who she's seeing?"

"I thought I told you. Nicky Hennessey. She's a photographer. She used to live here."

"I've heard of her. When are you going to call your cousin?"

Callie glanced at her watch. "It's five thirty in California. He'd probably tell me not to call back and hang up."

"What are you going to say?" Smudges of mascara gave Vicki a haunted look.

Callie had been thinking about that. "Do you need someone to manage the rental of the cottage? Someone to make sure it's clean for the next renter, that the windows are shut and the water pump and hot water heater are turned off, that there's no food left in the fridge, that all the outside things, like chairs, are put away, the boats are tied securely, the sail and paddles and other stuff locked in the boathouse." Had she forgotten anything?

Vicki looked impressed. "That's good. He really does need someone at this end. But I don't think you should start with a question. Tell him he needs someone and then tell him why. You could drop the 'Do you need someone' and say I'd love to help you manage the rental of the cottage and go on from there."

That's what she said when she called Bobby at eleven o'clock. She spoke quickly, nervously. After a long silence, Bobby said, "Who is this again?" He sounded sleepy.

"I'm sorry. Did I wake you up? This is your cousin, Callie. I rented the cottage a couple of weeks this summer. I'd like to check on it for you before and after rentals. I wouldn't charge."

He broke in. "Why? There has to be something in it for you."

"Yes, well, I want to be able to rent it a few weeks in the summer. I don't want you to sell it, and somebody needs to make sure the buildings are locked and everything's put away and the place is clean."

Another silence followed by a long yawn. "I'm paying somebody to take care of those things. You'd do it for free? Are you rich, Callie?"

She snorted a laugh. "I'd have bought the place if I were rich." She was watching Meg and Vicki, who were out by the barn. Vicki had said she was going to ride Tawny down the road with Meg.

"There is someone who wants to buy it. Frankly, I'm too far away to keep an eye on it or to use it."

Her hopes sank, creating an almost unbearable ache. It hurt to breathe. "I'll keep an eye on it."

"You know the family has first option to buy if I sell? That was a precondition your dad insisted on. How are your mom and dad anyway?"

"They bought an RV. Right now they're up north."

"I always had a soft spot for you, cuz. You'd do anything I told you to do. Remember when I handed you that snake?" He guffawed. "You actually took it. Your eyes were big as plates. Then you let it go."

She did remember. It had been a huge pine snake and had wound itself around her arm. She'd set it down and watched it zip off into the grass with amazing speed.

"Listen, kiddo, I've got somewhere to go this morning. I'll think about your offer and let you know. I have to notify everyone in the family and give them first chance to buy if I'm going to sell anyway. So it isn't going to be tomorrow."

Only her dad called her kiddo these days. "Okay. Good. Thanks, Bobby."

"I haven't said yes yet. Talk to you later."

She gathered Bill in her arms and went to the porch. He licked her hand, his body vibrating with purrs. Meg and Vicki turned the horses into the ditch at the end of the driveway. Tawny was prancing, tossing his head. She watched the two women dismount and change horses. She smiled to herself, satisfied that Vicki was no braver than she was.

§

Her parents returned on Friday, right after she arrived home from school. Lucy had just gotten off the bus and was walking toward the house when the RV roared up the driveway. Callie parked her car. She got out of the vehicle and waited for everyone. Tony, who had been riding to and from school with friends, wasn't home yet. Callie had wanted to tell him he couldn't ride with these boys, but she'd been unable to think of a good reason. He was still mad at her for cheating him out of moving upstairs, even though he liked Meg. He always perked up and spoke in complete sentences when Meg was around.

Not yet worried about being cool, Lucy threw herself at her grandparents. "Grandma, will you make dinner tonight? I'll gag if I have to eat any more spaghetti."

"Of course, I will—that is if your mom lets me and you help. It's her kitchen." Her mother raised her brows at Callie. "Well?"

Callie had never liked to cook and had learned as little as possible when her mom tried to teach her. "You'll get married and have kids some day, and then you'll wish you'd paid attention to me," her mother had often said when Callie was a teenager.

After she married and had kids, she sometimes wished she had shown more interest. Her sister, Phoebe, had been their mom's right hand in the kitchen, while Callie had helped her dad change the oil in the mower and shovel the walk.

"Hi, Dad, how was your trip?" she asked.

"Expensive. You know what kind of mileage we get with this thing?"

"Single digits?"

"Yeah. I think we're through running around the country. Can't afford it." He held his arms open to Lucy, who moved into them. "How's my pumpkin seed?"

"Good, Grandpa."

"Are you acing your classes?" He kissed the top of her head.

"Yeah, and I'm going on a trail ride with Meg Saturday. Dad said I could stay home for that. Tony's mad about it."

"Where is Tony?" Callie's dad asked.

"With his hoody friends probably," Lucy said.

Callie's parents threw her questioning glances. Was this true?

"They're not hoodlums." Even as Callie denied Lucy's assertion, she realized that she didn't know if they were or not. They all wore jeans that hung down around their hips, so their underwear showed. She'd never had a conversation with any of them. She never had a conversation with her son anymore. He spoke in grunts.

"Everybody says they are."

"Who's everybody?" Callie wanted to know.

"One has a younger sister in my class and another has a younger brother. They say their brothers don't even go to school half the time."

Callie would ask Tony when he got home, but she had an awful feeling that Lucy was telling the truth.

Her dad hung back with her while Lucy and her grandma went inside, arms loaded with food from the RV. "Do you think he's been skipping school?" her dad asked.

Her first impulse was to protect her son, but she knew she didn't have to defend him against his grandfather. "I don't know, Dad. He's a different kid. He talks in monosyllables if he talks at all. He spends most of his time on the computer or with these friends, who all have drivers' licenses."

"You better find out, sweetie." He put an arm around her shoulders.

"And then what do I do? Take away the computer? Make him ride the bus? Follow him around?"

"Good questions. He does have a dad. If he won't listen to you, will he pay attention to him?"

"He hates his stepmother. He's rude to her." She told her dad about the argument when Tim had slapped Tony.

"I know how you itch to smack them sometimes, but you can't."

"He might hit me back," she said.

"Let's go out and see the horses." He nodded toward the field where Brittle and Tawny stood side by side, hind legs cocked, soaking up the late afternoon sun. The two goats were hanging around the gate. "How's your roomer?"

"Meg?" Just saying her name moved something inside Callie. "The kids like her. Tony talks in sentences when she's around."

Her parents stayed after dinner, helping to clean up while waiting for Tony to come home. Meg had fed the animals, come inside and talked a bit, and gone upstairs. Lucy was doing her homework on the kitchen table. The sun had set when they heard the tires on gravel, the voices and the slam of the car door.

Tony looked surprised when he came inside, although he'd surely seen the RV parked next to Meg's trailer. "Hey, Gram and Gramps, how are the traveling duo?"

His grandmother crossed the room to hug him. "You're a hunk."

"Yeah, sure, Grandma." Tony actually smiled.

He wasn't a hunk. He had the usual zits. He was gangly and bony and he dressed like a gang member. Callie finally admitted the last part to herself.

"Hey, grandson, give the old man a hug too." He smiled over Tony's head at Callie.

"Where've you been?" Callie asked, knowing this was the wrong thing to say.

Tony's face shut down. He shrugged. "The car broke down."

"I think you better take the bus from now on."

The boy glared at her. "Only losers take the bus."

She wished she hadn't started this battle, because now she had to finish it. "Then you can change that. You're not a loser." Because Lucy was listening, she said, "We'll talk about this later."

"Sit down and eat." His grandmother put a heaping plateful of food on the table.

Tony stared at it. "I'm not hungry anymore."

"Sure you are, son. Sit down."

Tony either couldn't disobey his grandfather or he was so hungry he was unable to resist. He tore into the food like someone might take it away from him.

"Doesn't your mother feed you?"

"She's the spaghetti queen," he said with his mouth full.

"Yuk," Lucy said.

"Want to see more food, toady?" He opened his mouth for Lucy.

"Hey, not in front of your grandparents," Callie said.

"How was the cottage?" Callie's father asked out of the blue.

"The same. Someone made an offer on it, Dad. I talked to Bobby. I told him I'd check up on the place for him. Make sure it was clean and everything was put away and locked up. I wouldn't charge anything. I want to be able to rent it."

They were all watching her. "Mom, don't let him sell it," Lucy said.

"What a jerk," Tony added. "Can't you stop him?"

"Nope, but he has to offer it to the family first. We have an option to buy." Callie felt a little desperate. Voicing the fact that she had no control over what happened to the cottage made its potential loss more real.

"How much is the offer? Did he say?"

"No, Dad. More than I can pay, I'm sure, even with this new job."

"Let's talk about your new job," Callie's mom said.

"I like it. It's a challenge. The days fly by, I'm so busy." She thought of the group of pregnant girls, not much older than Lucy. They broke her heart every time they giggled like the fourteen-year-olds they were. By the time they reached high school, they'd be irrevocably changed.

Chapter 7

"Come see my home," Vicki said Saturday morning.

Tawny and Brittle had just disappeared down the driveway, carrying Lucy and Meg on their backs. Lowering clouds threatened rain and a slight breeze blew cooling air their way.

"I can't go till I take Lucy to her dad's." Tony was already gone. Tim had picked him up. Callie had called Tim after she'd phoned the school and been told that Tony hadn't been attending regularly. She thought Tony's friends were bad news, and she wanted Tim to talk to him.

"We'll go when they get back. You can stay over." Vicki's smile brought out the gold in her eyes.

Callie shook her head. "I don't do sleepovers." The kids would be gone. She'd be alone with Meg, too great a temptation to miss.

"Okay. Just come have dinner with me."

Around noon, Meg and Lucy returned, riding double on Brittle, leading a limping Tawny. Callie's first thought was the cost of calling the vet. Lucy slid off, tears marking her cheeks.

"What happened?" Callie asked.

"I don't know. He just started to limp." Lucy began to cry.

"I couldn't see anything in his foot, but it's a soft hoof." Meg shrugged.

"Should I call the vet?" She stared at the sore foot at the end of a white stocking, the one Tawny was favoring.

"Let's see how he is on the grass."

Once the little horse was off the stone driveway, he seemed all right. Meg cleaned his foot with a hoof pick and found nothing. She turned him out with Brittle and the goats, and he trotted off.

"He needs shoes if he's going down the road," Meg said, hands on hips.

"Why don't you get ready to go to your dad's, Luce?" Callie said.

"Thanks, Meg." The girl ran off toward the house.

When she was gone, Callie said, "I've been thinking about selling Tawny. School has started. Winter is on the way. It seems like Lucy rides Brittle more than Tawny." Callie looked for Meg's reaction to this news. Would she think her cruel?

Meg watched her without expression. She nodded her head. "Good luck. You might have your hands full, but I know how expensive it is to keep a horse."

She thought how she already had her hands full with Tony. Did she need that with Lucy? "I'll talk to her about it." That would do a lot of good. Lucy would howl. She'd bought the horse to placate Lucy for the move away from friends. She'd bought Tony a dirt bike, which he had totaled within a month. He'd also broken his arm. She refused to buy another. Bad for the earth, she'd told him, and too dangerous.

After dropping Lucy off at her father's house, she followed Vicki to her place. Vicki had invited Meg too, but she was going out, so it wasn't like Meg would be available. She might return at nine at night or in the morning. Callie never knew.

Vicki lived in a new house in a subdivision at the edge of town. Stone posts stood on either side of the drive into the complex. The brick, ranch-style home was built at the end of a cul-de-sac with new trees in the front yard and surprisingly old trees in back.

It wasn't what Callie expected. She parked next to Vicki's car in front of the garage and got out. The air was warmer here, probably due to the blacktop and lack of open fields. She got out of the car and walked into the garage with Vicki. "Nice and private."

"It's a new subdivision. Mine is one of the smaller houses." Vicki opened the door, and they walked into a large kitchen with an island and modern appliances. A booth built into a windowed nook looked out onto the backyard.

"You like to cook, don't you?"

"If I have time." Vicki shrugged.

"Hey, I wish I did. The kids call me the queen of pasta, but I guess you know that."

"I'll start dinner. Okay?"

"Can I help?"

"Why don't you look around?"

"Why don't you show me your home?"

When they were back in the kitchen, Vicki said, "Well?"

"Really nice. Cozy." It made her house look rundown and old, which it was. There wouldn't be any mice running around here. The place was relatively modest with only two bedrooms, hardwood floors, one and a half baths. There were no massive pieces of furniture that looked like they'd been made out of moose racks, as there were in Vicki's brother's summer home. Fireplaces rose back-to-back between the living room and the den, which had shelves of books whose spines actually looked like they'd been read. "Maybe you can lend me a book once in a while."

"Pick something out. I'll fix you a drink."

Callie stood before the bookcases, looking for a novel she hadn't read and wanted to. She finally picked up Jodi Picoult's *Change of Heart* and was reading the flap when Vicki came into the room with two drinks.

"If you liked *Keeping Faith*, you'll like that one. Take it home with you."

"It might be a while before you see it again. Since I started this new job I've been falling asleep five minutes after my head hits the pillow."

"You never say much about your job."

"Neither do you."

"I know. I like to separate the two, my life and my work." Vicki sat down in a leather chair.

"I'll have to. Otherwise, this job is going to eat me alive. Pregnant fourteen-year-olds, kids who need a hug but you can't give them one. Makes me worry about Lucy. Will she be one of these girls in a year or two?" She stood with the book in hand, looking down at Vicki.

"She dreams about being a horsewoman, like Meg."

She sighed. "Yeah. Stupid of me to buy her a horse, but she was so lost after the divorce. The horse was a bribe. I wrenched her from her home and friends and moved into that wretched farmhouse because it was cheap."

"Not every place has mice to entertain the cat or a hot woman on the second floor." Vicki laughed when Callie glared. "Hey, I like your farmhouse. It has character. I wish I was Meg."

She sat on the leather sofa next to Vicki's chair and took a swig of her vodka and tonic. She wasn't going to touch the remark about Meg. "Good drink. Thanks. I've made a lot of mistakes in my life. One of the biggest was probably buying that farmhouse, thinking it would be good for the kids to live in the country. I couldn't afford to stay in the house where they were born and buy into the store too, which proved to be an even bigger mistake."

"What is this? Bash Callie night?" Vicki's eyebrows arched.

"Did you ever wish you could go back to when you were twenty-one and start over?"

"Sure. Everyone does. What would you do differently?"

"I'd keep the kids. Everything else I'd change." She smiled wryly. "Hindsight. What about you?"

"I would have been driving the night my parents were killed. Then maybe it wouldn't have happened. But I had a date with someone. I can't even remember who she was."

Stunned by this admission, Callie was at a loss for words. She looked down at her drink and felt foolish for the shallowness of her mistakes.

Vicki stood and patted Callie on the shoulder. "Hey, I don't want to put a damper on the evening. It probably would have happened had I been there."

Callie looked up. "Want to tell me about it?"

"My dad hit a patch of ice and went off the road. I was in bed with this other woman when the police called."

"When did this happen?"

"Two years ago this coming January."

"I'm sorry, but how can you be responsible?"

"They asked me if I wanted to go with them. I didn't."

"Oh. But the patch of ice would have been there anyway."

"You're right, of course." Vicki's smile was a grimace. "I'll go finish dinner. You can stay here and read if you like."

"I'll help." Callie followed Vicki into the kitchen.

Dinner was a Vietnamese dish with grilled pork, rice noodles and vegetables. Callie was savoring the food, the wine and watching the birds at the feeders in the backyard when her cell phone vibrated in her pocket. She glanced at the display.

"Excuse me." She put the phone to her ear. "What is it, Marc?"

He sounded panicky. "There's a discrepancy in the sales and the inventory and the cash in the bank."

"How did that happen?"

"Ronnie said…" A pause. "Do you think he's been pocketing some of the proceeds?"

"Already? He's only been there a few weeks."

"I'll wring his scrawny neck," Marc whispered.

"Talk louder. I can't hear you."

"Never mind. I'll call you later. Where are you anyway?"

"At Vicki's house. Don't kill him, Marc. He's not worth going to jail over."

"Don't worry. I'll just beat the shit out of him. Say hi to Vicki."

The phone began vibrating again as she slipped it into her pocket. When she saw it was Tim, she experienced a vague sense of unease. "Sorry," she said to Vicki, who mouthed, "It's okay."

"Hi, Tim. What's up?"

"Tony just took my car and left. Do you have any idea where he might go?"

The unease twisted in her guts. "To his friends?"

"What are their names?"

"Ask Lucy. She'll know."

She heard him talking and Lucy answering and realized she didn't know all the last names of Tony's friends. What kind of rotten mother was she anyway? Tim came back on the line.

"Are you home? You better go if you're not. I'll keep in touch."

"Don't call the police, Tim. Let's see if we can find him."

"I'll let you know before I do anything like that, but he can't go around stealing cars, not even mine." The line went dead, and she was sure he thought she was at fault.

She looked across the table at Vicki. "I have to go home. Tony took Tim's car. He only has a beginner's permit. If he gets stopped, he'll lose that."

Vicki reached across the table and covered her hand. "You go ahead. I'll clean up here and follow."

"I'm sorry about the dinner. It's delicious."

"Hey, I'll pack it up and bring it out. We can eat it later."

On the drive home she realized that not only was she glad that Vicki was going to follow her home with the food, but that she expected it. Was she that demanding, she wondered as she bounced down the driveway.

No one but the cat waited by the door, his tail curled around his feet as if he'd been expecting her. She swept him up in her arms. The best thing about animals, she realized, was their unconditional acceptance as long as their expectations were met—food, shelter and a little attention. With that thought she hugged him a little too tight and he squeaked and wriggled to be set free.

Unable to sit down, she paced the rooms. She'd tried to call Tony on his cell phone every few minutes since she'd talked to Tim. He'd turned it off. Looking through the phone book, she found the name of one of Tony's friends, a Joe Seidl. A woman answered on the first ring.

"Hi, Mrs. Seidl? My son, Tony Adamson, is a friend of your son. I'm Callie. We need to find Tony. Have you seen him?" She rushed the words.

"I know Tony. He's not here. His dad called looking for him, too. What's going on?"

She decided to be honest. "Um, he took his dad's car without permission. He has a beginner's driving permit. I don't really know what happened. I wasn't there. So, you see, it's urgent that we find him soon."

"I don't know where my own son is. Why would I know where yours is? What's your number? I'll call you if he comes here."

Callie gave her cell phone number. "Do you know the last names of his friends? He hangs out with Chas and Sammy and Peter."

"I can't remember off the top of my head."

"Well, thanks." She wanted this woman on her side. She had to sound respectful.

Next she called her parents. Her dad answered and listened without interruption, then said, "He's here. I'll put him on."

"Dad, why didn't you call and tell me?" But her dad was gone.

"Hey, Mom." Tony's tone was surly.

"Have you phoned your dad? He's worried about you." She knew it was the wrong thing to say, but she was suddenly mad. "Are you all right?"

"He's worried about his car, not me."

"Well, I'm worried about you, son. You can't take your dad's car without permission. You don't even have a driver's license. It's called stealing."

"Yeah, I suppose he'll call the cops on me."

"Call him or have your grandpa call him. I'll come and get you."

"Mom? I don't want to go to Dad's anymore. Shirley hates me, and I hate her."

"We'll talk about it. Okay? Let me speak to Grandpa again."

She told her dad she was on her way. When she went out the door, she bumped into Vicki. "I have to go pick up Tony. He's at my parents'."

"Want me to come with you?"

"No. I need to talk to him alone."

"Okay. I'll leave some food in the fridge and call you tomorrow."

"Really?"

"Sure. What are friends for?"

"Thanks."

When she got to her parents' house, Tim's Lexus was parked in the driveway. She saw Tim and Tony and her parents through the kitchen window. Even before she opened the door, she heard Tim's voice raised in anger.

"You're lucky I didn't call the police."

"You'd do that to your own son, wouldn't you?" Tony said.

"We're going in the other room," her dad said, and he and her mom left as she walked into the kitchen. The TV came on in den.

Callie looked from her surly son to her angry ex-husband. "I came to take him home with me. Tell your dad what you told me, Tony."

"I don't want to go to your house on weekends." Mumbling, Tony looked at the floor. "I want to stay with Mom."

"Is that okay with you, Callie? It's sure okay with me. I don't want him in my house either."

Callie shot a look at Tony and saw the hurt flash across his face. He clenched his fists and glared at his father. "Okay. That's settled for now. Let me talk to your dad alone for a few minutes."

Without a word, Tony went out of the room.

"Well?" she asked. "What happened this time?"

"He told Shirley he hated her and wanted to go home. Then he stomped out of the house and took my car."

"There has to be more to it than that."

"Ask him. I don't know who said what, but I have to live with Shirley and she is his stepmother. He owes her some respect."

"I know. I'll take him home. Is Lucy all right?"

"Of course, she's all right. You think we abuse them?"

"No, I didn't mean that. It's just..." But she didn't know what she meant.

On the way home, she asked Tony what had happened.

"You think it's all my fault too, don't you?"

"I'm asking for your side."

"She said I looked like I was put together by a committee. And then she laughed."

"Did you say something to annoy her?"

"Yeah. I said I didn't want to be there. I wanted to be at my mom's. I don't know why Dad married her. You're prettier than she is."

"You said that?"

"No, Mom, do I look stupid? What does being put together by a committee mean?"

"You're just growing into your hands and feet, that's all." She was seething, but she was sure Tony had said more than he admitted. "Listen, though, you can't take your dad's car or mine or anyone's. You don't have a driver's license, and besides, that's stealing."

"You already told me that, Mom. I've heard that about a zillion times tonight." They were turning into their driveway, where Vicki's Audi was parked next to Meg's truck. "Do they know anything about this?"

"Vicki does. I was having dinner at her house when your dad called. She probably told Meg."

"They're okay, though. Cute chicks. You know how to pick

them, Mom." He got out of the car before she could say any more.

She followed him into the kitchen, where Meg and Vicki were sitting at the table with a couple of beers. Vicki asked, "Hungry anyone?" Her eyes rested on Callie.

"Me. I am," Tony said.

Callie sat down. "I am, too."

Vicki put two plates of warmed food in front of them, and Tony dug in without even asking what it was.

"Wow, this is good," he said, stuffing his mouth.

Callie smiled. "It is indeed. I didn't expect to find you here, Vicki."

"Yeah, well, Meg came home and we got to talking." She put a glass of merlot in front of Callie.

"Thanks. Anything interesting?"

Vicki looked at Meg, and Callie's heart bumped along unevenly.

"My blacksmith put shoes on Tawny," Meg said.

"What do I owe you?" Callie asked.

"Nothing. I told Lucy I would have it done."

"Meg asked me to go on a trail ride next weekend," Vicki said nervously.

"Where?"

"Out where you and I went." Meg's voice was soft.

Her appetite disappeared. It had been a hard enough evening without this. Vicki and Meg would sleep in the trailer. She was tied in knots with jealousy, the one emotion she detested. Looking from one to the other, she tried a smile but it failed, and she glanced down at her food.

"Got any more?" Tony asked, his plate empty.

"Sure. Want some dessert?"

"Thanks. I never got to eat. My stepmother tries to starve me to death."

Callie said nothing. Shirley probably didn't care whether he starved or not. She wondered how she would behave under the same circumstances.

"I have to go to the store anyway." Appalled because she was fighting back tears, she continued staring at her plate. No one spoke. She jumped when Tony put a hesitant hand on her shoulder.

"You all right, Mom? I'm sorry. I won't do it again."

Of course, he thought he was the reason she was so upset. Kids always did. She covered his hand with her own. "I'm okay. What won't you do again?"

"Take the car. I promise."

She blinked and chanced a glance at him. "I'll hold you to that."

"Don't cry, Mom. Okay?"

"I won't." She sniffed and finished eating. When she drained her wineglass, she was in control again, able to look at Meg and Vicki. "Have fun."

"You could go with us," Meg said after Tony left.

"And do what?" she asked as she filled the dishwasher.

"Read." Vicki got two more beers and refilled the wineglass. "Or you ride and I'll read."

"Yeah, sure."

"You could take turns. One could ride in the morning. The other ride in the afternoon," Meg said.

Callie shot a look at her, briefly meeting her eyes and glancing away. They were patronizing her and she hated it. She just couldn't bear the thought of them sleeping together. "Are you staying overnight?"

"No." Meg cocked her head and smiled as if to ask, *Is that what is wrong?*

Relief flooded her, so that even her legs felt weak. "Wish I could go. Do you know what happened at the store, Vicki?" She kept forgetting that Vicki owned a third of the shop now.

"Marc told me. After you left, he called. I figured you forgot to say anything because of Tony." She lowered her voice when she said Tony's name.

"I did. Want to sell?" Maybe one good thing would come out of this. Because Vicki had made the store profitable, it might tempt a buyer.

"I'll let you and Marc decide that one."

At the store the next day a spinning class was in full pedal with Ronnie instructing. Marc was writing up a charge for biking shorts for a customer. Callie slipped behind the counter and waited for the sale to be completed.

When they were alone, she said, "Why is there a spinning class and why is Ronnie on a bike? Why is he even here?"

"We have spinning classes when there are enough people who want to ride. He's doing your job. Someone has to. Do you know how many stationary bikes we've sold? No wonder he's pocketing a little money."

"What?" She couldn't believe his defense of Ronnie. "I want him out of here, and I want to sell the place. I can't be here, you can't be here, and obviously, he can't be here. That's the only solution." They spoke in heated whispers.

"What about Vicki? Doesn't she have a say?"

"She told me whatever we decide is okay with her."

He lifted one eyebrow. "Since we brought in the exercise equipment, we've grossed more than we made in a year. You don't pay any attention to what's going on. We're going to get rich. I'm thinking of expanding."

Her whisper rose an angry decibel. "We can't even find an honest employee to run the place, and you want to expand?"

"Okay. I'll buy you out. Maybe Vicki will stay in."

She felt deflated and relieved at the same time, like she was giving up something valuable but risky. She stared at him for a moment. "I'll tell you what. I'll stay in and be a silent partner like Vicki. I won't work here. You manage the place, but I want to see the books every month. And I want Ronnie out of here."

Sandy tapped her on the shoulder. "Am I interrupting?"

She turned toward Sandy and her anger began to abate, even though her hands still shook.

"I'm going to marry Scott." Sandy smiled. "I wanted to tell you in person."

She felt a twinge of guilt but not a bit of jealousy, not like she experienced when Meg and Vicki went off together. How long had it been since she'd seen Sandy long enough to talk to her? "That's wonderful. Let's go out to lunch and celebrate."

"I'd love to, but I'm going to meet Scott's family over lunch." Sandy's brown eyes momentarily looked troubled. "I've been neglecting my friends."

"No, you haven't. I think it's the other way around."

"I'm so happy, Callie. I never thought this would happen."

Scott, who'd been riding and was dripping sweat, came over and put an arm around Sandy. "Did she tell you?"

"Not the date." Callie smiled at their happiness, thinking at the same time that she'd never be able to put an arm around Meg or Vicki like that.

"Thanksgiving weekend," Sandy said. "I want you to be a bridesmaid."

"I'm not a maid anymore." This did not appeal to her. "Why don't you find some other use for me, like serving punch?"

"All of my bridesmaids are matrons. You'll fit right in. No frilly dresses. I promise."

They both laughed, and Scott turned to talk to someone behind him. "Thanks, Callie," Sandy said quietly.

"For what, my friend?"

"For breaking up with Scott. It would be you marrying him instead, otherwise."

"No way. He didn't want to marry me." She'd never let him get that far, nor did she want Sandy to think she was second choice.

Tony wanted to spend the next weekend with his grandparents. Callie's dad offered to come for him when he finished mowing the lawn. Callie wondered when she'd trust him enough to leave him alone. Lucy had gone to her dad's. Meg and Vicki had left early for the trail ride. She'd promised Marc she'd do the group cycling classes Saturday morning. That was the price of getting rid of Ronnie.

No one was at home when she got there, except the two goats hanging around the gate and the cat, lying in a patch of sunlight on the kitchen floor. Was this going to be her fate? Coming home to an empty house. It was only noon, and she pictured Meg and Vicki stopping for lunch by the stream. Maybe they would stay overnight. There was no reason they couldn't change their minds.

When her phone rang, she grabbed it and looked at the display—Bobby. "Hi, cousin. What's up?"

"How are you?"

"Good. And you?" Her heart pounded with the thought that he might have accepted the couple's offer, but why would he call her if he had?

"Terrific. Three guys rented the cottage for a week. They're supposed to be gone by noon today. Do you have time to run over and check it out?"

So he hadn't sold it yet. She jumped at the chance. "Sure. I'd love to."

"Stay and swim or catch frogs or something." He laughed.

"I never saw a frog this summer."

"They're telling us something, aren't they? Like the canaries in the coal mines."

"It's not like it was when we were kids."

"I know." They reminisced for a few minutes before he said, "Got to go, kiddo. Call me if you need to."

She phoned her parents to see if they and/or Tony wanted to go with her. No one answered. After filling the cat's bowls, and packing a few clothes, she left a note for Vicki and Meg and joyfully headed for the lake.

It was a lovely end of September day, warm and dusty. In the woods, the orange and red maples and yellow aspens stood out against the green pines. The fiery red sumacs along the roadsides were beginning to drop their leaves. Asters nodded in the ditches.

When she parked behind the cottage, a full trash bag lying next to the back steps alerted her to what she might find.

Inside, the floors were sandy and sticky, beer cans overflowed the wastebasket, and food had been left to rot in the fridge. Unwashed dishes filled the sink, and the windows were open. A flash of anger surged through her at such thoughtlessness. A note on the table read—*Sorry. We had to leave in a hurry. Here's an extra fifty dollars for cleanup.* She nearly called Bobby there and then, but instead, she started to clean.

It took her nearly an hour to sweep and wash the floors, cleanup the dishes, empty the fridge, bag up the cans. And she loved every minute of it. The warm wind whistled through the screens, blue jays screamed from the trees, squirrels scolded, honking geese flew over. She wanted to stay.

When she was satisfied the place was clean, she walked down to the lake. Most docks had been taken out of the water. Boat lifts and rafts and piers and canoes and kayaks littered the shore. A few fishing boats dotted the otherwise empty lake.

She walked around and climbed over the paraphernalia on the beach. When she reached Kate and Pat's place, she found Kate sitting in a chair on the shore.

She looked up from the book she was reading and said, "Callie! Are you here for the weekend?"

"Not really. Bobby asked me to check up on the cottage. The place was a mess." She went on to elaborate.

"I'm not surprised. Those three young guys tore around the lake in a speedboat with speakers blaring. We were glad to see them leave."

"Well, they won't be staying there again after I talk to Bobby." She sat in the beach chair that Kate was patting. "Where's Pat?"

"Shopping. Would you like to have dinner with us?"

"Are you sure?"

"I'm sure. I'm cooking. How is it going these days?"

Callie talked about her new job, about the group she'd started for pregnant girls, about some of the problems the kids faced who were sent to her office—never naming names, of course. She even told her about Tony taking Tim's car and how he hated his stepmother. The more she talked, the more she had to say and the more she realized how much she missed Kate. After a few minutes, she made herself stop. "I'm sorry. I haven't even asked about you."

Kate laughed. "You've got a lot on your mind, woman. My life is pretty predictable these days. I retired and there's not much to talk about, really. I had similar problems with my son, Jeff, when he was young. Once he took the car, skipped school and rear-ended another car. We grounded him for a month. For him there was nothing worse than having to stay home."

"I let Tony spend the weekend with his grandparents, which is what he wanted to do."

"I think that's great. How are Meg and Vicki?"

She snorted. "They went on a trail ride together. I hope that little horse's rough trot turns Vicki's legs to mush."

Laughing until she gasped, Kate said, "My, aren't you a sympathetic friend? Why didn't you go with them?"

"I had to go to the store and lead the group cycling because the guy who was supposed to do it was absconding with the money."

Kate studied her out of eyes that looked like the color of the lake on a sunny day, and Callie realized she was half in love with her. "You've had a hard time of it."

"I guess I'm feeling pretty sorry for myself. At least, Bobby didn't sell the cottage."

"That's one good thing."

Kate and Pat lent her a flashlight to walk home, and she made her way around the litter on the shore, only banging her shin once. She muttered a muted, "Fuck," and stepped more carefully. Once in the cottage, she washed and bandaged her leg before undressing and lying down to read. It was too late to drive home, and she'd had too much to drink.

When a voice said, "Hey, I was almost asleep," she let out a high-pitched scream.

"It's only me." Vicki laughed.

Her heart banged against her ribs. "What are you doing

here?"

Vicki hobbled barefoot across the room toward her. "I thought you might like some company."

A laugh burbled out of Callie. "Rough riding, huh?"

"Yeah. Miserable. I hated every minute, except getting off. That is the roughest little horse."

"Didn't Meg change horses with you, at least at first?"

"No. Wish she had."

"Why didn't you stay overnight?"

"Because Meg wanted to come back."

"The mystery woman." Callie burst into laughter every few minutes at Vicki's obvious discomfort. "I'm sorry. You look like I felt after riding Tawny." She was more amused than sorry, though.

"Where were you? At Kate and Pat's?"

Callie nodded. "Why didn't you come over?"

"Because I just got here and saw the flashlight bobbing along the beach." A wry smile pulled her mouth up on one side. "I want to get under the blankets with you. Don't we know each other well enough yet?"

"If you stay on your own side. That way we'll only have to change one set of sheets." But she knew Vicki never took a backward step. That's how she got what she wanted. She was as open as she was bold. No finesse, no nuances. What you saw was what you got. "And keep your hands to yourself." Callie turned her back.

"Yes, ma'am." Flopping on the side away from Callie, Vicki let out a sigh. "How are Kate and Pat?"

"Good. I ate there. Maybe we can walk over and see them in the morning."

Backed up against Vicki, Callie began to drift off. She felt Vicki's weight and her own merge into one. When she wakened in the night, they both lay on their backs, hands crossed on their chests. She had to pee and carefully straddled Vicki, reaching for the floor with one foot. She half expected Vicki's arms to snake out and grab her, but her expression was placid. Callie almost pushed the hair back from Vicki's sleeping face. It looked so thick and luxuriant.

When she climbed back over Vicki, she lay quietly watching the trees and stars outside the window before falling asleep again. Once she felt Vicki leave the bed and return, pressing up against her.

When they awoke, the sun was streaming in the windows. A warm breeze bathed Callie's face. She turned her head and looked into Vicki's eyes. "Morning."

"I don't think I can move," Vicki said with a sweet smile. "I'll just have to stay here."

"Actually, moving around helps." Callie looked at her watch—seven thirty. "I bet Kate and Pat are up."

"Maybe they'll feed us breakfast."

"Well, I think I'll eat a couple pieces of toast. The pigs that rented the place left bread and butter behind."

"Be sure to tell your cousin. He'll appreciate you more."

"Yeah, well, he just might decide it's easier to sell than rent."

"You need to look on the bright side, Callie."

She gazed into the warm, hazel eyes shaded by thick lashes. "Why do you like me, Vicki? I mean, I've never encouraged you. In fact, I've pushed you away more than once."

"I'm an eternal optimist. You must think I'm a fool. I know you're in love with Meg."

"I know you're not a fool. You're very innovative. You saved the store. You suggested I call Bobby and offer to keep an eye on the cottage, so that maybe he wouldn't sell it."

"I'm in marketing. That's how I make a living by coming up with ideas like those. It's not hard."

"Well, thanks for being smarter than I am."

Vicki got up on one elbow and gave Callie a serious look. "I know how to problem solve when it comes to businesses, but you help kids survive under difficult circumstances. You set up the group for pregnant girls. Sandy said you were very good at your job in child protection, persistent when you thought some kid was being abused at home. I don't think I could do that."

"Well, I got burned out at Child Protection Services, and I'm not very good with my own kids. Look at Tony."

"He's a teenager—a little lost. Yearning for his dad's approval. Resenting his stepmother." Vicki lay back down.

"You have really nice hair, do you know that?"

"I thought you liked blondes."

"Meg reminds me of the sun."

Vicki sighed. "I suppose that means it's time to get up."

She'd expected Vicki would come on to her. It puzzled her that she hadn't.

Swinging her legs over the side, Vicki stood and stretched. Her hair was tousled, her eyes still sleepy. She looked sexy. She walked to the windows and stood looking out, her back to Callie. "I love fall. Don't you? Look at those trees across the lake. It's like they're on fire."

Callie scrambled out of bed and stood beside her. A fishing boat floated in the mist rising off the water. "It's going to be a nice day."

"What time do you have to be home?"

"Tim's dropping Lucy off at my parents place around five. Tony's already there."

"I envy you those kids."

"Well, it's not too late. You could have one of your own. They were a lot easier when they were little."

"I don't think so," Vicki said, and Callie realized she was serious. "I spend too much time traveling."

"Want a piece of toast? There isn't any coffee. I never thought of staying overnight."

"Sure. I'll bet Kate and Pat will give us coffee."

The mist had evaporated to thin wisps by the time they reached the lake. "Look at all this stuff cluttering the shore," Vicki said, starting down the beach. "We should take your pier down."

"It's not my pier, but you're right. It has to be done. We can put it in the boathouse." She took Vicki's outstretched hand and jumped up on some pier sections next to her. A warm wind fingered her scalp. "If it could only stay like this for the next seven months."

"I love it when it snows every few days like last winter. I come in from cross country skiing and make a fire, have a drink, look out the window at the falling snow." She grinned at Callie, but something was different There was no wink, no sexual intimation. Had she changed tactics or given up or lost interest?

Kate and Pat were finishing breakfast on their porch. Pat opened the screen door. "Hey, come on in. The coffee is on."

"And we need it." Vicki gave them both a hug.

"We don't want to barge in on you," Callie said.

"Sure, we do." Vicki grinned.

"When did you show up?" Pat asked Vicki.

"Last night. Callie was on her way back from your place."

A small silence followed while Kate and Pat looked at each other. Callie felt her skin grow hot, knowing what they were thinking and unable to deny it.

Before they left for home, they put on their swimsuits and dismantled the pier, carrying the poles and crosspieces and sections into the boathouse. Callie looked over the empty lake. The end of summer was a poignant time for her. She didn't love autumn as Vicki had professed to, because it signaled the end of the season she loved most.

Vicki beeped and waved an arm out the window of her car as Callie turned off toward her parents' condo. Tim was taking Lucy there. She pulled into the driveway behind her parents' car. The RV was parked on a patch of cement next to the garage. She slung her purse over her shoulder and went through the side door, which led to the kitchen.

Her mom stood at the stove, while Lucy cut veggies at the island. Callie gave Lucy a quick hug and kiss. "How was your weekend, sweetie?"

"Not nearly exciting as when Tony ran off with Dad's car."

She ignored Lucy's answer and turned to her mom. Hugging her, she said, "Thanks for the invite. I'm starving. Anything I can do to help?"

"Pour us a glass of wine and set the table."

"Where are Dad and Tony?" she asked after she was done.

"Your dad's in the den."

He was watching the news. "Hey, Dad. Where's Tony?"

"On the computer or his cell. Where else? He's a secretive guy, but I guess we all were at that age."

She sat down next to her father. "What were you like, Dad?"

"I had a wild hair up my ass. Couldn't settle until I met your mom."

"How would you compare yourself to Tony in the wild category?"

"Hard to say." Her dad grinned and put an arm around her. "You were a pretty wild one yourself."

"I don't know why. Now look at me. I'm in bed by ten." She snuggled close. "What did you and Mom and Tony do all weekend?"

"Not much of anything. He slept and ate and was glued to either the computer or his cell phone."

"Didn't you talk about anything?"

"That's sort of confidential, honey. Your mom tried to tell him how hard it must be to be a stepmother, especially a hated one. He really does dislike Shirley. Is she that bad?"

Callie looked around to see if any of the kids were nearby. "She's sort of a whiner."

The doorbell rang and her dad got up. "That's for me."

Callie wandered into the kitchen and sat on a stool. "You've lost your assistant. Now do you need help?" Lucy had disappeared.

"Nope. I've got everything under control."

"Smells good, Mom." She glanced out the front door when she heard the sound of an engine. "Is Dad going somewhere with the motor home?"

"Nope. That must be someone else. We're having pulled pork. It's one of the kids' favorites. Lucy made the potato salad. We've got slaw, too."

"Where is that person taking the motor home?"

"Wherever he wants, honey," her dad said, coming inside. "He bought it."

"What? I thought you loved traveling."

"Not at four dollars a gallon."

Her dad got a beer out of the fridge and sat on the adjoining stool. "You gave me the idea."

"What idea?"

"To rent the cottage instead of traveling. We can take a trip somewhere a couple times a year."

Tony slouched into the kitchen, his hands in his pockets. "Smells great."

Callie said hello to Tony but still stared at her dad. A shred of hope teased her.

"Now I've got news tonight that will probably make you all happier. Maybe that's what we need." He raised his voice. "Where's Lucy? Lucy!"

"What?" Lucy appeared in the room, her phone pinned to her ear.

"Say goodbye and hang up."

"Jeez, Grandpa." But she did it.

"I've got a toast to make." He lifted his beer bottle. "To having the cottage back in the family."

"You bought it back, Grandpa?" Lucy said, throwing her arms around him.

"We're half owners with your cousin, Bobby. We'll rent it out when we're not there. Callie can see to the cleaning part and I'll schedule renters."

Callie stared at her dad, her mouth slightly open in surprise. She could hardly believe her parents had done this. Even so, she asked, "Do we have to rent it? These last people were slobs."

"It's an investment. That's the only way we can justify spending the money. Bobby still expects to make money off renting. We'll require a deposit that any slobs will forfeit." Her father gave them a huge smile, and she hugged him and her mom.

The kids jabbered all through dinner, and her dad, who had really sprung to life, talked about how he was going entice renters.

Callie remained quietly joyful, savoring this piece of good luck. The first person she wanted to tell, she realized, was Vicki.

Chapter 8

When Callie drove in the driveway, Meg was out in the pen with Brittle and Tawny. The goats milled around the gate, bleating, obviously nervous, leaving clumps of hair on the aluminum crosspieces. The sky glowed an odd green. Lucy took off in Meg's direction, Tony vanished into the house, and Callie stood for a moment in the yard, feeling the change in weather before following Lucy out to the pen. "It's going to storm." The wind was picking up.

"I'm not going in the basement," Lucy said.

"Did Vicki catch up with you yesterday?" The wind spun the hair and dust away as Meg brushed her horse. Usually calm, Brittle pawed and moved from side to side. Meg had tied Tawny to the fence and he was trying to get loose.

"Yes," Callie said.

Strands of Meg's hair came loose from her ponytail and whipped against her face. "Stand still, Brittle," she snapped.

"I've got good news. My parents bought back half the cottage."

"Hey, that's great."

Lucy let herself into the pen.

"Slip Tawny's halter off, Lucy." Meg released Brittle and turned both horses out. As they tore off with the goats in hot pursuit, lightning pointed a jagged finger toward the earth, singeing a spot of grass in the field. It was immediately followed by a terrifying crash of thunder and drenching rain.

The rain turned the burn to smoke. "We better go in the basement," Callie said. "Run, Lucy." Lucy churned up the ground.

"I'll stay in the barn."

"You can't, Meg." They were shouting over the rain and wind, both soaked to the skin.

"No, *you* can't, Callie. You have to go to the kids."

She did, she knew. She'd have to leave Meg. She ran toward the house through the battering wind, hardly able to see where she was going. A branch off the maple fell with a thud near her path. She screeched.

She fought with the wind to shut the door. Tony and Lucy huddled in the mudroom. "Downstairs, downstairs!"

"You don't have to yell, Mom. We're not deaf." Tony held a flashlight. There were two others at the top of the stairs. Callie handed Lucy the smallest and took the last for herself.

"Where's Meg?" Lucy asked.

"She's in the barn." The power flickered off and they felt their way carefully down the steep stairs into the room below, the one with the low overhead pipes hung with spider and cobwebs, the dank cement walls that harbored scurrying millipedes and the damp, slippery floor. Lucy shook all over and Callie put an arm around her.

"It'll be okay, honey. We're lots bigger than the bugs. And remember spiders eat all the nasty insects, like flies and centipedes."

"Like that's going to cheer her up, Mom." Tony stopped suddenly and they bumped into him as he pointed his flashlight in a corner where a rat crouched.

Oh, God, she thought, as Lucy screamed and the rat vanished into an uncovered drain. Spiders and mice she didn't mind, rats she did.

Lucy buried her face in Callie's shoulder. "Please, Mom, let's get out of here."

"Okay. We'll take our chances in the bathroom." The kids fell all over each other climbing the steps. She glanced out the door at the lashing wind and rain, which was all she could see—no barn, no trailer, not even the garage.

She and the kids ran around closing the open windows till they were only cracked. They'd have to mop up later. Water was everywhere. The blinds were sopped, the floors and furniture soaked. Window glass rattled in the panes as if it might break. She looked again for Meg and saw nothing beyond the storm.

"Is it safe in here, Mom?" Lucy asked as they sank to the floor in the bathroom.

"Well, it's safer in the basement."

"Yeah, along with the rat. Did you know we had rats, Mom?" Tony eyed her.

"No, but the creek is close by. Rats and water go together. It could have been a muskrat."

"I want to move."

Callie regarded Lucy with a questionable glance. "We'd have to sell Tawny."

Lucy crossed her arms and leaned into her mother. "I hate rats, Mom."

"We'll keep the basement door shut." Had they closed it? All she could think of was Meg outside in the storm. Hail began to fall, hitting the walls and roof with frightening force. She told the kids to stay put and slipped out to the kitchen, but still she could see nothing beyond the thick hail. She thought it an odd time of year for a storm like this as she searched under her bed for Bill.

"C'mon, Mom," Tony called and she carried the cat to her children, where the four of them huddled on the floor till the wind and rain abated.

The temperature dropped nearly fifteen degrees. Hail lay in piles on the grass. The earth steamed, and through the ground fog, she thought she saw the horses lying on the ground. Patches of burned grass smoked around them. She turned to Tony before she began running. "Keep your sister here."

Meg was kneeling beside Brittle. Soaked through, her hair and clothes clung to her. Tears streamed down her face and sobs shook her frame.

Callie dropped next to her and covered the hand that lay on Brittle's neck. She glanced over at Tawny, who was trying to get up, and wondered why it was he and not Brittle who had apparently survived.

Meg whispered. "I should have put him in the barn."

"How could you know?"

Tawny staggered to his feet and stood with his head between his knees. That was when Brittle began to stir, legs churning and long neck and head partway off the ground.

Callie took her cell out of her pocket. "What's the vet's number?"

Meg's sobs became a choked laugh. "He's alive."

And Tony was chasing Lucy through the sodden field, yelling, "Get back here."

They all stood around the horses, as Dr. MacIverson checked them over. Tony and Lucy had run back to the house and brought jackets for everyone. MacIverson listened carefully to the animals' hearts.

"Lightning does strange things to the living. They may seem unharmed. They may be disoriented. Horses can't tell us how they feel, so we have to guess." Brittle's head tilted weirdly and he snapped at his neck as if a fly had landed on it. Tawny's nose hung nearly to the ground.

Lucy began crying. "I'm going to sleep with him tonight."

"Not after that storm," Callie said in a knee-jerk reaction. She put an arm around the girl, who promptly pulled away.

"We'll put them in the barn," Meg said. "That way we can watch them."

There were two makeshift stalls in the lower level of the building, accessible from the pen. Tony helped bed the ten by ten foot areas with straw. Their footsteps echoed on the stone floor as they silently worked. Meg placed her sleeping bag on a pile of straw in a corner and Lucy ran to get hers. Callie set up a cot. Only Tony slept inside that night. Lucy had assiduously swept the cobwebs from their area, cringing at the clinging dirt and screaming at the occasional spider, till she could no longer keep her eyes open. She slept sandwiched between her mother and Meg, little snores emitting from her open mouth. Light came from an aisle of small, dusty bulbs, all but three burned out.

Callie and Meg shared a bottle of red wine and talked. Meg spoke mostly about Brittle, telling Callie he'd been such a great show horse that he'd been kidnapped to keep him out of competition and then sold to a boys' camp, where Meg had found him months later. She'd thought that she'd never see him again. She sat with arms wrapped around her long legs, her hair a blond halo. Callie stared at her in a sort of admiring trance, till she felt herself slipping into a dream.

In the morning Brittle was still shaking his head and neck, although slowly now. He looked exhausted. Tawny slept on his side. Lucy slept on hers. Meg was leaning against the wall, watching her horse. Callie pushed herself up, testing her aching muscles. She had to go to work. Lucy had to attend school. "Hi."

Meg turned a tired look on her. "There's something terribly wrong with him." The smudges under her eyes made them look enormous. "He's suffering."

"It may go away. Sometimes it takes weeks, the vet said." Glancing at her watch, Callie saw it was just after six. Outside the goats bleated and Randy clanked on the gate with a leg. "Damn goat." She gently shook Lucy's shoulder.

Lucy awoke immediately. "Are they all right?" She sat up, alert, and then wailed. "Is Tawny dead?"

"He's sleeping." Callie glanced quickly to make sure that was the case. "C'mon, honey, you have to get ready for school and I have to go to work."

"I'm not going to school. I have to take care of Tawny."

Callie glanced at Meg for help.

"Go to school, Lucy. I'll stay with the horses." Meg forced a smile. She looked gray and utterly washed out as if she'd aged ten years.

"Thanks." Callie rolled up her bag and left it on the cot. Although she felt guilty that she'd wanted to sell Tawny, she now wished she had.

"It's okay. I won't go anywhere till Brittle is all right."

"Look, there's food in the fridge. Help yourself."

On the way toward the house she realized that she hadn't heard from Vicki. How unusual was that? Her last glimpse of Vicki had been through her car window yesterday as they went different ways.

In her hurry to get ready for work, she forgot to ask Tony if Vicki had called the house. The kids were standing at the bus stop when she drove out. She fumbled for her cell and pushed number seven, which was Vicki's number, and listened to Vicki's bubbly voice. "Hi. You have reached Vicki's cell. Please leave a message after the beep and I'll call you back."

"Hey, remember that horrible storm last night? Well, Tawny and Brittle were hit by lightning. Neither looks good. Maybe you should call Meg. She's at the barn. Where are you anyway?"

It was unreal for Vicki to stay out of touch even for a night, unless she was traveling overseas, and she'd said nothing about going anywhere.

At school, Callie was immediately involved in a meeting, after which kids began coming into her room. One was a girl from her pregnant group. A sweet-faced kid with a slightly bulging belly. She'd gotten into an altercation with one of the guys.

"What happened, Francine?"

Francine dropped her dark head, stared at her feet and mumbled. "He wanted to know who knocked me up. I told him it was none of his business, and he said I was a whore, only he said 'a hole.' I hit him in the face with my pen."

Callie thought she was justified, but of course she couldn't say that.

"What would you do, Ms. C?" That's what these girls called her—Ms. C.

She dodged the question. "You can't hit somebody, Francine, because of what he says, and just about everything is considered a weapon." The girl had enough going against her without being badgered and maybe suspended.

"How is it at home?"

"I don't know who's going to take care of the baby when it's born. I won't be able to go to school."

"I'm looking into that, Francine." Callie thought maybe she could set up a special classroom where these kids could bring their babies. So far, she hadn't convinced anyone of anything except her good intentions.

"I know you are, Ms. C, but they ain't gonna let you do it."

"We'll see." There were always the charter schools. Maybe it would work at one of them. Otherwise, they were going to have a bunch of high school dropouts. She glanced at her watch as the bell rang. "I'll see you at group." Callie stood and opened the door for the girl.

"Thanks for rescuing me from detention." Francine gave her a wry smile.

The principal called her into his office at three, just after she'd seen her last student of the day. "Sit down, Callie."

Anxious, almost frantic, to get home, she tried not to fidget. At four o'clock she could leave the building, and she still had to enter some data in her computer.

"I'm meeting with the superintendent after school. I told him about your hope to provide childcare for mothers who have none. I wondered if you'd like to give your views in person."

She jumped at the chance. "Sure."

That's how she found herself nervously explaining her idea. "These girls have no one to watch their infants while they attend school. I thought we could set up a room for the babies with sufficient child-care, using the mothers during their study halls and lunch hours. Maybe we could even allow kids who are in childcare classes to take a turn. Otherwise, these girls will probably have to drop out once they have their babies. Most have single parents, mothers holding down two jobs to keep everything afloat." It was a good idea she thought, maybe not put as well as she could have done. Of course, there was always the liability issue.

"Thanks, Callie. We'll certainly take it under advisement." The superintendent, Ron Grossman, stood and shook her hand. "Won't we, Alan?"

"Callie's full of good ideas." Alan smiled at her and lifted his eyebrows.

She was dismissed and left the room feeling as if she'd somehow failed Francine and the other girls. It was close to five when she drove in the driveway, expecting to see Vicki's car parked in its usual spot.

The trees had dropped a lot of leaves, but because of her new job, she dreaded winter's coming less. Another lonely winter at the store would have done her in, or she would have done herself in, she thought. She hurried in the house and changed into jeans and a sweatshirt before going out to the barn. She could see the goats hanging around the pen. No horses were in sight.

Meg and Lucy were sitting on her cot, both looking beat. Brittle lay on his side, his long neck and head stretched out in front of his mounded body. He was asleep, as was Tawny. She stood with her hands on her hips. "Well?"

"No change. The vet was out here again. He has no prognoses, good or bad."

"Has anyone heard from Vicki?"

"No. She did say something about going to Europe last time I talked to her."

"She never said a word about that yesterday when I was with her." Callie was taken back.

"Didn't she?" Meg said disinterestedly and gave Callie a haunted look before staring again at Brittle. It was obvious her horse was the only thing on her radar screen.

"I'll go fix some food." She started away and turned back, nodding at the horses. "Did they eat or drink?"

Meg shook her head.

They needed Vicki to cheer everyone up, she thought. That's what Vicki did best, after all. How could she go to Europe and never say anything about it? Hell, even Callie's parents hadn't called. She punched in their number and got her dad.

They had phoned. Tony just hadn't passed on the information, nor had he said anything about the horses except that everyone was out in the barn.

"They were struck by lightning or it came damn close."

"Want us to come out?"

"No, Dad, maybe later in the week. I'll keep in touch."

She phoned Marc next, thinking perhaps he would have talked to Vicki. "Hey, girlfriend. We miss you at the shop. Everything is selling like tomorrow won't wait."

"Yeah? Well, that's great. Have you talked to Vicki?"

"Vicki? No. Should I have? I've talked to your friend, Sandy, who wants to know where you've been."

She felt a stab of guilt. Some friend she was. "I'll call her."

"You'll have to catch her at Scott's. They moved in together."

"That's wonderful. And what about Ronnie? Is he still working at the shop?"

"Nope. I found another guy to take his place, a real cutie. Why don't you come in and see us?"

"I will, as soon as everything settles down out here. Lightning struck the horses. They're not doing well."

"No shit!" He sounded shocked. "What about Randy? Did he take a hit?"

"No, of course not!"

Marc sighed loudly. "There's no justice in this world."

"I've got to go." She phoned Kate. If anyone else had heard from Vicki, it would be Pat or Kate.

Pat answered. "Hey, how are you? When are you coming

back?"

"On Saturday. I'm in charge of checking up on renters."

"There's a couple with two kids at your place."

"Have you talked to Vicki, Pat?"

"Yes. She's in Europe on business. Would you like to say hello to Kate? She's right here."

"Hi." Kate's voice always calmed her. "Are you okay?"

"I'm looking for Vicki. She never told me she was going to Europe, and something terrible has happened." She was talking too fast.

"What happened?"

"The horses were struck by lightning during the storm yesterday. If you talk to Vicki, will you tell her? I called and left a message on her cell."

"Are they all right? The horses?"

"One has been sleeping ever since and the other looks like his head is on crooked. Maybe I'll see you Saturday. I have to come over and check up after some more renters."

She made a sandwich for Tony and herself and took two out to Lucy and Meg. She ran a hand over Lucy's hair. "Eat your sandwich and go do your homework. You can't sleep out here tonight, Lucy. Kids who don't get enough sleep do poorly in school."

Lucy began to cry. "But what if Tawny needs me?"

"I'll be here if he needs something."

"I'm going to call Dad."

"Go ahead. Maybe it would be better if you stayed with him for a few days."

"I can't leave, Mom." Lucy's voice rose in alarm and Callie caught sight of Meg's raised eyebrows. What was the matter with her? Of course, Lucy was upset. Her horse wouldn't wake up.

"Okay, but you have to sleep in your own bed tonight."

Callie and Meg once again shared a bottle of wine as they watched over the horses that night. The storm had changed the weather dramatically. The humidity had dropped, and it felt downright cold. They huddled under blankets.

Both horses were still sleeping. Tawny had been knocked out since Sunday. Meg leaned into Callie. Her eyes had sunk as the flesh seemed to fall away from her face, emphasizing the high cheekbones, the firm chin.

Callie wrestled to control her feelings. Meg was feverishly hot. She put a cool hand on her forehead, "You're burning up. Were you struck by lightning, too?"

Meg smiled so sadly that she kissed her cheek. "If he wakes up, I'm going to turn him out."

Callie nodded. "I'll turn Tawny out with him."

When the horses struggled to their feet, Meg led Brittle outside into the cool night. Tawny staggered after him. Stars glittered overhead. Fog floated across the cooling ground, waist high. Meg put her arms around Brittle's neck and leaned into him, then she let him go, and he lurched off into the meadow with Tawny glued to his rump and the goats following.

"Are you sleeping inside?" Callie asked when Meg turned toward the barn.

Meg shook her head. They lay down on their sleeping bags, half-tanked, and Callie slept like the dead. When she awoke in the morning, Meg was gone, the bottle was empty, and she had a fierce headache.

She reeled to the gate and slipped into the field. The sun had dispersed the ground fog. Under a nearly denuded maple tree at the far corner of the field, she saw them. The goats were eating, the horses lay on the ground, and Meg was on her knees.

She called Alan and said she wasn't sure she'd make it to work, that Lucy's horse had died in the night. Lucy was hysterical, crying until she threw up. Meg wouldn't let the vet call the people to haul the large animals away. She wanted to rent a backhoe and bury them under the tree.

"I'll pay for it, Callie. I can't let them turn him into fertilizer or dog food."

Lucy screamed. "Mom, don't let them feed Tawny to a dog."

Callie wanted to throw up herself. It would have been bad

enough without being wasted from wine and lack of sleep. She held her head in her hands and tried to think, but the easiest thing to do was to go along with Meg.

The rental company delivered the backhoe. Meg locked the goats in the pen and climbed up on the high seat. The deliveryman showed her how to drive the huge machine, how to set the stabilizers down, how to work the hydraulics that controlled the boom and bucket. She tried to dig, jerking the bucket back and forth and up and down.

When Dan showed up, he drove his pickup to where Meg sat high on the tractor seat, got out and stared at the horses for a few minutes before climbing up on the backhoe with Meg. He put an arm around her and she sort of melted into him, her mouth open in a wail that couldn't be heard over the engine. Callie's heart constricted painfully.

Tony came out in the field to see what was going on and tried to talk Lucy into going to school. Instead, Lucy called her dad to say that her horse had died. Callie's dad and mom showed up about the time Tim drove into the driveway. The only missing person, the one who Callie felt should be there, was Vicki.

Dan dug the hole wide and deep enough for both horses. Then as gently as possible, he picked them up with the forks on his loader tractor, the one that carried the big bales of hay, and lowered them into the depths. Meg stood by the edge of the hole. Lucy broke away from her dad and ran to the grave.

"Don't cover them with dirt. Maybe they're still alive," she shouted, and Meg pulled her close to her side.

When the hole was filled, mounding over in a hillock, so that Callie wondered why the dirt that came out seemed so much more plentiful than the dirt that went back in, they stood around its edge.

Tim cleared his throat. "Well, I think I'd better go to work." He hugged Lucy. "Your mom and I will talk later. Are you going to be all right?"

Lucy cried and clung to him, and Callie wondered why. Tim hadn't wanted to buy the horse in the first place. She was the one who had been here for Lucy while Tawny was dying, not her father.

Her own dad put an arm around her, and her mom leaned in on the other side. "It's okay," her dad whispered in her ear. "Dads aren't much good for anything else."

She laid her head on his shoulder. "You're good for a lot more than that. I'm all right, Dad. They weren't my horses." It didn't seem to matter, though. She felt terrible. When her dad released her, she walked up behind Meg, whose shoulders slumped, her halo of hair wild in the sunlight.

Meg was quietly telling her horse goodbye.

Early afternoon Callie broke away and went to school. She couldn't stay there anymore. Lucy had gone home with her grandparents. Dan had loaded up the backhoe and the deliveryman had taken it away. Meg stood alone by the mound of dirt.

"Are you going to be all right, Meg?" she asked before leaving. It seemed like everyone was always asking that question.

Meg looked at Callie as if surprised to see her. Her face was dirty from wiping away the tears with her hands. She nodded, and Callie guessed she wanted to be alone.

As Callie backed around to leave, she saw Meg's distant figure sitting by the hill of dirt, and she almost turned back. But she was too afraid she'd lose her job and too sad to stay, not even for Meg. She needed some distance.

When she returned, Meg's truck was gone. It turned cold as darkness set in. Only Bill met her at the door, a half-live mouse in his mouth, which she removed and freed outside. It perked up and scampered into the bushes, and she felt good about saving something.

She picked the cat up and went looking for Tony. She found him in his room, lying on his bed. "Hey, Mom, where is everyone?"

"Lucy's at grandma and grandpa's. I don't know where anyone else is." She put her face into Bill's fur, thinking she should turn on the heat.

"They died, huh?" Tony followed her into the other room.

"The horses? Yes."

"Are you going to buy Lucy another one?"

"I don't think so." She turned to look at him. "No."

"I could use a car. Do you think Dad would buy me a car? I'll have my license soon. I'd run errands for you. Go to the store and stuff like that."

She shook her head in disbelief. "After you took his car without asking?"

"I know he only cares about Lucy."

"Oh, Tony, that's not true." She didn't have the strength for this, she thought. "It's been a long, sad day. Let's not argue. Are you hungry?"

"I fixed a frozen pizza." He slouched back to his room. It was the lengthiest conversation they'd had since he'd taken his dad's car. She had to find a way to reach him but not tonight. Tonight she wanted to eat and go to bed.

Peering into the fridge, she saw the open bottle of chardonnay and poured a glass. Just this morning she'd sworn off wine, but the headache had dissipated during the day. Besides, chardonnay was less likely to give you a headache than a red wine. She liked the red wines better, though. Eating leftover pasta with Bill on her lap was a trick. She had to hold him in place with one hand, but after a while he slid to the floor anyway.

When the phone rang she jumped for it, certain it would be Vicki. "Hi, friend, I heard from Marc about the storm and the horses. I'm so sorry. How are you anyway?" Sandy said.

"They died, Sandy. We buried them today." She started to cry.

"How is Lucy?"

Callie told her about the last few days, culminating with the digging of the grave. "It was awful. You know what it is about animals, Sandy, that makes it all so sad? They don't complain. They just give up, like they know when their time comes." She was crying in choking sobs now.

"Are you alone?"

"Tony's here, but he's not what you call company."

"I'll come, just give me a minute to pack."

"You stay with Scott. I'm happy for you both. Really. I'm going to bed just as soon as I finish eating."

From under the covers, she stared at the ceiling fan. Bill didn't want to snuggle. He lay on her feet instead, his twelve pounds ridiculously heavy. After a while, he left the room and she slept.

The alarm clock woke her at six and she sluggishly got out of bed. Looking out the window, she saw that Meg's truck was still gone and wondered if she'd ever see her again. Or Vicki.

The week went by in a blur of kids and meetings and coming home to her kids and Bill. Lucy remained silent and lifeless. She sat and stared a lot, like she was seeing something—probably the horses. Tony was surly as usual. Bill piled up mice corpses in the kitchen. Every time she looked out at the field, she saw the mound covering the horses. Sometimes the goats stood on top of it. Her stomach hurt, especially in the evenings.

She was throwing a little grain to the goats on Friday afternoon when Dan drove in. She hadn't seen him since he'd dug the horses' grave. "How old is that boy of yours?" he asked, striding toward her.

"Tony? Almost sixteen."

"Think he'd like to work for me? I need help with the corn and beans. He could work weekends and after school. Or does he have a job?"

"I'll go get him," she said. "That's just what he needs." Her heart expanded a little.

When Dan offered Tony a job, the boy toed the ground and avoided eye contact. Finally, Callie could stand Tony's apparent indifference no longer and said, "It's a great opportunity."

Tony looked up. "I'll get to drive?"

"Depends on how well you can stay in the rows," Dan said. "Come with me. I'll show you what you'll be doing." Dan whisked him away before he could change his mind.

She called Vicki's number and listened to her voice message. Perhaps something had happened to her. She would ask Kate on Saturday. She curled in a ball in bed, trying to ease the pain in her belly.

Saturday arrived, a warm, breezy day carrying the dry, nutty odor of fall. Everything had turned golden—what leaves were left, the crops, the dust kicked up from the chaff as the combine moved slowly across the field, emptying its load of corn in the truck parked by the road. Dan would drive the truck to the elevator and Tony would take over the combine. Tony loved it when his turn came and was surprisingly good at staying in the rows. Dan took to letting Tony run the combine, while he worked elsewhere on the farm, returning only when Tony called to say the truck bed was full.

Callie had dropped Lucy off at her dad's the night before. She never heard Tony get up and head out the door in the morning. When she awoke, the day was in progress and she was once again alone. She hadn't heard from Vicki, which was so out of character for the Vicki she knew. Meg hadn't returned since Brittle's death either. At least, Callie hadn't seen any sign of her. She had called her cell once and been greeted by a message. She hadn't left one of her own. What would she say? "Where are you? Why don't you come home? It's lonely?" She'd cut out her tongue first.

She left a message for Tony saying she might be late and headed toward the lake at ten. The renters were given till eleven to clear out, so that the next group could move in at three. That gave Callie a few hours to clean up if she had to. The first time she'd done this, when the three guys had left such a mess, there'd been no one scheduled for the next week. It was that way on this October day. The plumber was coming the next week to drain the water for the winter months. She would take home anything that might freeze, empty and unplug the fridge, prop the door open, and turn off the propane and electricity. It was time to close the place until spring. She could have stayed overnight and done all this Sunday morning, if Tony hadn't been home alone.

A feeling of peace settled over her as she pulled into the sandy driveway. She parked under the white oak and paused to smell the pines before unlocking the back door. Inside, the place was spotlessly clean. No windows left open, no food or garbage in the fridge or trash can, no sand on the floors, no dirty counters. From the porch windows, she saw a lone sailboat plying the waters. She quickly changed into her swimsuit and went down the stairs to the shore.

She'd never understood why fall left her feeling bereft. Most people loved the beauty of the season, but for her it marked the end of summer and the beginning of winter. There was something heartbreaking about the leaves turning different colors and falling, leaving the branches bare and black and rattling in the wind under a pale sky.

The frigid water took her breath away. Nevertheless, at chest level, she plunged in and swam out where she could tread water and look at the shoreline. She never heard the sailboat, only saw it when it came abreast of her. Startled, she turned toward it as the sail flapped and Pat and Kate slid over the sides of the Sunfish.

"Hey," she said, delighted. "You bought a sailboat."

"Pat did." Kate gave her a wet hug. "Did the horses recover?"

Callie's smile vanished. "No. They died."

Kate looked shocked. "How is Lucy?"

"Lucy is quiet. Meg is gone, like Vicki." She glanced at Pat, who looked away.

"You've heard from Vicki, haven't you?"

"Once." Pat's smile was strained.

"Is she still in Europe?"

"No."

"Well, can you tell me why she won't return my calls?"

"I don't know." Kate's eyes met Callie's.

Callie nodded and looked away. She told them about the cottage.

"That's wonderful. We'll have you for a neighbor again."

"I know. I can hardly believe it myself."

Kate said, "Do you want to sail, Callie? Pat would love to

take you out."

"No. Thanks, though." She wanted to address what no one was talking about. What had happened to Vicki?

"I'll take the boat home," Pat said.

"You go with Pat, Kate. I don't want to keep either of you from sailing."

"That's okay. I like going alone. Kate prefers a safer ride." Pat raised the sail and lifted herself over the side of the boat. She pulled the sheet tight and sped across the lake. When the boom dipped toward the water, she leaned back against the force of the wind. Callie felt regret stirring. She wanted to sail, but with Kate, not Pat.

She met Kate's eyes again. "Well?"

Kate sighed and took a deep breath. "Vicki let you go. She said you really didn't want her. You wanted Meg, and she wasn't going to muddy the waters anymore."

"Why doesn't she answer my messages?" She stood halfway submersed, the sun warm on her upper body, the water cool from her waist down. "Doesn't friendship mean anything?" She sounded like a petulant child and changed her tone. "I thought I could always count on her." This she said more to herself. She squinted at Kate, thinking that life for Pat must be easy, realizing again that she was half in love with her.

"Could she always count on you?"

Callie looked away. Kate knew the answer to that. "It didn't seem to matter to her."

"She's traveling for her job. She'll be back."

"I thought she'd come back when she heard about the horses, at least for Meg's sake."

"You were there for Meg. That must have been hard, Callie. I remember when Arthur died. People who don't have pets discount the grief that those who do feel when an animal dies. They only think the death of a friend or relative matters."

Vicki had told Callie that Kate had lost a brother to AIDS. Surely, that loss couldn't compare to the death of her dog. Perhaps loss was different only in perspective, though. How would she feel when Bill died? Marc would tell her to get another cat, but she would mourn Bill anyway. Would buying another horse take away the haunted look in Lucy's eyes?

She began to talk about these things as Kate edged toward the beach. Callie got a couple of chairs from the boathouse.

"I don't have any answers, Callie. I thought you wanted to sell Tawny."

"Horses aren't really pets. Their upkeep is expensive. You have to use them for more than riding down the road. Meg's horse was once a valuable show horse. Tawny wasn't even a good trail horse, and Lucy hardly rode him at all. Her dad called to say maybe we should buy her another horse, though, and her brother thinks if we do that, we should buy him a car."

"What do you want to do?"

"Neither. I told Tim that. Winter is coming when Lucy never rides but the horse still has to eat, and I don't want Tony to have a car yet—not one of his own anyway. I want some control."

"What did Tim say?"

"Okay. We don't usually argue about the kids."

"That's good."

"But Lucy's moping around like Tawny was her best friend. I think it was traumatic to see him die like he did. It was for me, watching the light go out of his eyes."

Kate met her eyes. "That's the spirit leaving, don't you think?"

"You must believe animals have souls."

"Definitely. Some are kinder than we are."

"Not Bill, my cat. He's a mouser."

"Ah, but I bet he loves you."

"Yep. I'm the one who feeds him." And she laughed.

"You must feel abandoned."

She looked away. Her voice was thick with tears. "I do. First Vicki disappears and then Meg. I expected it from Meg but not from Vicki. She could have said goodbye." She was angry, too.

Kate patted her on the knee. "Well, why don't you come over and have lunch with us and spend the day? We don't see enough of you. Are you staying the night?"

"I can't. Tony will be home alone. I don't trust him. Yet," she said, pulling shorts and her sun shirt over her swimsuit. She handed her towel to Kate to wrap around her shoulders, picked up her book bag and started down the beach.

"Do you like fall?" Around the lake, some maples were still clothed in orange and red while the aspens sported yellow leaves and the oaks had taken on a russet hue. It was like a contest, the colors contrasting with the more numerous white and red pines. A blue jay screamed from an overhead branch and another answered.

"It's lovely, isn't it? But I like spring and summer better."

"Me, too." She was dreading the coming winter now that both Vicki and Meg were gone.

They climbed over the long piers on wheels and the boat lifts that cluttered the beach.

Pat had anchored the sailboat and put out another chair. After Labor Day weekend a quiet fell over the lake. A few fishermen were hunched over their poles or stood casting toward shore. The sounds of summer were gone—the kids laughing while swimming or shrieking as they whipped across the waves on a ski tube, people's voices carrying across the water late into the night. No roar of motorboats speeding by with skiers behind them, nor the whine of Jet Skis.

"I could get used to this silence," she said.

"That part is nice." Kate turned to Pat. "We were talking about fall."

"I love fall, but then I like winter, too." Pat leaned forward in order to see Callie. "Do you cross country ski?"

"I do, not a lot, though." She didn't like narrow trails and steep hills.

"Vicki and I go out for hours."

"I believe it," Callie said. "You're both athletes."

Pat laughed. "Vicki will be back. She can't stay away forever."

What Callie feared was that Vicki would find a job elsewhere or maybe she'd find someone else. The question she kept asking herself was why she cared? It was true she desired Meg, but she also knew that Meg wasn't available. What had made her think Vicki would hang around no matter how many times she pushed her away? She told herself it was better this way. How would she tell the kids anyway, which made her wonder what Kate had told her kids.

When Pat said, "You two stay right here. Okay? I'm going to fix lunch," she jumped to her feet.

"Let me help. You're always making me something to eat."

"This is my treat." Pat strode off to the house.

Kate smiled. "She thinks we want to talk."

"I do have something to ask you, but it's pretty nervy." Her face grew hot.

"Now I'm curious. Spit it out."

"How did you tell your kids about Pat and you?" Then she wondered if she'd gotten it right. Were they a couple or just good friends? She doubted her certainty for only a moment.

When Kate spoke, it was as if she was trying to remember. "They guessed. My girls were pretty much okay with it. I think it upset them more when my husband married a younger woman. They liked Pat, and they loved my brother, who was gay. It was my son who gave us a hard time at first, but he got over it. It's not an easy thing, telling your kids. It wasn't easy for me to admit it to myself." She smiled ruefully at Callie. "Are you worried about telling your children?"

"What's to tell? Vicki's boldness scared the hell out of me. And then I got hooked on Meg. And now there's no one. But the thing is, if there was someone, Tim might try to take the kids away from me—especially Lucy. He wouldn't want Tony, because Tony hates his stepmother. I don't think I could stand losing primary custody."

"My kids were over eighteen. Surely, yours are old enough to decide for themselves."

"Probably, but then they'd feel guilty for choosing one of us over the other. I'd probably run out and buy the first horse I saw to ensure Lucy's vote."

Callie caught sight of Pat coming down the path from the house with a tray and rushed to help her. Sandwiches and chips. Callie tucked the bottle of beer under her arm and took the glasses of iced tea.

"Did you want a beer or a glass of wine? I should have asked."

"No. This is great."

She walked back down the beach with Kate and Pat late in the day, wishing she could stay overnight. Tired from too much sun and water, she said goodbye on the shoreline.

"Next time plan to stay overnight."

"I will, but that'll probably be in the spring when the cottage is open again. I'll call you when you move to town for the winter. I owe you dinner." She wondered what they would make of the farmhouse.

"Sounds good."

She stood at the top of the hill for a long time, tucking the lake away in her mind for the coming months. After checking the cottage again, she closed the windows, locked the door and drove away.

She'd called Tony twice during the afternoon and gotten his voice mail. "Hey, I'm busy. Leave a number and I'll get back with you later." On the way home, she called again and got the same message. She told him she was on her way home.

When she passed the combine trundling across the field with its headlights on, she pulled off the road and got out of the car. Tony was leaning against the truck. "Hey, Ma, I already ate. Dan's wife can really cook."

"Yes, I know. She owns a restaurant."

"Yeah? I won't be home till late. We're putting this stuff in the silos."

Tony looked different somehow—taller, more confident, happier. "What would you say if I became a farmer?"

"Whatever turns your crank, kiddo." A nearly full moon

floated over the field. She was in shirtsleeves, as was Tony. How different from the night the horses died when it seemed as if winter had arrived.

Meg's truck was still gone, and she wondered briefly where she was spending her nights. She turned on the kitchen light and blinked in its brightness. The cat brushed against her legs and she picked him up, looking around for any carnage he'd left behind. Nothing. Amazing.

"Losing your touch, guy?"

He rubbed against her face before struggling to get down. She fed him and headed for the shower, stopping to listen to a message from Marc on the way.

"Hey, girl. I quit my job at the print shop. We're making enough money to pay me a decent salary with insurance benefits. I think we should discuss this, the three of us. Where the hell is Vicki?"

The store would be closed by now, and she didn't care what Marc paid himself. It couldn't be much. She'd talk to him on Sunday.

She was in bed with a book when she heard a vehicle in the driveway, followed by the door opening. Figuring it was Tony, she kept reading. Tony would see the light if he wanted to talk to her. Bill lifted his head and stared at the open bedroom door.

"Come in," she said at the knock on the frame and looked up to see Meg standing in the opening. She sat upright and said the first thing that came to mind. "Where have you been?"

Meg waved the question away. She had lost weight, if that was possible. Her pale hair was carelessly piled on her head and her eyes, smudged by shadows, looked too large for her face. "Is it okay if I leave some of my things here, like the trailer and my stuff upstairs? I came to get some clothes. I've run out and I'm tired of washing every couple of days." She gave Callie a grim smile. "I'm sorry, Callie. I just can't be here right now. I left a check in the kitchen for two months rent."

"You don't need to pay any extra for…" Her voice trailed off. Her heart was leaping around her chest as if looking for an exit.

What she really wanted to say was, "Please stay. Sleep with me," but she couldn't get the words out and, besides, she knew Meg wouldn't.

"I know."

"You don't have to pay anything if you're not going to be here."

"Yes, I do." Meg had been leaning against the doorframe in a sexy slouch. She stood and braced herself with both hands. "I'll be in touch. Thanks for letting me bury Brittle." Her voice caught like a sob on the name.

Callie threw the covers back and started to get up. Pain swept through her middle in hot waves.

Meg put out a hand. "Stay there. You're a good friend, Callie, a good mom, a good person. I just can't look at that mound of dirt for a while." She scooped up Bill who was purring against her and put him back on the bed before leaving.

Callie stared at the closed door for as long as it took Meg to leave the house. Then she turned off the light and pulled the blinds to watch Meg stride to her truck and drive away.

Both Meg and Vicki were gone. She lay flat on the bed, gasping a little. If she breathed deeply, sometimes it helped relieve the ache in her midriff. Then she went to the kitchen and took a bottle of merlot to bed with her. She never heard Tony come home.

She drove to the shop the next day, despite feeling terrible. Tony was working in the fields. Lucy was still at her dad's. When Marc caught sight of her, he grinned and spread his arms wide. She looked around and saw that, indeed, the place had changed. There was an order and busyness to it that hadn't existed when she'd last gone through its doors.

"How do you like it?" he asked.

"Exciting," she said. "You've done a terrific job."

"Thanks. There are money matters I need to discuss with you."

"That's okay, Marc. Send me a financial statement, or

whatever they're called. I just wanted to see the place, I guess, maybe take a spin on a bike. You still doing that?"

"Yeah, but we don't have classes on Sundays."

She realized she didn't really want to ride one of the bikes after all. Her stomach hurt clear through to her back. She tried to contain the pain with a hand, but it was too widespread.

"You don't look good, Callie," he said.

"I'm okay. You asked about Vicki. I haven't seen her."

"Is that what's wrong? What happened?"

"I don't know. One day everything seemed fine. The next she was gone."

"What about your roomer? You're not all alone, are you?"

"She's gone, too. The horses died. Lucy is still mourning. Tony has a job, though, working for Dan, our neighboring farmer. He loves it. So it's not all bad news." She realized she was here because she felt friendless. She wanted to reconnect with Marc. "How is Sandy?"

"Happy as a clam. I never understood that saying. What makes clams happy?" His thumbs were hooked in his belt loops, his wolfish smile disarming. "How is the job?"

That was another thing. A couple of her pregnant girls were close to giving birth, and there still was no resolution on her childcare proposal. If she didn't push for it, she'd disappoint her girls. If she did, she might endanger her job. She almost wished she'd never thought of a daycare for babies of schoolgirls in the first place. She had two kids of her own to look out for.

A short, muscular guy walked up to them, a big grin on his face. Callie knew by the way he was looking at Marc that they had something going on between them.

"Callie, meet Dave Carlson, my right-hand man. He does the classes now. Callie was our first spinning instructor. She wants to ride."

"Good. Let's do it."

"I'm really kind of out of shape." She hadn't ridden a bike since the last class she'd led. That seemed months ago, but thinking she needed to get back in shape, she'd worn her padded shorts and a T-shirt under a jacket. "I just have to put on my biking shoes."

On the bike she straightened her back and took a deep breath. She'd forgotten to bring any Tums. The now familiar pain, the one that swept through her middle unrelentingly, seized her. She swallowed rapidly as the two pieces of toast she'd eaten for breakfast climbed up her throat.

They pedaled slowly for a few minutes before beginning a sitting climb, putting on resistance every few seconds. That was followed by three thirty-second sprints and five jumps, after which came a standing climb. Dave apparently assumed she was fit, that this was easy for her. After fifteen minutes, the room began swimming. She wiped the sweat out of her eyes and said nothing. Then everything went black, just like that. One minute she was conscious, the next she was lying on the mat with Marc and Dave standing over her.

"I'm all right." She struggled to get up, but there was something wrong with her left leg. It hurt like hell.

"I'll call an ambulance," Marc said, his face white.

"No, don't. Just help me up." A crowd encircled her. Faces she didn't recognize, staring.

Marc and Dave put their arms under hers and lifted her to her feet. When Dave let go, her left leg gave out and she leaned heavily on Marc. "We're going to the ER," Marc said firmly.

"No. Take me to the clinic." Her insurance would cover that. She put a little weight on the offending leg, testing it.

"Hey, girlfriend, what happened?" Sandy asked, appearing suddenly and looking worried.

Marc filled her in.

"I'll take her. We've got lots of catching up to do anyway, don't we?"

They waited an hour at the emergency clinic to see someone. She wasn't sure what hurt more, her leg or her stomach.

"So why did you fall off the bike?"

"I passed out and my cleats caught in the pedal."

"Ouch! But why did you pass out?"

"I don't know. It happened so fast. I'm out of shape."

"Me too, but that doesn't mean I faint. Something must be wrong."

"Well, I've had this stomachache that won't go away." She wriggled in the chair, but the pain remained constant. It responded to neither pain relievers nor change of position. "It's gobbling me up. I eat a ton of Tums, but I didn't have any with me today."

She changed the subject and started talking about her idea for childcare when her pregnant girls delivered. "These girls are going nowhere if they don't finish high school."

Sandy looked fascinated. "Sounds like a great idea, if only it were that simple. I suppose the school doesn't want the liability. If something happened to one of the babies while it was in childcare, the school district could be sued."

"I have to think of another way to work this. You're always full of good ideas." She looked hopefully at her friend.

"Some businesses run daycare centers for their employees. Why don't you talk to them?"

"Businesses have money. They can afford insurance and daycare employees."

"If you miraculously were allowed to do this during school hours on school property, some parents would say you were encouraging kids to have sex."

"I know."

The nurse called for Norah Callahan, and Sandy patted her arm. "That's you, Callie. Let me help."

Leaning on Sandy's arm, she hobbled down a hall to a room and sat heavily on a chair. Sandy took the other one. When the doctor came in, she took the rolling stool. She seemed much too young to be a doctor.

"What can I do for you?" she asked, looking from one to the other.

Callie told her about her leg, because that was what she saw as the immediate problem. Surgery lurked as a possibility in the back of her mind. When would she have time for that? Then Sandy said that Callie had fainted and fallen from a stationary bike.

"Did you eat this morning?" the doctor asked.

She had. Breakfast was her favorite meal.

"Did you sleep well last night?"

"As well as I usually do."

"She's had a stomachache for weeks."

Callie frowned at Sandy. She could speak for herself.

"Can you get up on the table?"

She managed with help. Lying back, she stared at the young doctor's face as the woman probed her midriff and asked her questions. "Are you throwing up? Do you take aspirin? Do you drink caffeine and liquor? Where does it hurt?"

"All the way through to my back," she said after answering the first four questions—no, no, yes, yes.

"Now we'll take a look at your leg."

After her leg was X-rayed and Callie was back in the doctor's office with Sandy in the other chair, the doctor came in and showed them the pictures. "There is no fracture. You probably tore a tendon when you fell, and that won't show up on an X-ray. Often tendons heal without any help. Why don't you wait a week and see if it's better? Meanwhile, make an appointment with your regular doctor, just in case." She handed Callie a scrip for Cimetidine. "For the stomachaches. A tablet twice a day, and lay off the caffeine and liquor for a while."

Sandy and the doctor helped her off the table.

"Invest in a knee brace and a cane." The doctor turned at the door and smiled. "Take it easy."

After filling the prescription and purchasing the cane and knee brace, Sandy drove Callie to her car at the shop. Theirs were the only vehicles in the lot. The store was closed. Callie assured Sandy she could drive home. It was her left leg after all. She asked Sandy to call Marc and assure him she was all right.

She phoned Tony on the way. No answer. Lucy picked up on the first ring. "Where are you, Mom? Dad's still here, because Tony isn't home. Where is he?"

"I'm on my way." She was in no mood for long-winded

explanations.

She struggled out of her car and, leaning heavily on the cane, moved at a snail-like pace toward the house.

Tim threw open the back door. "For Christ's sake, Callie, what now? Everything's a crisis with you."

Was that true? She looked up at him, standing on the stoop, holding the door open.

Lucy pushed her way past her dad. "What happened, Mom?"

Tim roughly helped her up the stairs. "Where's Tony?"

"Working in the fields." Inside, Bill rubbed against her leg in welcome. She couldn't pick him up. "You can leave now, Tim."

"What happened?" he asked.

"I fell," she said tersely. "I'll be fine." Tomorrow she had to go to school. How would she do that when she moved at the speed of a turtle?

To her amazement, the tendon slowly healed itself. In two weeks she put the cane and knee brace away. Her stomach was better. No more hot flames coursing through her. She was glad she'd put off calling her doctor.

When she talked to Alan again, he said the superintendent had reservations and some of the school board members thought a childcare center for babies of students would encourage other students to have sex. Anyway, there was no money in the budget for a daycare provider or insurance.

"We're on our own," she told her group of girls. "They're not going to allow a childcare facility on school grounds. Too costly and too much liability."

Francine got up and walked agitatedly around the room. "If they give us a break, other girls will decide to get pregnant, like it's so much fun carrying around all this weight. That's what they think, isn't it? They don't want us setting any examples. We're supposed to pay for making a mistake. Right, Ms. C?"

"That could be part of it, but liability insurance is a big hurdle. So is paying a daycare person."

Gloria, a girl who seldom spoke, said, "My aunt loves babies. She lives across the street and down a block. She watches the neighbor's baby. She used to work for a daycare place before she went on the disability."

"Well, why didn't you say so a long time ago, Gloria?" Francine's hands were fisted on her hips. "You coulda saved us a lot of worry." She sounded like fifteen going on thirty, and Callie smiled.

"Can we go talk to her after school, Gloria?" Callie asked, trying not to let her hopes soar. They'd have to find some way to pay this person even if she had a license. And then there was the disability issue.

"I'll ask her tonight."

There were four girls. Before the school year was out, there'd be four babies. How much did daycare cost for four babies?

Gloria's Aunt Tiffany's house appeared small and rundown from the outside. Tiffany looked like she should be in high school. "I want to be a Web designer," Tiffany said, leading the girls through the tiny rooms with brightly painted walls. "I take care of the neighbor's baby, but that only pays for one course. I have to buy Dreamweaver. It's a software program and costs about three hundred dollars."

"How are you going to study and care for babies?"

Tiffany gave Callie a lovely smile. "That's the beauty of it. Little babies sleep most of the time. You just have to give them a bottle once every few hours and change their diapers, and their mamas are going to come over during study hall and lunch hour. There'll be time."

Tiffany showed Callie her daycare license, cheaply framed and hung on the living room wall.

"Gloria says you're on disability."

"I've got fibromyalgia, but babies aren't that much work."

"How much do you charge?" Callie said. "We have to raise money."

"A hundred apiece. That's twenty days a month, five dollars a day. That's cheap." Tiffany's almond-shaped eyes met Callie's gaze straight on as if trying to convince them both this was a good price and she was a great choice.

"We'll see what we can do. Do you have a husband, Tiffany?"

"No. My mom lives here with me. She helps when she's not working."

On the way back to school, the girls talked excitedly, while Callie thought about ways to raise money. They could ask for a food stand at a couple of games, but that wouldn't bring in much. They could sell something, like candy bars, which would produce pennies compared to what they needed. They could do a car wash. It wasn't too cold yet. She sighed and stopped in the middle of the sidewalk to present these possibilities to the girls. They responded enthusiastically. This was when she needed Vicki, the queen of marketing.

She would call Marc. He said they were making money hand over fist.

Chapter 9

April. Spring break. The cottage was open. The kids were going to Florida for ten days with their father. Callie was home alone, sitting on the front porch with Bill on her lap and a vodka and tonic at her elbow, grateful that winter was over. Her pregnant girls had all delivered. Now came the question of what they would do for daycare next year. Tiffany only watched babies. However, there were influential forces at work to continue and expand what Callie and the girls had started—childcare for student mothers, which was the new coinage defining the girls of these babies.

Callie had spent every penny she got from the shop on the daycare center, which was kept alive through donations and fund-raising. The student mothers knew how to raise money. It was heartening how even the shyest kid, like Gloria, turned bold when her baby's welfare was concerned.

An Audi turned into the driveway and bounced over the ruts. Her heart bumped with it. Vicki drove an Audi. Callie sat very still for a moment and then, forgetting Bill, stood abruptly. The cat landed on all fours and meowed aggrievedly.

She picked him up to apologize and carried him to the kitchen door.

Vicki was rummaging around in her trunk. She held up a beer and smiled. "I was hoping you'd be home. It's happy hour, isn't it?" She walked toward the stoop and stood on the bottom step, looking up at Callie, as if she'd seen her yesterday, as if she hadn't been gone six months. "You look wonderful."

Callie stared at her. Surprise paralyzed her vocal chords. She'd never expected to see Vicki again. These last difficult months—after Brittle and Tawny died and Meg left, the scrounging for funds for daycare, the cold, snowy winter—she had often wondered why Vicki had left with no warning. At some point, though, she had let that question go, along with Vicki, and now here was Vicki on her doorstep.

Vicki looked the same—tan as if she'd spent the winter on some sunny beach, her brown hair highlighted with blond streaks, her body slender and fit. The dark-lashed hazel eyes with their specks of gold smiled when she did. Callie found herself looking at Vicki's white teeth and wide mouth. She said what she'd said to Meg the last time she saw her. "Where have you been?"

"Traveling for the company."

"Why didn't you say you were going?" Anger edged her words.

"Where are the horses?" Even the goats were gone. Dan had taken them home to give the field a chance to recover from being eaten to the ground.

"See that mound out there in the field?" Callie pointed. "That's where the horses are."

Vicki stared and slowly turned back. "Why didn't someone tell me?"

"Didn't you get my messages?"

"I couldn't find my cell just before I left to catch the plane, so I left it."

"You talked to Pat. I know that."

"I called her when I got to Texas." The smile was gone. "How is Lucy?"

"It was hard for her."

"And Meg?"

"Meg left. She couldn't bear to look at the mound." The one that reminded Callie every day of what had happened.

"Her trailer is here."

"So are her things. She pays rent to keep them here."

"Damn. I'm sorry, Callie. I didn't know."

"Well, if you ever find your cell, you'll hear the messages." She turned and went inside. She was still mad. Why hadn't Vicki called her?

Vicki followed. "Can we talk?"

Unable to imagine what Vicki could say that would right her vanishing act, Callie shrugged and headed for the porch.

Vicki sat next to her and twisted off the beer cap.

Not so fast, Callie thought. You're not out of the woods. Part of her wanted to tell Vicki to go and not to come back. What kind of friend went off like Vicki had, and then suddenly appeared six months later as if nothing had changed? The other part, the part she was trying to squelch, was secretly glad to see Vicki. Callie practically inhaled her drink and went to make another, leaving Vicki on the porch. When she came back, the cat was settling down on Vicki's lap.

"Why did you go and say nothing about it? Why didn't you at least call?" It had been so unexpected.

"I thought I'd give you and Meg a chance to make a go of it. I was always around, and nothing I did seemed to please you, Callie."

"But why did you come to the cottage that last night and then just disappear?"

"I got the message. I mean if you can climb in bed with me and nothing happens, no vibes or anything, there's no hope. I thought if I went away long enough, I'd get over you. Everyone says that's the only way to do it." She put Bill on Callie's lap. "I'm going to get another beer."

"Well, you didn't exactly make a move that night either." Callie met Vicki's gaze and held it for a few seconds.

"I didn't think you wanted me to."

Callie chewed on her lip, knowing that Vicki was right. "Since when did that ever stop you?"

"It suddenly seemed hopeless." She smiled tightly. "I'll be right back."

Staring out at the only color, a streak of red across the western horizon, Callie remembered that night. The occasional touch of bodies in the narrow bed had been both comforting and disturbing. It had left her confused. It was so easy just to be with Vicki, who demanded nothing and gave everything. How selfish she'd been to just take.

Vicki sat down again. "I put a couple bottles in the fridge. I'll leave when they're gone."

When the sun set, the night took on a chill, but she wasn't ready to go inside yet where she'd have to talk to Vicki face-to-face. And why was that? She'd never been in awe of Vicki. "Have you talked to Marc?"

"Yes. I told him to plow my profits back in the store. I hear you had better things to do with yours."

"The daycare center. I couldn't think of another way to keep my student mothers in school." She thought of them as hers. They would leave her behind soon.

"Hey, that was a great thing to do. I'd love to contribute to the cause."

Vicki was always ready to donate. "The daycare needs all the help it can get. Thanks, Vicki, for offering."

"I mean it. I can write a check tonight."

"How nice it must be to have so much money." A small silence followed and she glanced at Vicki and found Vicki looking back.

"I don't know how to respond to that."

"Of course, the girls would appreciate whatever you want to give," she said quickly. "I didn't mean…" What had she meant? It must have seemed like a slap in the face. "I'm sorry."

"No. That's okay. I'd rather you be honest. Listen, I better go. I've got a lot of stuff to do before I go into work tomorrow. I'll just get my checkbook. It's in the car."

Callie hadn't expected to feel the way she had when Vicki arrived, excited and angry, nor was she prepared for the loss she experienced when Vicki said she was leaving. She knew instinctively that Vicki wouldn't come back, that this was it. She set the cat on the floor and walked through the dark house to the kitchen where she turned on the lights.

Vicki gave her a tight smile and blinked in the glare as she handed Callie the check. "Talk to you later."

"Don't you want your beer?" Callie asked, feeling a little sick. She glanced at the check—a thousand dollars—and wanted to cry.

"Nah. Give it to Meg when she comes back." Vicki turned away.

When she was halfway to her car, Callie tore out the door. "Wait, Vicki. Don't go. Please." It seemed like everyone and everything had left her, even the damn goats.

Vicki stood with her back to Callie, her arms hanging at her sides.

Callie stepped off the stoop. "Can't we start over?"

"From day one?" Vicki put her hands in her jacket pockets and turned to face Callie.

"Yeah."

"I don't know if I can just be a friend, Callie."

"We never gave anything more a try, did we?"

"I did."

"Come inside, Vicki. Eating crow isn't easy."

Vicki nodded and closed the distance between them. "Here I am. What are you going to do with me now?"

"Appreciate you." Nearly in tears, Callie was grateful for the cover of night. "I didn't know how." She pulled Vicki's hands out of her pockets and looked her in the eye. She had never been bold like this, but she was desperate. "They're cold."

"That's why they were in my pockets." Vicki's face remained impassive, impossible to read. Maybe she was having trouble believing Callie was serious.

She pulled Vicki into the house, stumbling on the last step so that Vicki righted her before she could fall. "Whoa, woman. Is this what you really want, Callie? What about Meg?"

"What about Meg?" There was a little twist of longing when she heard or spoke Meg's name, but she was more afraid of losing Vicki again than Meg. She wanted the old Vicki back, the one who was always around no matter what.

"I thought you wanted to be with Meg." They were back in the kitchen, assessing each other through unwavering eyes.

Callie held tight to Vicki's hands, as if she thought Vicki might try to escape. "Sit down. I'll get you a beer."

"You sit down. I'll get you a vodka and tonic." One of Vicki's eyebrows arched.

She almost laughed at this brief glimpse of the old Vicki. "You can't always be in the driver's seat, Vicki."

"I can try." Vicki stepped closer, near enough to lean forward and kiss Callie on the mouth. A gentle, tentative kiss, one that asked if this was okay.

Callie dropped Vicki's hands and slid her palms up Vicki's arms to her shoulders. Why had she been so scared of this? It was nice. Vicki's tongue traced her lips and Callie met it with her own. Briefly, she wondered if she should turn off the light. Instead, she maneuvered them both into the shadowy living room, which wasn't easy to do because Bill was twining around their ankles.

Breathless, Callie broke away. Their foreheads touched and Vicki kissed her eyes and eyebrows, her face and neck. Callie followed suit, still moving her feet, propelling them toward the bedroom. She was no longer sure of Vicki, and she thought some real sex would keep her from leaving again. It occurred to her that this would have scared the hell out of her a few months ago.

Vicki looked around when they were in the doorway. "When I slept with you that night at your cottage, I was waiting for you to make a move like this. You so obviously didn't want me. Why now?"

"I missed you. I couldn't believe you left without even saying goodbye. I'm still mad about that."

A laugh caught in Vicki's throat. "Well, you must be pretty conflicted right now." She sniffed Callie's neck, nibbling at the skin. "God, you smell good, like fresh air. Can we take this off?" She tugged on the hem of Callie's T-shirt, pulling it over her head, then wriggled out of her own and dropped it on the floor. She leaned over and put her tongue in Callie's cleavage, then backed Callie toward the bed. When Callie stiffened, she stopped. "Are you all right with this?"

"Just once, let me." Callie pulled Vicki down next to her on the mattress. She slid a finger into Vicki's cleavage, which was warm and slightly damp, and hesitantly met Vicki's gaze.

"Let me help you." Vicki unclasped her bra, then reached behind Callie and unhooked hers. "You can do anything you want, Callie. You can look, too. I, for one, am going to memorize you." She smiled mischievously, dispelling Callie's inhibitions.

"Wow," Callie said softly. Vicki's breasts were lovely—lying one on top of the other, the blue veined skin pale, the nipples dark. She raised her eyes to Vicki's. "I noticed them even when you were leaning over the side of your boat after you nearly ran me over," she said with wonder, "and I still didn't guess."

"Guess what?" Vicki kissed her mouth.

"That I liked breasts."

Vicki laughed. "You could have fooled me. You were mad as a hornet. I think I fell for you when you struggled into that little sailboat half full of water and flew across the lake." As she talked, Vicki worked Callie's panties off and kicked her own out of the way.

Callie gasped when Vicki's hand slipped between her legs. At first, she was unable to respond, but after a few moments of pure narcissistic pleasure, she began to caress Vicki. She found as much enjoyment in touching the smooth, taut skin and rousing a response—a low moan very much like a growl. When they pressed against each other, hands and mouths and breasts and bellies, it seemed almost possible that they could become as one.

They fell asleep finally. When Callie awoke in the night, the cat was stretched out between them, and she moved him to the end of the bed. Vicki lay on her back, covers up to her chin. The house was cool. Callie lay next to her, so that their arms and hips and legs touched. Vicki sighed and turned toward her, throwing an arm over her midriff.

In the morning, she was sandwiched between Vicki and the cat. Quietly, she slipped out of bed and went to the kitchen to feed Bill and to the bathroom where she brushed her teeth, then slid just as silently back between the sheets.

"Hi," Vicki said sleepily, putting her arms around her and giving her a big kiss. "You even smell good in the morning."

"Hi, yourself."

"How do you want to spend the day? I know how I want to start it."

"It's raining."

"Good. That makes it easy."

They got up around ten and ate a big breakfast. Callie looked across the table at Vicki and wondered how they were going to work this out. Who lived with whom? Or did they just get together on the weekends when the kids were at their dad's? Then they wouldn't have to tell anyone, not her children, not her parents, nor would Tim find out.

"What are you thinking?" Vicki's hair was rumpled, her left cheek lined from the pillow, her eyes puffy. Callie thought she looked cute.

"I'm wondering what we do now."

"What do you want to do now?"

"Don't answer a question with a question. You know more about lesbian protocol than I do." Annoyed, she knew she sounded ridiculous.

Vicki laughed. "That's a new one—lesbian protocol." She leaned her arms on the table. "It's up to you, Callie. You have kids. You have parents. I know it can be very sticky telling the truth. What is the truth anyway? Are you as nuts about me as I am about you?"

"I'm getting there." Callie panicked at the thought of telling her mother but laughed when she imagined the expression on her mom's face. "Are we supposed to move in together, because I don't think you'd want to live here and there isn't room at your place for me and the kids and the cat."

"Why don't we play it by ear and see how it goes?"

"You're not going to disappear again, are you?"

"Not on your life." Vicki ate the last of her toast and honed in on Callie. "What's going to happen when Meg comes back?"

Callie shook her head with some regret. She was letting go of a fantasy. "She doesn't want me."

"Do you want her?"

"No."

"Be honest."

There was something so exciting about Meg, so sensual, so irresistible. "I can only handle one woman at a time. You're the winner. Lucky you!"

Vickie smiled and reached across the table for her hand. "Yeah, lucky me."

Callie didn't know when her mom guessed. She sometimes wondered what the kids thought, because Vicki often stayed over during the week. She'd start out in the guest room and end up in Callie's bed, then move back to the other room early in the morning. The kids liked Vicki. However, Lucy asked if Vicki didn't have a home and Tony asked why she was always at their house. She told both of them that Vicki had no family at home, and she liked sharing theirs. Lucy bought it, Callie thought, but doubted that Tony did. He was so busy helping Dan after school with spring plowing and disking that he probably didn't give Vicki's staying over much thought.

However, one Sunday late in April when Vicki was outside talking to Callie's dad and the kids were with their father, her mother confronted her. With hands on hips, lips compressed, she said, "Now is as good a time to talk as any. What's going on between you and Vicki?"

"What do you mean?" Annoyed that she was stammering like

a guilty kid, Callie forced herself to look her mom in the eye.

"Did she take advantage of your loneliness? Is that it? I mean why did Scott marry Sandy? He used to be your boyfriend."

"Oh, Mom. You make me sound like a loser. Scott and Sandy love each other. I never loved Scott."

"Did you love Tim?"

"I thought I did till he took up with Shirley."

"I always knew you were different."

Callie heaved a sigh and gave up. "I guess I am. You could say Vicki and I are a couple."

It wasn't a look of surprise on her mom's face. It was more an expression of dismay. "What will your father say? This will kill him."

"I don't think so." Her father had always been her champion. "Let's call him in and tell him. You might be surprised. It's not a terrible thing, Mom. A lot of people are this way."

"A lot of people are what way?" her dad asked, coming into the kitchen with Vicki.

Vicki looked at Callie and away but not before Callie caught her nervous smile.

"Gay, dad. A lot of people are gay and lesbian."

Her dad looked puzzled. "I know that. Why…" And then he caught on. She saw it register, first as surprise, then as if he were trying to digest it. "Well, at least we got our grandkids first."

She laughed nervously. "Do you still love me?"

"Hey, kiddo, love isn't like a cake of soap. You can't wash it away."

It was an odd thing to say, but they'd run out of time to talk. Tim's car drove into the driveway and the kids spilled out of it.

Her mother had been cooking dinner as she usually did when she and Callie's dad came over. Chicken and mashed potatoes and green beans. Comfort food. They needed it, Callie thought, as the kids' voices flooded the kitchen.

"We went fishing on Lake Winnebago. It was hot." Lucy's face was burned like the sun.

"Nah. It was the most fun thing we've done all year. I'm not going next weekend, though, because I'm helping Dan in the fields. We're going to plant. Dad said it was okay."

"Why didn't your dad come inside?"

"He had to get home. They were having company." Tony got along better with his stepmother since he'd been working with Dan. "Hey, Gramps, I caught a huge walleye. Twenty-four inches. We measured."

"Isn't that a keeper?" Callie's dad said. "Your grandma could have fried it up."

"Dad said the big ones aren't that good to eat."

"They get kind of mealy," his grandpa agreed, putting an arm around him.

Callie watched as her kids talked to their grandparents and to Vicki, who jumped right into the fishing conversation to say that northern pike were tasty if you filleted them right. Her mother cast a wary eye on Vicki but seemed won over when Vicki started talking recipes with her.

Waiting for it all to blow up, Callie only relaxed when her parents left, their taillights winking at the end of the driveway. The kids went to their rooms, leaving Callie and Vicki alone. "Are you staying?" Callie asked.

"I'd like to."

"Well, do then." Callie took her hand. "We'll finish off the wine."

"We could get a place of our own now that the news is out." Vicki said. "Give it some thought, sweetie."

Callie loved it when Vicki called her by some endearment when they were by themselves.

On a Friday in May, Callie noticed Meg's horse trailer missing when she came home from work. Her heart jumped. Lucy's dad had picked her up from school. Tony was already gone to Dan's, so she couldn't ask him.

She went into the house, but there was no message on the table. After changing her clothes, she went outside. Scraggly grass grew in the field, but on the mound stood a patch of violets, blue as the sky. She looked in the barn first, before walking out to the horses' grave to see if Meg had left any clues. Nothing.

Vicki would be late tonight. She had a four o'clock meeting. Callie knew she worried about Meg coming back, but after the last few weeks, Callie no longer thought about Meg. She was besotted with sex and with Vicki and sometimes wondered why it had taken her so long to get this way.

As she left the field, Meg's truck and trailer pulled slowly into the driveway. Meg parked by the barn and waved as she got out of the truck and headed back to the trailer. Her hair as usual was piled loosely up off her neck, a golden crown.

When Callie reached the trailer, Meg had opened the tailgate and was clucking to the horse inside. "Come on back, fella." The horse took a step backward, but when it felt nothing but air behind it, jumped forward. Meg stepped into the other side of the stock trailer, took hold of the lead rope and backed the animal out onto the stone driveway. The horse was a leggy, sorrel gelding with white on its face.

So far, neither woman had spoken to the other. Meg was the first to break the silence. "How do you like him?"

"He looks like Brittle, except younger."

"He's Brittle's baby brother. I'm going to show him." Meg glanced toward the field. "Where are the goats?"

"Gone home." Would she have to put up with Randy again? "How are you, Meg?"

Meg's eyes glowed. "Good. I have an offer to make. Let me just put him in the pen and give him some water and hay. Calm him down a little. It would sure help if Randy was here."

She didn't want Randy. The little goat would be okay, but she couldn't recall its name. "I'll call Dan. Maybe he can bring one of the goats back when he comes home. He works for Dan now."

"Good for him. Thanks, Callie." She put a hand on Callie's shoulder. "I missed you."

Her heart took another leap. "You were gone a long time." She called Dan's cell and after five rings, he answered. She told him she wanted the little goat, not Randy, if it was okay with him.

"Meg's back?" he asked, disbelief in his voice.

"Yep. With another horse."

"No bull?"

"Nope, none." She hung up.

The horse was restless in the pen. He ran from side to side, head high, nostrils flared, neighing rather pitifully. Meg talked quietly to the animal. She called him Tango. After fifteen minutes, the gelding stopped his running and walked up to her. She rubbed the white strip between his eyes.

"Are you moving back in?"

"I'd like to." Meg looked gravely at her.

Callie's heart was pounding now. She listened, ears pricked for Vicki's arrival. She thought she should say something about the two of them but didn't know how to phrase it. When she heard two cars on the gravel, she began to sweat.

The little goat bleated from Tony's arms. He set the animal down. "Hey, Meg. Big horse."

"Hey, Tony. Little goat," Meg replied and added as if seven months hadn't gone by, "Hi, Vicki."

"Should I put him in the pen? What if the horse creams him?" Tony asked.

"I'll go in with him."

Meg held the horse's lead rope, while Tony hung on to the rope around Pete's neck. The two animals sniffed noses. The goat bleated, the horse whinnied, stamped one foot and sniffed again.

"I gotta get back in the field," Tony said.

"Take Pete out of the pen and release him. We'll let them get acquainted through the gate."

"When did Meg show up?" Vicki looked stunned.

"About a half hour after I got home." Callie gave Vicki what she hoped was a reassuring smile.

"Is she moving back in?"

"I guess." Callie studied Vicki's eyes, seeing her worry, knowing that her own was mirrored there.

When Tony was gone, Meg slipped out of the pen and joined

the other two women. "I want to talk to you about something, Callie." She looked from Vicki to Callie.

"What?" Callie breathed deeply, trying to act as if Meg's return was anything but exciting.

"I'd like to make an offer on your place. Would you consider selling? It's not that I mind living upstairs. It's just that I'd like to make some changes, and I have the money."

Taken by surprise, Callie stared at the smiling gray eyes. She knew in that moment that she couldn't live in the same house with Meg anymore. Meg was a lightning rod as far as she was concerned. She turned to Vicki.

"It's your call, Callie," Vicki said magnanimously. Callie knew she was silently urging her to say yes.

She nodded. "Sure. Vicki and I were just talking about getting a place together."

Meg smiled. Beatifically, Callie thought. "Congratulations, you two. It's about time."

Meg stayed for dinner, after walking the fence line with her new horse. Pete trailed after them, sometimes trotting to catch up. The three women sat at the table in the kitchen, sharing a bottle of champagne that Vicki had brought and eating a pasta tuna salad.

It was a perfect deal for Callie. She would look for a house while closing on this one with Meg. She could always move in with Vicki, which made her think of Tony. He wouldn't want to move. Maybe she and Tim could buy him a used car, so that he could drive to Dan's.

"Or he could stay here with me," Meg said. "I hope to give Lucy lessons if she wants them."

Callie thought he could probably live with Dan, but she wanted him with her, at least until he was eighteen when she hoped he would go to college and maybe major in agriculture.

After dinner, Meg went out to check on the horse. Callie heard her come in and go upstairs. She and Vicki were driving to the lake the next day. A small surge of excitement shot through her. The cottage was back in the family, she was going to move from this rundown place, she and Vicki were going to buy a house together. Or were they? They sat on opposite sides of the bed, shedding clothes. Callie pulled an old T-shirt on and swung her feet up on the mattress.

"Are you buying a place with me or are you keeping yours and living in mine?"

Vicki rolled next to her and met her gaze. "I thought we were buying together."

"What will I tell the kids?"

"That we're doing this for economic reasons, if you need an excuse."

"Were you surprised?"

"Oh yes, and relieved. I thought it was going to be same old."

"And what was same old?" Callie ran her fingers through Vicki's thick hair.

"You know, you lusting after Meg." Vicki took Callie's face between her hands and kissed her. "The thing is, I understand. She's very lustable." Another kiss.

Callie kissed her back. "That's not a word."

"It should be." Vicki rolled on top of her and nipped her ear.

"Hey, watch it. Biting is prohibited." She buried her face in Vicki's neck.

"It's the vampire in me."

"You're no vampire. You don't take. You give." She ran her hands over Vicki's backside, down to her thighs. Rolling Vicki off her, she lightly traced her curves with her hands and mouth till Vicki squirmed.

"It takes two to make love," Vicki said hoarsely. "Come back up here."

Was it the anticipation that made lovemaking so exciting, Callie wondered before she succumbed to Vicki's touch, or was it the actual contact that sometimes, like now, was so intense that she lost herself in the ecstasy of the moment?

On Saturday, they threw open the windows to the cottage

to rid it of the musty, closed up smell. Callie looked down at the restless lake as the breeze blew in around her. If Vicki asked her what was her favorite place in the whole world, she would say the small cottage, the lake at the bottom of the hill, the soaring pines, the ferns that grew beneath them, and the lilies of the valley whose scent filled the moving air of which Vicki was now a part.

"It feels very different from when I slept on that bench out there." Vicki encircled her with an arm. "Want to go for a swim?"

She'd never thought she'd end up with a woman. It was still a wonder to her. "I'll teach you how to sail."

Publications from
Bella Books, Inc.
The best in contemporary lesbian fiction

P.O. Box 10543, Tallahassee, FL 32302
Phone: 800-729-4992
www.bellabooks.com

SIDE ORDER OF LOVE by Tracey Richardson. Television foodie star Grace Wellwood is not going to be golf phenom Torrie Cannon's side order of romance for the summer tour. No, she's not. Absolutely not. $13.95

WORTH EVERY STEP by KG MacGregor. Climbing Africa's highest peak isn't nearly so hard as coming back down to earth. Join two women who risk their futures and hearts on the journey of their lives. $13.95

WHACKED by Josie Gordon. Death by family values. Lonnie Squires knows that if they'd warned her about this possibility in seminary, she'd remember. $13.95

BECKA'S SONG by Frankie J. Jones. Mysterious, beautiful women with secrets are to be avoided. Leanne Dresher knows it with her head, but her heart has other plans. Becka James is simply unavoidable. 13.95

GETTING THERE by Lyn Denison. Kat knows her life needs fixing. She just doesn't want to go to the one place where she can do that: home. $13.95

PARTNERS by Gerri Hill. Detective Casey O'Connor has had difficult cases, but what she needs most from fellow detective Tori Hunter is help understanding her new partner, Leslie Tucker. 13.95

AS FAR AS FAR ENOUGH by Claire Rooney. Two very different women from two very different worlds meet by accident--literally. Collier and Meri find their love threatened on all sides. There's only one way to survive: together.
$13.95